In the pages of *Cast a Road Before Me*, Brandilyn Collins not only delivers a captivating story, she literally draws you into the lives of the characters. As those characters become real enough to touch, suddenly Bradleyville becomes your town.

Sally E. Stuart,
Editor, *Christian Writer's Market Guide*

What a page-turner! The character of Jessie is wonderfully vulnerable yet feisty. The Mayberry-like town of Bradleyville is both homey yet mysterious. This is *not* predictable Christian fiction! *Cast a Road Before Me* contained all the elements of a gripping story—tension, romance, inspiration, and yes, even humor. I read it in a single sitting.

Holly G. Miller,
Contributing Editor, *Clarity* magazine,
Travel Editor, *The Saturday Evening Post*

Brandilyn Collins's *Cast a Road Before Me* is an intense tale of one woman's confusion over God's role in the universe, in her life. Ms. Collins's characters are portrayed with realism and candor. A thought-provoking story.

Lyn Cote,
Author, Blessed Assurance series
and *Hope's Garden*

Brandilyn Collins writes with a depth and clarity that makes the sights, sounds, smells, and the just plain folks of the South spring to life! She breathed life into her characters and fanned the flame of faith in this reader—just wonderful!

Annie Jones,
Author, *Deep Dixie* and *The Snowbirds*

Cast a Road Before Me is an engaging and sensitive story of a young woman's coming to faith. Full of drama, romance, and subtle humor, it has all the makings of a good read.

Ann Tatlock,
Author, *A Room of My Own*
and *A Place Called Morning*

Brandilyn immediately transports her readers back to a slower, and what seems from the outside, a more gentle time, then jars you with one of those tragedies that changes a life in an instant. You cannot stop reading as you have to see what happens next. Her lyrical use of language evokes emotion and compels the reader into the heart of the story, the heart of her characters, and makes them come alive in the heart of the reader.

Lauraine Snelling,
Author, Red River of the North series,
Daughter of Twin Oaks, and *Sisters of the Confederacy*
(Secret Refuge series)

cast a road before me

Books by Brandilyn Collins

Eyes of Elisha
Dread Champion

The Bradleyville Series
Cast a Road Before Me
Color the Sidewalk for Me
Capture the Wind for Me

Book One of The Bradleyville Series

cast a road before me

BRANDILYN COLLINS

ZONDERVAN™

GRAND RAPIDS, MICHIGAN 49530 USA

ZONDERVAN™

Cast a Road Before Me
Copyright © 2001 by Brandilyn Collins
Previously published by Broadman & Holman Publishers, Nashville, Tennessee.

Requests for information should be addressed to:

Zondervan, *Grand Rapids, Michigan 49530*

Library of Congress Cataloging-in-Publication Data
Collins, Brandilyn.
    Cast a road before me / Brandilyn Collins.
      p. cm.—(Book one of the Bradleyville series)
    ISBN 0-310-25327-6
    1. Strikes and lockouts—Fiction. 2. Women pacifists—Fiction. 3. Labor
movement—Fiction. 4. Kentucky—Fiction. I. Title.
PS3553.O4747815C37 2003
813'.6—dc21

                                                                    2003002414

Interior design by Susan Ambs

Printed in the United States of America

---

03 04 05 06 07 08 09 /❖ DC/ 10 9 8 7 6 5 4 3 2 1

For my husband, Mark.
For all you've done and all you are.

For I know the thoughts that I think toward you,
saith the Lord,
thoughts of peace, and not of evil,
to give you an expected end.

Jeremiah 29:11

~ 1960 ~

chapter 1

The last time I saw my mother alive, she was on her way to serve the poor.

She was wearing one of her favorite dresses, a blue cotton knit with a sash at the waist. She'd had it for years. It was her favorite not because of style, but because it was comfortable and easy to wash. "This dress will do just fine," she would say whenever I bewailed the notion that she wore it so much to Hope Center, people might think she slept in it. She was far more careful in dressing for work, starching blouses and skillfully mending old skirts so they would not bespeak her lack of a wardrobe. She'd add one of her three pairs of dime-store earrings, sometimes an inexpensive necklace. But any jewelry was out of the question at the Center, where it would only get in the way or, worse, remind the homeless and hungry that their needs were far beyond our own. As for the blue cotton dress, it had been spit up on by mewling babies, dirtied by the spilled soup of children, even torn by the clutching hand of a frightened young mother. Mom would drag home from another long evening at Hope Center, her beautiful face lined with fatigue and a thick strand of her dark auburn hair straggling out of its rubber band, and shake her head good-naturedly over the day's ruin of her dress. Then she'd wash it by hand and hang it up to dry for the next time.

I often volunteered alongside Mom at the Center. After my homework was done and her workday as a receptionist at an insurance firm was finished, we'd hurry through a simple meal, then drive to the two-story brick building in downtown Cincinnati that provided room and board to the poverty-stricken. Saturdays, I always went with her. Except *that* Saturday. My high school sophomore finals were the following week, and Mom had insisted I stay home to study. "You stay home too," I'd pleaded. "You're exhausted, and you haven't given yourself a day off in weeks. Let somebody else fill in for you just this once."

"Oh, but I can't," she'd replied softly. "I promised little Jianying and a whole group of children I'd read to them today, and then I've got to teach that class on how to interview for a job. And besides, Brenda's sick, so I've got to oversee cooking dinner." Brenda Todd had founded the Center ten years previously and acted as manager. Mom had been her "right-hand woman" for eight years.

And so, on that horrific Saturday, my mother kissed me good-bye and walked out the door of our small rented house and down our porch to leave. I followed, still protesting. "Then at least let me come with you. Maybe I can help with dinner, and you can come home after the class. I'll get somebody to give me a ride home. I can study all day tomorrow."

She placed her hands with firm gentleness on my shoulders. "No, Jessie. Stay here and study. And maybe I can find someone to replace me tomorrow. I wouldn't mind a day in bed." She smiled, trying to hide her tiredness as she slid into our battered Chevy Impala.

I will always remember that smile. It is cut into my brain like a carved cameo. I can picture her blue dress; the paleness of her cheeks, void of makeup; the warmth of her brown eyes. She'd placed her worn white purse beside her on the seat, its bent handle flopping forward. Something about that old purse tugged at my heart. I thought of the long hours she was about to put in— again—for no pay. How many dresses, how many purses could she have bought had she spent as much time earning money?

Mom hadn't led an easy life herself, yet she was always thinking of others. Her husband—my father—had wandered away when I was a baby, leaving her with nothing but dark memories of his alcoholism. Years later, he was killed in a drunken fight in some bar halfway across Ohio. Her one sister lived in a tiny, remote town in Kentucky, and they rarely saw each other. And Mom had been estranged from her parents for years before their deaths. After the one and only disastrous time we'd taken a chance and visited them, I'd declared with all the righteous indignation a ten-year-old could muster that we'd *never* go back again. Within four years of that visit, my grandfather had died from cirrhosis of the liver, and my grandmother from heart disease.

As Mom slipped the keys into the ignition, the smile I've held in my memory faded from her lips. Then, for the briefest of moments, her eyes slipped shut, and I watched an expression of despair spread across her features. Anxiety for her hit me in the chest, and I was just about to argue with her further about staying home when her eyes reopened. She noticed me gazing at her, and the expression vanished. She smiled again, a little too brightly. The car started and she began to pull away from the curb. I saw her left hand come up, fingers spread. It was a small wave, intimate. "Thanks for caring," it seemed to say, "but you know I'll be fine." I lifted a hand in return, managed a wan smile back.

I sighed in worry as I watched Mom ease down our street and turn right. Then she was out of sight. Two blocks from our house, she would turn left and begin the climb up Viewridge, which curved to become visible from where I stood.

I fervently wished she had stayed home to rest.

The distinctive sound of a mail slot opening clanked through my thoughts. I turned to see Jack, our mailman, pushing envelopes into the Farrells' house next door. Calling out a greeting, I waited near the curb for him, shielding my eyes against the sun.

"Hi, Jessie," Jack said as he drew near, pulling our mail from his cart. "Almost done with school for the year, aren't you?" He folded the envelopes inside a magazine and held the bundle out to me. I raised my hand to take it. That's when the squealing began.

It was a long keening, the unmistakable sound of frantic brakes. It's not the noise itself that immediately draws your eyes, it's the expectation of what's to follow. Jack's head jerked up. I whirled around, scanning Viewridge, and caught sight of my mother's car. Then I saw the vehicle reeling toward it, pulling a trailer. Fishtailing badly. Dread bolted me to the sidewalk.

Time slowed, suspended in the suddenly suffocating air. In the next second it looked like Mom swerved onto the shoulder toward safety, but she had little room. I remember the nausea that seized me at that moment, even before the inevitable crash. I felt as if I were watching a horror movie, shouting "No! No!" at the screen. Then I heard the words yelled and realized they were my own.

Jack murmured a prayer. Vaguely, I registered the sound of mail hitting the sidewalk.

The crash played forever. There was the smash of impact as the truck hit the side of my mother's car, a grinding of metal and gears, the lingering screech of twisted vehicles careening to a halt. Then utter, dead silence. My feet still would not lift from the sidewalk. Screams gurgled in my throat.

My next memory puts me a block away, breaths ragged with sobs, running, running. . . .

chapter 2

S he had such a good heart."

"Your mother was the most giving person I've ever known."

"Dear child, you can know she's in heaven, for all the loving things she did."

Words of solace poured from the mouths of all who attended my mother's funeral. Hope Center's large gymnasium, cleared of its overnight cots for the homeless, was filled with men, women, and children who wept with me for my mother. Little Jianying Zheng, her doe-brown eyes brimming, wordlessly pressed a white rose into my hand. Her mother placed both palms against my cheeks, her gentle fingertips conveying what her tightened throat could not. In that simple motion I understood the depth of her gratitude. My thoughts, numb as they were, flashed to the recent night this tiny Chinese woman and her five children had come home with Mom to sleep on our floor, the Center being too crowded to take them in. Mei Zheng and her children were immigrants, her husband recently dead from an illness he'd picked up in a filthy overseas refugee camp. Mom had seen that they all were fed and bathed, patiently trying to understand their broken

English as they told of their troubles. After dinner, Mei Zheng had pulled a small statue of Buddha from her ragged knapsack, and the entire family knelt before the statue on our checkered kitchen floor to give their thanks. I had never seen such outward religious obeisance before and was touched by it. As long as I could remember, Mom had instilled within me the understanding that one's soul is more important than earthly matters. How one reached God was up to the individual, she said; people throughout the world found him through differing religions and beliefs. Mom taught me that the way was not important. Her personal way was living a life in service to others.

"They're so content, even when they have nothing," Mom had whispered to me as we tiptoed from the kitchen out of respect for the Zheng family while they worshiped. "Theirs is a wonderful religion—peaceful, revering all life, never violent." Mom abhorred violence, her burning aversion long ago forged at the lightning quick hand of her intemperate father. From my earliest days, she had taught me never to raise a hand against anyone. As she lingered to look back at the threadbare, kneeling figures, her lips curved at their serenity.

During the funeral service, that scene—the tiny frame of Mei Zheng bowed low, her dark hair spilling onto the kitchen floor, and my mother's loving, accepting smile—rose before me again as Ralph Crest, the minister from the Unitarian Church two doors down from the Center, spoke his eulogy. Mom's closed casket was covered with flowers, from expensive arrangements sent by nearby business owners to hand-picked daisies and day-old bouquets foraged throughout the city by those whom Hope Center sheltered. I knew without a doubt which ones Mom would have liked best. I sat on the front row of hard folding chairs between Aunt Eva Bellingham, Mom's sister, and her husband, my Uncle Frank. I had seen them only once before, also at a funeral; that one for their only child, Henry, who had been killed in the Korean War. I was only seven at the time, yet had felt the weight of the grief from those around me pressing down on my own small shoulders. I had wanted to comfort my aunt and uncle then; now they were trying to comfort me.

"Marie Susanna Callum was a deeply religious woman," Mr. Crest was declaring in a voice of hushed reverence. "She gave wholeheartedly and unceasingly here at Hope Center, yet asked God for nothing for herself. And because of that, she has certainly found her salvation today, now that she has passed from this world.

"You know, every once in a while, Marie would visit our services. And I want to tell you of a day a few years ago when she came with her daughter, Jessie. Marie looked so tired, and I knew she had been working even more than usual here, preparing meals and serving. I believe you'd lost one of your volunteer cooks at the time. After the service she shook my hand and thanked me for my words. Seeing the lines on her forehead, I said, 'Marie, don't you ever get tired of giving?' I said, 'Some people would insist you've already done enough good for one lifetime.' And you know what she replied? She looked me straight in the eye and said in her soft voice, 'Well, Minister Crest, I'm afraid I'd have to disagree with those people. No amount I can do will ever be good enough.'"

Never good enough.

A knife cut through me at the words. All too well I remembered the day they had been hurled at my mother through the gritted, tobacco-stained teeth of her hateful father. How *furious* I'd been at him that day. And how hurt I had been for Mom, my eyes suddenly opened to the childhood abuse at which she'd only hinted. I struggled to push the memory away as a sob rolled up my chest. I could hear others crying behind me, the shaky whispers of women shushing their young children. I thought at that moment that I would simply die, for the sorrow was more than I could bear. It was going to split my chest wide open. How could my wonderful, self-sacrificing mother be *dead?* I squeezed my eyes shut, swooning in my seat. Uncle Frank hastened his arm around me and held me tightly.

"What a marvelous testimony for one who had already done so much," Ralph Crest concluded. "Yes, Marie Susanna Callum was forever compassionate to the needs around her. She was always ready to do more."

I shuddered against Uncle Frank's broad chest. Despite the minister's interpretation of Mom's words, they spoke to me only of wrath and judgment. How could she even have formed those words with her own tongue, especially in reference to herself?

After the service, I rode to the cemetery in a solemn black limousine with my aunt and uncle. I barely remember the journey. Only that Aunt Eva hugged me so hard I could barely breathe, weeping, "My poor chil', my poor chil'; Lord Jesus, help us take care a her." It was a fitting day for a burial, the air oppressive with humidity, a light drizzle beginning to fall as we stood before the grave site. When they lowered my mother's casket into the earth, taking what was left of her away from me forever, I sank to my knees, wracked with sobs. I cried for the loss of her, then cried harder that I wouldn't even be able to tend her grave. I was to leave the next day to live with my aunt and uncle in the tiny town of Bradleyville, Kentucky, a town I'd seen only once, when their son had been buried.

The ceremony finally complete, I still could not get up. Aunt Eva and Uncle Frank knelt beside me, oblivious to the rain, and prayed aloud for God's comfort, long after everyone else had gone. Still, I could not leave. Finally, Uncle Frank rose, gathered me tenderly in his arms, and carried me from the grave, my head lolling against his starched white dress shirt, now wet and wrinkled from the rain and my tears.

chapter 3

Nothing could have prepared me for the change in atmosphere and pace that I found in Bradleyville. The town was even smaller than I remembered. It contained all of two stoplights, both on Main Street. The first was upon entering the town along Route 622 after a series of stomach-dropping hills; the second heralded the one-block downtown area. In between the two was the post office, in which Aunt Eva worked. Past the second light were the grocery store, the Laundromat, Miss Alice's sewing shop, and Mr. Tull's Drugstore on the right. Across the street lay the hardware store, dime store, and bank, plus a small police station that included a tiny holding cell (hardly ever used), the fire station, and the doctor's office. There were two churches at strategic locations on different side streets off Main—a Baptist and a Methodist. I soon learned that both prided themselves on being the cleanest, preaching the purest gospel, and boasting the best cooks, who would go to great lengths to outperform each other at the annual townwide potluck supper, which was held at each church on alternating years.

Aunt Eva and Uncle Frank attended the Methodist church, a white wooden building with matching steeple and, above the entryway, a small stained glass window of Jesus tending lambs. I remembered that window from Henry's funeral, although in the dead of winter its panes had seemed lifeless in the pale sun. The first time I attended services at the church on a sunny June day after I'd moved to town, the window sparkled with a brilliance that left me standing in awe, head tipped back and lips parted. Jesus' face radiated love, his hand lying gently upon the back of a tottering lamb. I stared at the picture with stabs in my heart; it reminded me of my mother's tender care of folks at the Center.

The entire town of Bradleyville embraced me as its own lost little lamb. In such a small place, naturally everyone knew everything about everybody. There wasn't a soul within the city limits and surrounding countryside who didn't know my name and my story before I arrived. They all were kind to me. They certainly talked differently, however—half Southern drawl and half what I'd have called plain old "hick." As for ambiance, Bradleyville was a pretty town in summer. Flowers bloom and ancient leafy oaks sweep the sky. Nestled in the foothills of the Appalachians in eastern Kentucky, Bradleyville proudly displayed some of the greenest lawns I'd ever seen. My eyes took in the town's charming beauty, my lips smiled at folks' generosity, but none of it registered. My mind was too full of anguish.

It didn't help that my aunt repeatedly gushed over how much I looked like my mother. I didn't believe it anyway. True, we both had the same wavy hair, although mine was a darker brown, lacking the red highlights. We both had brown eyes and were petite, small-boned. Mom had only stood five feet, four inches, and I wouldn't be much above that. There was also some resemblance in our heart-shaped faces and upturned lips. But I would never be as beautiful as my mother. Not in face or in soul.

During my first few months in Bradleyville there was one person who could raise my spirits: Thomas Bradley, town patriarch and war hero. His father, Jonathan, founded the town by building the sawmill on the banks of the Cumberland River a year before Thomas was born. Upon his daddy's death in 1955, Thomas had inherited the mill and so was boss to my uncle and most of the men in town. Fortunately, everybody loved Thomas.

Thomas was fifty-seven when I met him, which sounded pretty old to me, but he was spry, feisty, and quick-witted. He wasn't a large man, but his presence lit up a room like an electrical charge. Thomas would regale me with a story, and his blue eyes would twinkle until I laughed in spite of myself. He was many things to me—wise, proud, and at the same time, humble enough to want to spend time with a bereft sixteen-year-old. What's more, he publicly cemented our special friendship by inviting me to call him by his first name. Many times during that first summer Thomas treated me to a milkshake at Tull's Drugstore, where he met almost daily with his two oldest friends, Jake Lewellyn and Hank Jenkins. Never could two people argue like he and Mr. Lewellyn, both pumping their egos by seeking to outdo the other. Theirs was a most enigmatic friendship.

Thomas's pride sprang from not only his daddy's accomplishments, but his own. You couldn't be acquainted with him for five minutes without hearing he was thrice decorated in two wars—the Second World War and Korea. That fact would earn him respect in any town, but in an isolated burg like Bradleyville, his feats—abroad and at home—ran legendary. All the same, while I admired his bravery, he and I learned early in our friendship not to discuss war, for the strategy of battle coursed as hotly through his veins as abhorrence to violence ran through mine.

It was Thomas who opened my eyes to the fact that my aunt and uncle needed me as much as I needed them. Not that Henry could ever be replaced, but they did view me as "another child brought to them by heaven," as he put it. From the outset, they lavished me with love and displayed only patient understanding at my self-absorption.

Although my aunt and uncle cared for me with one mind, the two of them were as different as night and day. Whereas Uncle Frank was carefully spoken, quiet and constrained, Aunt Eva was chatty, easily set off, her freckled hands often flitting to pat red curls into their ill-contained bun. If gossip was the official sport of Bradleyville, Aunt Eva was the referee. "Now So-and-So, sittin' two pews in front of us," she'd whisper before church started, "I tell you he's had the hardest time with. . . ." And she'd go on to tell me of So-and-So's wife or child or physical ailment—until she'd catch herself and abruptly snap her lips shut. "There I am, at it again," she'd breathe, eyes tilting skyward. "'Whoso keepeth his mouth and his tongue keepeth his soul from troubles.' Proverbs 21:23. Forgive me, Lord."

Looking back on my first summer in Bradleyville is like staring into a deep, dark hole. Often, alone in my bedroom, I would cry until my tears ran dry. Weekdays, Aunt Eva was busy at the post office, and Uncle Frank worked at the sawmill. To keep me busy while they were gone, my aunt and uncle had made a point to introduce me to girls my age, and they all tried to be my friends. They'd invite me over for an afternoon or to slumber parties, but I rarely said yes. My grief was sucking me dry; I had no energy for people.

When I wasn't crying, I spent hours slumped upon my bed, trying to sort things out. I was obsessed with the harsh finality that my mother's life, so charismatic and unselfish, had been cut short within an instant. She'd been only thirty-five years old. The memories of her death were enough to wrench me from nightmarish sleep, sweat-drenched and shaking. How to describe that mindless, wobbly-kneed run ending at the twisted crunch of metal that had been our car? My mother inside, bent and bloodied, with no way to reach her because the doors were flattened, handles gone.

"Sweet chil', only Jesus can help you through your grief," Aunt Eva would croon to me. "I know, because he surely helped me when we lost Henry. I'd sat in church every Sunday since movin' here, but not until Henry died did I accept Jesus as my Savior. That terrible loss drove me to my knees."

I knew she was trying to help. But her words of faith and encouragement sounded like such platitudes, even though I didn't doubt she bore deep sorrow—over Henry's death and my mother's.

I didn't mean to be selfish, but I couldn't believe anyone really understood the depth of my pain, not even Jesus himself. Besides, I didn't want Jesus to "help me through my grief."

I just wanted my mother back.

In the fall, I began my junior year of high school. Bradleyville's high school was a fraction of the size I was used to attending, consisting of one small building on the same campus as the elementary school. I flailed my way through eleventh grade, barely able to concentrate in class. Eventually, I had to repeat the whole year. The nightmares still pursued me, and grief over my mother had swelled into a smoldering resentment against God for taking her from me. Although Mom had taught me to pray when I was young, I no longer cared to talk to God. As far as I was concerned, my mother was the best person who'd ever walked on this earth; yet he'd let her die, while criminals and all manner of selfish, nasty people still lived.

Every Sunday I went to church with my aunt and uncle, fixing my eyes upon our pastor, Jeffrey Frasier, during his sermons but hearing little. The Bellinghams were joyful in their worship, and I admired their faith. Sometimes I wished I had what they did, for they seemed well grounded and content. I'd look at them and then think of Mei Zheng and her children, praying to Buddha. As my mother would say, both families had certainly found their ways to God. There had been times, when I was serving at Hope Center alongside my mom, that I'd felt close to him too. But now he seemed so distant, his ways impenetrable. My anger at him left me feeling all the more alone.

One Sunday about a month after Christmas—which was the hardest day I'd faced to date in Bradleyville—Pastor Frasier preached from the third chapter of John about a man named Nicodemus. "Verily, verily I say unto thee," he quoted Jesus as saying to Nicodemus, "except a man be born again, he cannot see the kingdom of God." For some reason, those words penetrated my distant thoughts, and I frowned, trying to make sense of them. The statement didn't sound right to me. I knew the kingdom of

God was heaven. And I knew my mom was in heaven. But I'd never heard her talk about being "born again," whatever that was. Nicodemus apparently was as confused as I, because he questioned Jesus about what the term meant. Our pastor quoted further verses from the same chapter, and the more I heard, the more confused I became. "Please understand, dear folks," Pastor Frasier continued, "Jesus says plainly in verses fifteen through eighteen that he is God's only Son, and that there is no salvation but through him. You can't be 'religious' enough; you can't serve the poor enough; you can't go to church enough or even spend time on your knees enough to save your own soul. You can only accept Jesus Christ as your Savior and Lord and live your life for him."

You can't serve the poor enough. The minister had actually said that. He might as well have accused my mother by name. He might as well have spat, *"Never good enough!"* like her horrible father. Anger caught fire and burned in the pit of my stomach. By the time his sermon was finished, my arms were crossed against my chest, my jaw set. After the final hymn, I informed my aunt and uncle they could go on home; I'd walk.

"But chil', there's snow on the ground!" Aunt Eva protested.

I tossed my head. "I don't care; I'll be fine in my coat. I have to speak to the pastor, *right now.*"

Uncle Frank placed his large hands on my shoulders, his gray eyes warm. "You hear some things that disturb you?"

I was too incensed to answer.

"That's all right, Jessie." His lips curved. "You go on and talk to the pastor. I'll take Eva home and come back for you. I'll wait as long as you need."

Jeffrey Frasier was a tall man in his late fifties with an amazing head of silver hair. His hazel eyes were enlarged behind thick-framed glasses, his complexion dark. He sat behind his wide oak desk clasping long fingers, regarding me with a kind expression that

I was in no mood to reciprocate. On one corner of the desk lay a well-thumbed Bible; on the other were scattered framed pictures of his wife and grown children. I perched across from him on the edge of a worn leather chair, my throat tight with defensiveness. Now that I was in his office, I regretted my impulsive request to talk to him. I should have waited a day or two, when I wasn't so upset.

"Well, Jessie," he said as he leaned back in his seat, "I've had lots a folks come into my office over the years, and I've seen that look you now wear on your face more than a few times. It seems I've offended you in some way."

I swallowed hard, resisting a sudden impulse to cry. A moment passed before I could answer. "It's my mother," I managed finally, twisting my hands in my lap. "You said something about Jesus being the only way to salvation. That serving the poor isn't enough. I just don't understand. I know Jesus was good and all that. But my mother always taught me there are many ways to God, and that each person has to find his own way. Mom's way was through serving others. And, besides, I know Jesus helped others all the time." A picture of Mom gently guiding the withered arm of a frail elderly woman into her coat sleeve flashed through my head. Tears bit my eyes. "My mom *died* on her way to a center for the homeless where she'd volunteered for years. She tended the lambs, just like Jesus on your stained glass window. She was such a good person, I *know* she's in heaven. So now you're telling me she's *not?*"

Sadness spread across Pastor Frasier's face. "Ah, young Jessie. The Lord has given you much to handle. Sometimes it's hard to understand his purpose."

I brushed at a tear with impatience. I did not care to hear more platitudes. "You're not answering my question."

He placed two fingers against his chin, his gaze drifting to a snow-dusted oak tree outside the window. Then his eyes closed, and I sensed he was praying. He turned back to me with an apologetic smile. "I did not preach this sermon to purposely speak against your mother, you know," he said gently. "Even if it might seem that way to you right now."

The compassion in his eyes surprised me. "I know."

He nodded briefly. "Okay. Well, then. Seems to me there are two issues here. One is your mother. But the most important is you. What do *you* need to do to find salvation?"

"No, it's the same issue, because I can't separate us like that. She was everything to me, and she did nothing but give to people. You don't know how much she was respected at the Center; you just don't know." My words began to tumble over themselves. "And she was very loving and patient with me. I've always wanted to be just like her. She worked really hard at the Center because she always felt like she wasn't good enough, that she had to do more. She never said it, but I think she felt she had this stain on her soul. It wasn't really there, of course, but she thought it was. I think it's because of the way her father treated her."

My mouth shut abruptly, and I eyed Pastor Frasier with a vague wariness. I'd never intended to say so much.

"We all have 'stains on our soul,' as you put it, Jessie. Even the best among us. Not because someone here on earth tells us we're not good enough, but because God says through his Word that we've all sinned and fallen short of his plans for us." He gazed at me, judging my response. "Is that somethin' you can agree with?"

"Well, I guess. Otherwise, I suppose we wouldn't need to seek God."

His face creased into a smile. "Well, see there. We're not on complete opposite ends of the pole."

My resentment lifted a little. It was hard to stay angry at this man.

"Let me ask you somethin'." He shifted in his chair, searching for the right words. "Do you think that by her service to others your mother was able to cleanse that stain away?"

His question took me by surprise. I leaned back slowly, pressing my arched shoulders against the cool leather. "Absolutely."

He showed no response to the indignant tone of my voice. "What tells you that?"

"Because she kept *doing* it. If it hadn't worked, she'd have . . . done something else."

"I see." He took a deep breath and let it out slowly. Suddenly, he seemed weighted, tired. "Will this also be your 'way to God,' Jessie?"

I thought for a moment. "I plan to help people, if that's what you mean. I'll never be as good at it as Mom was. Probably never work that hard. But as for finding God, yes, I think that's what it will take for me." *If I was ever ready to talk to him again.* "I do believe in him," I added, as if I'd spoken the thought aloud. "I'm a good person. Now I'm even coming to church every Sunday. What more could you ask?" I lifted both shoulders in a deprecating shrug, smiling ruefully. "But that's not the problem, anyway. I didn't come here to talk about me. I came because I felt you'd attacked my mom, and I just . . . I couldn't let that be." My throat tightened. "I can't believe the things you said in your sermon, because if they are true, all her work—even her death—would be for *nothing.*"

"Jessie," Pastor Frasier leaned across his desk, "please understand me. Nothin' I ever say—in a sermon or anywhere else—will be aimed against your mother. Only God can judge how she lived her life. So I leave her in God's hands. All right? My sermons are preached for those of us still on this earth. For myself, for you, for the person sittin' in the front pew and the back. And I'll tell you somethin', Jessie. I believe God brought you in here today for both of us. First—you. He's placed within your heart a yearnin' for the truth—a yearnin' that you may not even fully discern yet. I pray he'll give me the words you need to hear so you can find that truth. As for me, it seems he's brought you here to reinforce my burden for this town."

I frowned, uncomprehending.

He regarded me thoughtfully. "I'm not quite sure what God has in mind, but I feel he's promptin' me to tell you this." He hesitated, choosing his words. "Although you're a newcomer in Bradleyville, Jessie, you—with your view of salvation—are a lot like other people in this town. I suppose you've heard how Jonathan Bradley pulled up stakes from Albertsville and moved here when it was nothin' but countryside? He was a wonderful Christian man, fed up with the immorality around him. He said God told him to build a town, and by gum, that's what he did. This was a town whose very foundation was Christian. My own father was the first preacher, here in this church. Later, the Baptist church was built as more folks came. In the young days of this town, folks lived their lives centered on Christ." Absently, he rubbed a nick on the edge of his desk. "But now that a generation's gone by, things have changed. People still go to church and talk about bein' Christian. And they still raise their children under strict biblical principles. The problem is, Jessie, they think this is enough. They've lost sight of what it means to have Christ as Lord of their lives. Now, I'm not talkin' 'bout everybody. Your aunt and uncle, Alice Eder, Martha Plott, and others are still firmly centered. But many more are not. That's why I preached my sermon today. And that's why I'm in deep prayer over this town. Because, Jessie, I'll tell ya somethin' I've learned. Bein' good and servin' others and goin' to church are all things we should do. But when the fryin' pan meets the flame, these things alone won't sustain you. For in choosin' to do *only* those things and not embrace Jesus Christ as our own Savior, we're choosin' to remain lords of our own lives."

Two minutes ago I'd been nearly mollified. Now, fresh defensiveness rose within me. How dare this man make such judgments. "Uh-huh." I managed a stiff smile. "Okay. I see where your beliefs are. But as I told you, Mom saw the good in many different ways to God. And so . . . I'll respect your beliefs, as I hope you'll respect mine." I stood, abruptly ending the discussion, then felt a twinge of remorse as disappointment flicked across his face. "I'm sorry to leave," I added, my back still stiff, "but my uncle's waiting for me so . . . I better go."

"All right, Jessie." The pastor rose gracefully. "I've filled your ear enough for one day anyway." He ushered me out of his office, then walked me down the hall and back into the sanctuary, where Uncle Frank sat with his head bowed, praying.

chapter 4

*T*hat afternoon in Bradleyville, an elderly widow fussed over the ivy plant on her kitchen table, watering it with care and wiping imagined dust from its leaves. That done, she shuffled across the black-and-white checked floor, her plastic watering can cradled in both hands. Humming the chorus of a hymn under her breath, she drew up before her small pots of herbs lining the window sill. A flash of red out in the street caught her eye, and she turned to set the watering can down on a nearby counter. Peering through lace curtains, she saw two neighbor boys throwing a ball back and forth. "Crazy kids," she chuckled to herself, "out in the cold."

She picked up the watering can in her right hand, gently pulling aside the leaves of a basil plant with her left to allow room for watering. She smiled, thinking how much she enjoyed the savory taste of sweet basil in spaghetti. Without realizing it, she started humming again.

What happened next came without warning. The cheery kitchen and plants faded, and a vision sprang to the widow's mind, as clearly as though the horrifying scene was spread before her. A vision of blackness. Violence. Death. Amid the raging bodies, she could see the features of only one face. The presence of this face, and the expression upon it, stunned her with fear and disbelief.

A small gasp puffed from the widow's parted lips. She froze, her back still bent over the plant, the watering can suspended. What on earth? Why had such a crazy thing entered her mind? She pondered it until her back began to ache, and then she straightened, shaking her head. Must have eaten too much Jell-O salad at lunch; the sugar was acting up on her again. She took a deep breath, mentally shaking herself back into place, then lifted the can to water her mint plant. Next, she moved to the parsley. After a moment, her humming resumed. A heater vent was in the wall below the window, and she took her time, relishing the warm air on her legs.

She was just about to water the rosemary when the vision flashed a second time into her brain, with double the clarity. "Oh!" she cried, nearly dropping the can. She froze again, mind reeling. Then, slowly, a new expression spread across her wrinkled face. With a slight frown, she set the watering can on the counter and turned her back to the window, facing the empty kitchen. "Lord?" she said aloud. "Is that you?" She listened intently, eyes lifting toward the ceiling. "You tryin' to tell me somethin'?"

She stood for what seemed a long time, until her legs started to get stiff and her right hip throbbed. She headed for the kitchen table, pulled out her wooden chair with the handmade red padded cushion tied to its back slats, and fell into it with a slight sigh. That's when the vision leapt into her head for the third time, clinging to her thoughts so forcefully that she could not pry it loose.

"Dear God Almighty," she breathed, shaken to her bones. "Please tell me. Is this fearful picture from you?" She tried to still her pounding heart, awaiting the reply, and the answer came as surely as though God had spoken aloud.

Yes.

"Oh, help us, Jesus." Automatically, the widow clasped her hands, leaning over the table to talk to God. It was a long time before she arose.

When she did, she walked purposefully into her small, neat living room and toward the phone. As she had prayed, she'd begun fully to grasp the *meaning of the vision. A terrible crisis was going to befall Bradleyville. She didn't know what or when or how. Only that God had called her— and a few others she was to tell—to intercede in prayer.*

Lips moving silently, she picked up the phone and dialed Pastor Frasier's number.

~ *1968* ~

chapter 5

A faint squeaking of brakes filtered through the open kitchen window and, reflexively, I jumped. Brushing aside the white sheers, I spotted a red pickup truck pulling toward the curb out front. Frustration twinged inside me. I hadn't been home for more than half an hour, just long enough to eat a hurried supper. My bags were still in my car. I'd made quite an entrance, twirling my tasseled college graduation cap, as if it hadn't been exclaimed over enough two days ago at the ceremony. I'd expected the three of us to linger over our meal, discussing how well my plans were going. Instead I'd found my aunt on tenterhooks, my uncle preoccupied.

"Oh, that'll be Lee Harding," Aunt Eva breathed, deftly slicing into her still-warm chocolate cake. "Will you get the door please, hon?"

"You didn't tell me we were having company," I called over my shoulder as I turned the corner into the living room.

"Well, just Lee and Thomas, but there was hardly time, and we didn't want to get into the subject...." Aunt Eva's chattering answer drifted through the hallway as I opened the door.

My gaze fell chest-high on the massive man standing before me, and I raised my eyes to take in broad shoulders, a muscular neck. Lee Harding was easily six-foot-five, with thick black hair combed over a wide forehead, eyes of dark chocolate. I was only five-foot-five myself and had to tip back my head to look him in the eye. One of his huge wrists was probably bigger than both of mine put together. For a brief moment we stared at each other, my hand still on the doorknob.

"Jessie," he said, pleasure in his voice. "I didn't expect to see you this soon."

I hesitated, searching for a response.

"I met you when you were down for Christmas, remember?" he said, automatically wiping his large booted feet on Aunt Eva's worn welcome mat. "And again in church at Easter."

"Yes, of course I remember," I smiled. "Nice to see you again. Come on in, they're expecting you."

Aunt Eva appeared around the corner, a crumb-coated server in her hand. "Come in, Lee, come in!" she cried, flitting toward me like an eagle joining her chick. "Thomas will be here any minute, and Frank's right on my heels. Just have yourself a seat. You remember Jessie. She's gonna be with us till August; it'll be so *nice* to have her around this summer, don't you think?" She beamed meaningfully at us both.

Oh, boy. It appeared Aunt Eva had plans of her own for me my last few weeks in Bradleyville. "I'll go get some iced tea," I said.

By the time I'd gathered three glasses of iced tea for the men and prepared three plates of cake, Thomas had arrived. I trotted to the door to hug him, feeling the thinning bones beneath his red-checked shirt. "Thanks again for coming to my graduation," I whispered, kissing his scruffy cheek.

"Ah," he waved a hand, "what's a bit of a drive for my best girl."

Uncle Frank and Lee stood to greet Thomas—my uncle with warm familiarity, Lee with a touch of reverence. Next to Lee Harding, my uncle looked diminutive, even though six feet himself. As the men settled into armchairs and the couch for their meeting, I excused myself, noting the look of concern in my uncle's eyes, the corners of his mouth dragging toward his rounded jowls. Aunt Eva was edging toward the couch, and he gave her a look. "Well," she exclaimed, smiling at no one in particular, "Jessie and I'll just . . . eat our dessert in the kitchen." She walked away with dignity, beckoning me to follow like an errant child.

The reason for the unusual meeting was evidently serious, indicated by the fact that Lee and Thomas had arrived on our doorstep at 6:00, a sacred time in Bradleyville. The mill shift let out at five, with wives putting suppers on tables by 5:30. Supper was a time for fathers to question children about their behavior, for mothers to "tell daddy" a toddler's newest word. Visiting hours did not begin until around 7:00—an unwritten rule, perhaps, but no less sacrosanct in a town founded on strong familial bonds.

Aunt Eva and I returned quietly to our seats at the kitchen table, out of sight of the three men but within good earshot. My aunt perched at attention, picking up her fork and gliding it through her piece of cake and into her mouth without a breath of sound. I suppressed a smile. She'd never change.

"Thomas, I hear congratulations are in order at y'all's house." Lee Harding's voice was deep but surprisingly gentle for a man his size. "How's the baby?"

"Hooo, you should see that grandson a mine!" Thomas crowed. "Kevin Thomas Matthews—ain't that a name! He's strong, smart. Just amazin' what you can tell in a person one week old."

I heard the slap of Thomas's fingers against his leg, could imagine his pleased-as-punch grin.

"And Estelle?"

"Fine, fine. Takin' care a her growin' family. And what a big sister little Celia's turnin' out to be. Won't let that baby outta her sight."

Aunt Eva scratched her nose impatiently as the "askin' after" pleasantries continued. We heard that Lee's mama was still mending slowly after falling and cracking her hip. And his younger sister was "havin' her ups and downs, what with bein' pregnant and suddenly husbandless and all." That comment wrought forth a shudder from Aunt Eva as she poked her fork in the air and turned it, skewering an imaginary Bart Stokes for his faithlessness. "That's what comes a marryin' an Albertsville boy," she'd sniffed when she'd told me the news. "They just don't have our morals."

When the men's conversation turned to business, my aunt was again all ears.

"Thomas," Uncle Frank began, "Lee and I been wantin' to talk to you 'bout the mill, and after today, figured it couldn't wait any longer. Blair Riddum just informed us he's not gonna raise wages again this fiscal year. The men're mighty hot over it."

"What's his reason?"

"Same as before," Lee put in. "Mill's not doin' well, cain't afford it, and on and on. It was hard enough hearin' that last year, but he promised things'd be different this year, so we all tightened our belts and waited it out. Not much else we could do; the mill puts food on our tables. Now it's the same thing all over again."

The discussion paused. I managed a bite of cake, upset for Thomas over the news. After his wife died four years ago, Thomas had sold the mill and retired, moving in with his daughter, Estelle, and her family. He'd never have wanted that sale to hurt his employees.

"Everybody was grumblin' somethin' fierce on their way out the door tonight," Lee continued. "It particularly don't set well, Thomas, seein' as how not two months back Riddum finished that big addition to his house. You must a seen it out Route 622. He's got a new wrap-around porch and a fancy-cut, heavy door, plus at least a couple a new rooms. So now he's got no money for us. I can tell you, that's hard to take when I'm addin' on to Mama's house for my sister and her baby. I was countin' on a raise to repay the bank for materials."

"What do the accountin' books say, Frank?" Thomas asked.

My uncle snorted in disgust. A boding wind blew through me at hearing such an atypical display of frustration from my patient uncle. "They been taken outta my hands. Riddum told me last week my title means assistant manager in production *only*. 'You got to get more work outta the men. They're gettin' lazy and slow,' he says."

"The men were never slow when I was there."

"And they ain't slow now, Thomas," Lee declared. "We already been workin' faster, hopin' for those raises come July. It ain't even safe around the blades now. Ken Beecham like to cut off his thumb the other day."

Someone sighed loudly. Probably Thomas. I'd been in Lexington attending the University of Kentucky when he sold the mill but had heard all about it from Aunt Eva. It was a major affair for Bradleyville, being the first time the mainstay of the town had passed into the hands of someone other than a Bradley. Blair Riddum lived about a mile outside of town and was no stranger, but neither was he Bradleyville born-and-bred. Some of the townsfolk had expressed their doubts about the sale, which is a nice way to say that the other mill in town—the gossip mill—ran wild. But Thomas had calmed everyone's fears, reminding them that buyers don't come often, and that one mile past the large wooden Bradleyville sign was a heck of a lot better than twenty-two miles—referring to the nearest town of Albertsville.

I heard an iced tea glass being set on one of Aunt Eva's glass coasters, then the creak of a chair.

"I been hearin' things for a while," Thomas said. "No way not to. I've tried to keep outta the way, thinkin' it's not my place now. But I cain't help but feel bad that sellin' for my own retirement is hurtin' the town."

"No one's blamin' you, Thomas, certainly not us," my uncle replied. Lee Harding voiced his agreement. "We didn't want to come to you, especially now, with a brand new grandson and all.

But there's not a man in Bradleyville who won't listen to you. So what we're askin' is for you to pay Riddum a visit. Let him know how serious the situation is."

"Just how serious is it?"

Uncle Frank cleared his throat. "Well, a few hot-tempered ones have even mentioned strike."

Strike.

Aunt Eva's eyes widened. "Frank didn't *tell* me," she whispered fiercely. I shook my head, brushing back a long strand of hair. It would never happen.

There had been a strike at a big sewing factory in Albertsville when I was seventeen. That town was five times the size of Bradleyville, yet it still had reeled from the impact. Violence erupted when "scab" workers were brought in to replace the strikers, and three people had been killed. More than three hundred families were without income for a month, and grocery store robberies were common.

"Strike," Thomas repeated.

"Don't worry, sir," Lee said quickly, "that's just a few loose cannons talkin'. Al Bledger always runs at the mouth."

"I tried to calm the workers down after the shift," Uncle Frank explained. "Lee came to my rescue—he's someone they look up to, even though he's been there less than a year. It was his idea that we see you." He paused. "What I'm tryin' to tell you, old friend, is that this here meetin's no secret. We're all countin' on your seein' Riddum, hopin' it'll knock some sense into him. If it don't, well, Lee and I'll keep tryin' for some sort a compromise. We don't want trouble."

"And we don't want a union either," Lee added. "Not yet, anyway. But if this don't work itself out, a union's promises are gonna look better and better."

"Always said I'd be in my grave afore a union got hold a my mill," Thomas said. "Goes against everything Bradleyville stands for, outsiders tellin' us what to do."

Aunt Eva's cake was forgotten. She leaned her elbows on the table, hands cradling her stricken face.

"So," Uncle Frank said, "you'll see Riddum?"

"I'll do what I can. And if it don't work, gentlemen . . . ," he paused, "we'll have some hard prayin' to do."

chapter 6

I unpacked my suitcases slowly, disturbed by the news I'd heard about the saw mill. Thomas had stayed a while after Lee Harding left, and his expression left no question as to how distraught he was. "I jus' cain't believe it's got this bad," he kept repeating as we sat around the kitchen table. I'd cleared away all the dishes. "Where've I *been?*"

"You been thinkin' 'bout a baby bein' born, that's what, Thomas." Aunt Eva patted his arm. "There's a lot goin' on in your household."

Thomas shook his head, uncomforted. "I shoulda been watchin'; maybe things'd never a gotten this far. I shoulda talked to Riddum weeks ago."

"They haven't gotten all that far," Uncle Frank put in. "That strike talk is just a couple a hotheads talkin', like we said. Most a the men ain't even mentioned it."

"All it takes is one hothead," Thomas rejoined. "One hothead, and the whole company can fall; I seen that enough in my battle days."

"*Which*, by the way, are behind you, Thomas," Aunt Eva declared, lightly hitting a fist against the table for emphasis. "Arguin' over wages is not a war, and Bradleyville's not Korea. So don't you go thinkin' in such ways. We're not talkin' here 'bout strategy or battles; we're talkin' 'bout the mill, which has been here a long time and will continue to be here many more years."

I threw her an odd look, wondering who she was most trying to convince. She squared her shoulders. "You ain't been here for a while, Jessie," she retorted, then caught herself and lightened her tone. "Things've been difficult at the mill; no one knows that more'n your uncle, who's treadin' the line, bein' both assistant manager and friend. But all the same, Thomas," she turned to him, "what we need to be doin' most of all is prayin'. God helped your daddy build that mill, and he's the one who's gonna protect it."

My eyes slid over to Thomas. Aunt Eva may not have been subtle, but her perception was right on the mark. Thomas's view of himself as town patriarch—and therefore ultimate problem-solver—reigned supreme. He slowly scratched the side of his mouth, quelling a defensive reply.

"'Course you're right 'bout that, Eva." He puckered his chin. "God's gonna help us, no doubt. But I'm the one here on earth who's gotta try to drill some sense into Riddum's head."

"And we're glad to have you," Uncle Frank interjected. "We're glad for your wisdom and experience. Eva's right too; we gotta be prayin'—for you and for the town's protection."

"I'm all for that." Thomas smacked his hands against his knees and rose to leave.

"Now you let us know, Thomas, soon as you come outta that meetin'." Aunt Eva stood and pushed her chair back into the table.

"No doubt, Eva, you'll be one a the first to know," Thomas replied with a twinkle in his eye. He knew her as well as she knew him. If Aunt Eva caught the intimation, she paid him no heed.

Now, alone in my room, I opened a dresser drawer and sighed. I knew I was being selfish, but I was as disappointed over the situation for me as I was for the town. Quiet was what I longed for, not turmoil. During my entire senior year, thanks to an overloaded schedule, I'd only been able to visit Bradleyville during Christmas and Easter, even though the University of Kentucky was only about four hours' drive away. Throughout my five years at college, I'd juggled thirty hours' work a week plus classes. This past year, in order to graduate, I'd had to add an extra class per semester. On top of that, I'd put in about five hours a week volunteering at a soup kitchen run by a downtown church in Lexington. I was exhausted. I'd so looked forward to coming home for two months' rest before starting my new job in Cincinnati. During that last, crazy week of finals, studying late into the night and repeating facts in my head as I sewed clothes alterations at Susan's Dry Cleaning, I kept telling myself, "Just a few more days. A few more days, and you'll have it easy in Bradleyville."

I shook out a wrinkled dress and hung it in the closet, looking at it askance. I was badly in need of a decent wardrobe for my new job as a social worker for Hamilton County, in which Cincinnati resided. My one goal for the next two months, other than to rest, was to sew at least six outfits, using some of my hoarded savings for fabric and patterns. My first day of work was August fifteenth. The apartment I'd leased would become available August first, which was perfect. I'd have two weeks to settle in to the large apartment complex, re-explore Cincinnati, and possibly make some friends. Most importantly, I'd have a few days to donate to Hope Center, which was still managed by Brenda Todd, who "couldn't wait to welcome me back with open arms," as she'd responded when I'd written her of my plans to return to Cincinnati. After my job commenced, I planned to work at the Center a few evenings a week and every Sunday. "I certainly can't fill my mother's shoes," I'd said in my letter, "but I can do my small part to help."

Carefully, I pulled my favorite photo of Mom out of my suitcase and placed it on my dresser. She was pictured in front of Hope Center in her heavy black coat, a winter sun glinting highlights in her hair. I lingered over the picture, smiling back at her smile, touching the filigreed gold frame. Even though I still missed her terribly, it warmed me to know that she watched me from heaven and that, most assuredly, she was proud of me—proud that I'd earned my own way through college and proud that I would continue in her footsteps, giving of my time and energy to others at the very Center she'd so loved.

A wave of sadness washed over me without warning, and tears sprang to my eyes. It still happened once in a while, the pain of missing her rising afresh, sometimes when I least expected it. I padded across the carpet and sank onto my bed, falling back to stare at the ceiling. Melancholy was the last thing I'd expected upon returning home. Evidently, I was more tired than I'd realized. Tears rolled out the corners of my eyes and down the sides of my face, wetting both ears. I let them come, not bothering to wipe them away. Soon, I knew, the sadness would pass, and I could go on about my business. I hadn't had time to cry in months; now, after all the hubbub of preparing to graduate, my body was simply letting down, that was all.

My nose began to clog. I breathed in deeply, exhaling through my mouth. The scene was familiar—lying in this room upon my mother's old double bed and blue spread, crying. How often had I done that the first year I moved to Bradleyville? How far I'd come since then! Things had finally begun to improve for me after "The Dream."

I shifted my position on the bed, folding my hands across my stomach. If I closed my eyes and concentrated, I could still relive that dream, feel the very aura of it, even though it had been more than seven years ago. It had been so real and so breathtaking in significance that it had shaken me from my grief-obsessed existence, redefining my life.

April 11: that was the night of my dream. It had been ten months since my mother's death. I still couldn't seem to grasp hold of myself. It was as if I were drifting—a lone, lost boat on a rocky sea. My conversation earlier that year with Pastor Frasier still haunted me. Even though I knew he was wrong and even though I found it hard to forgive him his words, something about them plagued me—a small, disconcerting voice whispering within me.

I was losing weight, yet did not care to eat; was tired, yet night-mares of my mother's death still nipped at the heels of sleep. Then in April, I dreamed of her. I dreamed I was sitting in church, listening to Pastor Frasier preach. Suddenly, the sanctuary disappeared, and I was alone on the pew in the middle of a vast, daisy-strewn field. The night was warm and moonlit, a hint of breeze lifting a strand of my hair. I felt light, trembling with anticipation for I knew not what. And then in the distance I saw my mother moving toward me. She seemed to float more than walk, although I sensed her legs gliding under her robe of palest blue. Moonlight spilled upon the filmy fabric that billowed out from her, and her very skin gleamed pearl-white. She was beautiful beyond words.

"*Mom!*" I cried, leaping to my feet and running to meet her. Grass and knolls moved beneath my feet, yet her image grew no closer. "Mom!" I cried again, straining for her, stretching out my arms as I ran until I thought they would pull from their sockets.

"No, Jessie!" she called. "It's all right."

Her voice, just as I remembered it, drifted over me with chiffon lightness, the color of sunrise. An ancient knowledge seemed to ride on her breath, which was translucently visible in the moon-light. It slowed my running feet, that knowledge, weighting me with a tingling as it settled over my head and shoulders.

"You're an angel," I said softly, knowing she would hear.

"Yes," she replied. "Your guardian angel. I watch over you."

I gazed at her, dumbstruck by the misty effluvium of awareness flowing between us. I remember raising my hand and watching it strand itself silkily through my fingers. "What should I do?" I asked lamely, feeling so basely *human.*

"Follow in my footsteps." The words glimmered through my hearing.

A whisper of disquiet trailed through my head. "What if some-one says I'm wrong?"

She smiled, and her lips shone, sending darts of light that hit me in the chest. My knees weakened at the sensation, my throat tightening with love for her. "I've shown you the truth; you need not heed others." Her first words rolled straight toward me, but the last undulated, weakening in sound.

"No, wait!" I shouted, even as she began to shimmer, her image breaking up to reveal patches of night sky behind her. *"Waaaait!"* I screamed in desperation.

Her final expression streamed with compassion and love. "I'm watching over you," she uttered, her robes rising to enfold her until her image melted and was gone.

I reached out for her and felt the weight of my arm, the incredible force required to lift it. It fell heavily, and bedcovers smoothed against my skin. My eyes blinked open in a darkened room, confusion filling my mind. My heart was beating hard enough to raise the blanket; my limbs trembled. When I realized I'd had a dream and understood its life-changing significance, my brain scrambled to recapture every image, every nuance. I could forget nothing, overlook nothing. Hardly daring to breathe, I relived the dream again and again, reveling in its beauty, feeling a lightheartedness that I had not known could exist. The judgmental words of Pastor Frasier crumbled away, and my soul seemed to rise in freedom. My mother *was* right. I *knew* she was right! Not even death had stopped her from calming my doubts. For as surely as I lived, she had appeared to me in that dream. It had been too captivating, too *real*, not to be so.

I did not sleep the rest of that night.

The next morning, a Saturday, I arose early, excited to tell my aunt and uncle what had happened. I related it all as we sat in the living room, tripping over words vastly unworthy of capturing the frothing essence of the dream. Neither uttered a sound until I was through. I took a hurried breath as I awaited their response, assuming their joy for me.

"Oh, my, no," Aunt Eva blurted from the couch, bringing a freckled hand to her cheek. "God's Truth lies only in Jesus. Satan has deceived you, chil'."

I stared at her in disbelief. *"What?"*

Uncle Frank spread his fingers over her hand, warning her to keep quiet. Their eyes met and held.

"What do you *mean*, Aunt Eva?" I could feel the heat rising to my face, my breath becoming shallow and rapid amid the anger. I'd never argued with her before; even in my lowest moments of frustration and loss I'd simply retreated to my room. But this was too much. How could she possibly call this wonderful vision of my mother something from *Satan?*

Uncle Frank's hand remained firmly on top of hers. I knew she was dying to answer me; I could practically see the words spilling out of her mouth. But she held her tongue.

"The dream you had," Uncle Frank said slowly, "it was wonderful for you because you saw your mother, whom you've missed so much. We understand that, Jessie. I know if I or your aunt had dreamed a seein' Henry after he died, we'd feel the same way. So we don't want to take that away from you. Our . . . concern is over what your mama said to you. I don't know anything 'bout interpretin' dreams, but I do think it's significant that you were first in church, listenin' to the pastor. I know your conversation with him has weighed heavy on your heart these past three months. I know that's been difficult for you, Jessie, but Eva and I believe that weight is from the Lord. He's been tryin' to talk to you."

"If he's been trying to talk to me, he did it through my mom last night," I interrupted. "He must have sent her to me." I searched his face, pleading for agreement.

Uncle Frank glanced at the carpet, his face drawn. I could tell he was struggling with an answer that he knew I did not want to hear. A sudden urge to get up and walk away spun through me. I would not let them spoil my dream for me, I would *not*. Just as suddenly, the urge to leave was replaced by the desire to make them understand. My mother's appearing to me was so important that I knew it would change my life. Already, I felt quickened, instilled with an energy I hadn't experienced for months. For the first time since my mother's death, I felt I had a purpose, even though I wasn't yet sure exactly what form it would take. I sensed my mother's words had set me in the proper direction, and now I was to take them to heart, use them to chart my course. The difference between this new feeling inside me and the aimlessness I had felt just twenty-four hours ago was immense. My aunt and uncle had worked so hard to help me find my footing. They needed to see that now I'd discovered it.

"Jessie," Uncle Frank replied, "please hear me. I won't tell you that your mama's words—and your entire dream—wasn't sent by God. I will ask you this crucial question. *If* you believed that the message you heard in that dream—even though it came from your mama—was opposite of what God would tell you, would you still want to heed it?"

I was nonplused. "But I know it's not, so—"

"All right, Jessie, but that's not what I'm askin' you. So just set that belief aside for a minute. What I'm really askin' you is, if your mama and God told you very different things, who would you follow?"

No answer arose in my mind, for I couldn't imagine it.

"Honey, can't you see—" Aunt Eva burst.

"Wait a minute now, Eva," my uncle shushed her. She pressed her lips together, agitation spilling off her shoulders.

"Jessie, let's leave it at this. We're glad for you that this dream has helped you feel better. You know we want you to go on with your life and be happy. And I know that deep inside, you long to know God. He has placed that desire within you. So I offer you a challenge. If you really want to know him and know how your mama's words fit with his direction for your life, read the Bible. That's the book that tells you all about him. I mean read it cover-to-cover. That's the only way you can see the whole picture—how God made the world, how man fell into sin, and how God provided a way of redemption through his Son. Read the Bible and ask God to open your eyes to its truths. Then, Jessie, *test the words* you heard in your dream against what the Bible says. If those words lead you to do what God commands through his Word, then you can know they are from him. But if they do not," Uncle Frank paused, "then you should not heed them, no matter *what* the source." He regarded me with a sad little smile, and I saw the depth of his love for me in his eyes. "Can you understand this?"

I nodded, unable to speak.

"Will you do it?"

"I'll try," I said tightly.

He rose from the couch to hug me. "Good."

"But I don't want to talk about it anymore, okay?" My throat hurt; I was afraid I would start to cry. "I mean, I know you both love me, and I know what your beliefs are, and, well, when you don't agree with me about this, it's hard for me. Because this is the best thing that's happened to me for almost a year, and it hurts not to have you understand."

"We do understand it, Jessie; we do," Uncle Frank responded. "And we will let you be. Just . . . read the Bible, like you promised. And we won't talk about it anymore." His mouth curved the slightest bit. "But you can't stop us from prayin'."

Somehow, I'd managed my own hint of a smile. "I don't think ten tons of horses could stop you from that."

Since that day, my aunt and uncle had not mentioned my dream directly, yet many times Aunt Eva's mouth had opened only to be snapped shut. The two were quite free with talking about Jesus Christ in their lives and living in the center of his will, but they didn't preach at me. After a while I was able to kid them lightly about my faith, reminding them that at least I went to church every Sunday, and Lord knew, I heard enough preaching there from Pastor Frasier. As for my end of the deal, I hadn't been quite as faithful. I started to read through the Bible with the best of intentions, really I did. But the laws in Leviticus were so boring, and then I couldn't understand God's supposed judgment through all the wars. So much bloodshed. It offended my pacifist beliefs. So I skipped to the New Testament and read about Jesus and how much he talked about helping the poor and doing what was right. He'd even told one man who'd asked him how to get to heaven to sell all he had and give it to the poor. That sounded relevant to me. Other things that I didn't understand, I simply discarded as well. All in all, I didn't find anything that told me my mother's command to follow in her footsteps had been wrong. Seemed to me I was living a good life, and that's all I needed to do. As for Aunt Eva's talk about "giving my life to Christ," well, that was *her* way to God. I respected that for her, but didn't want it pushed upon me. At any rate, after reading the four Gospels, I figured I'd read enough and quit.

Blinking away the memories, I slowly arose from the bed. I'd wasted enough time and still had unpacking to do. Thank goodness Aunt Eva, who was usually so chatty whenever I first arrived home, was enough in a dither over the sawmill situation to leave me alone. She and Uncle Frank had said they were going to retire to their room early to pray for Thomas's meeting with Blair Riddum, which he hoped would occur tomorrow, on Saturday. I figured it wouldn't hurt to say my own little prayer to my guardian angel. If Thomas could put an end to this problem quickly, I'd enjoy the restful two months in Bradleyville that I so needed.

chapter 7

*T*he following morning, across town, two middle-aged women stood in a sweltering kitchen, canning green beans. Tackling the task together made the hot work more enjoyable, and the opportunity to gossip was just too good to pass up.

"You hear Jessie Callum's back in town? Got here yesterday."

"Eva must be happy."

"Sorta sad too. 'Cause once she leaves again, it'll be for good." The woman stood at her sink, expertly popping beans as her eyes wandered occasionally over the rolling farmland out the window. In the distance, formidable and smoky blue, rose the Appalachians.

"I like Jessie. So dainty and sweet."

"And one strong girl, after all she's been through." The woman glanced at her neighbor, who was carefully placing canning jars and lids into boiling water with a long pair of tongs, face shiny over the heat. Steam wafted from the stove and hung like a damp, hot cloud, making both women sweat. "She got that job she wanted, you know. Plus she's bound and determined to volunteer in that poorhouse where her mama worked her fingers to the bone. Least that's what Eva tol' me."

"Well, Jessie's always wanted to go back to Cincinnati, anyway."

"I know. I suppose we should be happy for her; she's come a long way. I do feel sorry for Eva and Frank though. Havin' to see her leave Bradleyville for good, an' all."

Her friend laughed. "If I know Eva, she's schemin' already to keep that girl in town."

chapter 8

Aunt Eva stuck her head around my bedroom door. "Well, Jessie, it's time for some visitin', what do ya say?"

I straightened up from making my bed. "Good grief, I only got here last night."

"And this is Saturday," she responded. "Everybody's home from work. People know you're here. They'll be expectin' to see you."

"Oh, brother." Under Aunt Eva's persistence, I knew claiming fatigue would get me nowhere. But I really didn't want to see anyone just yet. Thomas had managed to schedule a meeting with Blair Riddum that morning, and according to Aunt Eva, who'd probably been on the phone since dawn, the town was holding its collective breath. It felt as though a cloud of doom had descended. I did not relish the thought of conversations about the sawmill problems.

"Don't you want to wait by the phone to hear what happens?" I asked.

"Oh, heavens, no!" My aunt fluttered a hand in the air. "Sittin' around and waitin' will drive me plumb crazy. Look at your uncle—he rode into Albertsville with a neighbor, sayin' he had to go to the big hardware store. Pshaw. He doesn't need anything he can't get right here in town; he's just full a worry and had to find somethin' to do."

"He didn't look all that worried."

She plopped onto my bed with a sigh. "You don't know your uncle as well's I do. He always *looks* calm, but he's worried, all right." Automatically, she leaned aside to fluff up my pillow. "And so am I, which is why I got to keep busy too." The pillow still wasn't quite right, so she punched it twice with her fist as she continued. "That's why I thought you and I could go see some folks."

A vague irritation washed over me. "Who do you want to visit?"

Her face brightened, the pillow forgotten. I could almost hear the wheels turning in her head as she geared up for my social re-entrance into Bradleyville society. "Let's see. You must drop in on Estelle Matthews. Little Celia's dyin' to see you again; it's been since Easter. And you haven't seen baby Kevin yet. 'Course," she tapped her cheek, "that requires takin' a present, so we'll have to stop by the dime store."

What a natural she was, I thought. Undeniably in line with social etiquette. But I knew her too well. Time it right, she knew, and we'd hit the Matthews's house just about when Thomas arrived home from his meeting. She'd be the first to hear. The Matthews's was the *last* house I wanted to be in that morning.

"And you know who else?" she continued. "You need to get over to the Hardings' and see Lee's sister, Connie; you remember her. Poor thing—not six weeks from her due date and without a husband. I'd say she's well rid a any man who'd run off with a neighbor girl, but she still pines for him. She's what, two years younger than you? I'm sure she could use a friend."

Lee's house. A second hidden agenda—and the other household directly involved with the mill situation. For an irrational moment I pictured myself retorting to Aunt Eva that I wanted no part in her machinations. But, of course, I couldn't say that. "I don't know. I thought I'd pick a pattern to start making a dress."

"Well, you need to go to the store then anyhow. You can see what the dime store right here's got, maybe avoid a trip to Albertsville." She glanced at her watch. "Come on, we can manage to visit both families if we get a move-on."

My eyes closed. "What do you think will happen in the meeting?"

She regarded me, her expression changing. "You're worried 'bout this too, aren't you?"

I lifted a shoulder.

"Well, honey, don't worry too much. Everybody listens to Thomas, you know that. Even Blair Riddum."

"I suppose you're right."

She smiled, then eyed me critically. "You certainly have lovely skin. And that high-cheeked face a yours has always been perfect. But perhaps you ought to comb your hair, put on a touch of lipstick. Lee might be home, you know. I'll fetch my purse."

I rolled my eyes as she flitted happily out my bedroom door.

We were at the dime store before 9:30, waiting for Gladys Winchet to arrive and unlock its doors. At 10:00 I was still dallying in the baby section, an impatient Aunt Eva at my side. I was vacillating between choosing an infant sleeper or a soft green blanket for Connie's baby. A sweet blue and white outfit for Kevin Matthews was already tucked under my arm. Finally I chose the sleeper.

"Jessie, you must tell me all about your graduation!" Gladys Winchet exclaimed as we paid for the presents. To Aunt Eva, she whispered, "Heared anything yet?"

Aunt Eva shook her head, but importantly informed Miss Gladys, "We're on our way over to the Matthews's right now."

Numerous people stopped us, hailing me with effusion and pumping my aunt for information. I was glad to see the townsfolk again, that familiar Bradleyville stability washing over me like warm rain. But the constant invitations to chat, normally welcomed by my aunt, were now driving her to near frenzy as she shooed me out the door and back into her old tan Buick. "Gracious," she exclaimed, hefting her purse onto the seat, "it'll be a wonder if we ever get off Main Street!"

We stopped at home to wrap the gifts. When we finally arrived at the Matthews's, Thomas was still at his meeting. Not a good sign, but none of us wanted to say so. Miss Estelle and William Matthews greeted me warmly, while six-year-old Celia threw her arms around me in unabashed adoration. Celia was a striking child—blond-haired, serious beyond her years. At times, she carried an air of sadness that I could not quite define.

"Celia," I said, pointing out the front window, "did you make all those designs out there?" Aunt Eva and I had been amazed at the chalked artwork on the front sidewalk. Almost every inch of it was covered in multihued hearts and flowers.

She stilled. "Yes."

"They're absolutely beautiful! Are they for something special?"

Her eyes slid away from mine. "I colored it for Mama when she brought Kevy home from the hospital. It was a present."

I ran my fingers over her hair, feeling its silkiness. "You must have worked a long time. I'll bet your mama really liked it."

"Mmm hmm," she replied distractedly. "Want to see my brother?"

Proudly, she showed me baby Kevin, sleeping in a small crib in his mother's room, one tiny fist against his cheek. Back in the living room, she clamored to open my gift herself, already pulling at the ribbon on the brightly wrapped box.

"Celia!" Miss Estelle's voice was sharp. "Mind your manners or go to your room." Purposely, she took her time unwrapping the gift, ignoring Celia's impatient jiggling. "Oh, Jessie, it's so sweet." Her fingers smoothed over the blue and white summer outfit. "He can wear it to church tomorrow."

Miss Estelle was a pretty woman, with light brown hair and satin skin. Her features may have been delicate, but an undeniable strength resonated beneath those smooth pores. She donned herself in simple dresses, her hair in a bun, but no doubt about it, she wore the pants in the Matthews family. Her control extended over her family's speech; no bad grammar allowed. Her husband worked as an accountant in Albertsville and was one of the nicest, quietest men I'd ever met, often holding up his hands in mellow contrition when Miss Estelle decided he'd overstepped his bounds. I often thought she reined her husband in so sternly to make up for the fact that she could do nothing to stop her father's shenanigans or his war stories, which he loved to recount. Not to mention that Thomas spoke like any other long-time resident of Bradleyville and was proud of it.

Aunt Eva settled herself on a small love seat as if she were there to stay. Miss Estelle and Mr. Matthews sat in their respective armchairs. Celia cuddled next to me on the couch.

"Jessie, have you found a place to live yet?" Mr. Matthews asked.

"Yes." Absentmindedly, I smoothed Celia's hair. "It's a great one-bedroom apartment in a large complex with a pool. Not too far from my job. I can move in August first, so I'll have two weeks to settle in before I start working."

"Good, good. Will you be back in your old neighborhood?"

"Close to it."

He nodded thoughtfully. Aunt Eva and Miss Estelle exchanged a glance. "No boyfriends hanging in the wings?" he asked.

The inevitable question. I was an old maid by Bradleyville standards. Typically, the town's young men and women linked up in high school, adhering to strict rules that allowed actual dates only after girls turned seventeen. After graduation, there was always a rush of weddings. Within a year or two most of the brides had babies, their eyes suddenly opened to the wary protection of their own mothers, their minds already calculating future enforcement of the dating rules they'd so hated.

"I didn't have time to go out much," I replied.

I answered more questions and posed a few polite ones of my own. Miss Estelle and my aunt took turns surreptitiously watching a clock hanging over the mantel as the hands inched toward noon.

"My, it's lunch time," Aunt Eva finally burst. "Where is that Thomas? Got me worried sick, bein' gone so long."

"I'm beginning to wonder myself," Mr. Matthews replied.

"Well, at least your family wouldn't be touched by a strike." Aunt Eva patted her hair distractedly. "I can't stand to think a Frank in the middle of it."

"Of course we'd be affected." Miss Estelle's tone held an edge. "You think Dad would keep out of it, with his grandiosity? Look at him already."

"Thomas has a good head on his shoulders," William put in mildly. "He'd know what to do."

Miss Estelle closed her eyes. "That's what I'm afraid of."

"Well, there *won't* be a strike," Aunt Eva insisted, waving an arm. "God forgive the first man who even spoke the word. Imagine what could happen to this town. Men fightin', families without a paycheck. It would be awful, just awful. I can hardly sleep at night, thinkin' 'bout it." She craned her neck, looking through the front window. "Where is that man, anyway?"

Not until we were nearly finished eating did Thomas return, the tires of his son-in-law's car crunching over loose pebbles in the driveway. He mounted the back stairs and entered the kitchen wearily, removing his brown felt hat to run stubby fingers through his white hair. Our questions were silent, displayed in Miss Estelle's worried eyes, the halt of a sandwich halfway to Aunt Eva's mouth. He nodded at me and winked but did not smile. Leaning against the kitchen counter, he swiped at his forehead with an arm.

"Got any more a that iced tea?"

"Sure, Dad, I'll get it." Miss Estelle moved with efficient grace.

Thomas took his time pulling out a chair, its wooden legs softly scraping across the linoleum floor. He swigged the tea, placed his glass on the table with a *click*. "Well." He stuck his tongue between his teeth and upper lip. "Riddum said, 'No.'"

chapter 9

I shot you; you're dead!"

"Did not!"

"Did too!"

"Hush up you two, you'll wake up yer little sister. Go outside and kill each other in the yard."

"Yessir."

Two small pairs of boot-clad feet rat-tatted across the bare wood floor and down the porch steps. "Lord love 'em," their father whispered to himself, turning his beefy face toward the clock. A fly buzzed his head, and he swatted at it with impatience, registering the clink of dishes as his young wife cleaned up after lunch. One-twenty and no word yet. He shot a disapproving look at the telephone as if it were to blame, and, by providence, it rang. Crossing the room in four strides, he snatched up the receiver. Sounds from the kitchen ceased.

"Yeah."

"Riddum said no deal."

His lips exploded air. "Why?"

"Said the money ain't there; he cain't spend what he ain't got."

"He ain't got it 'cause it's sittin' in that fancy new porch a his."

"Yep." The voice on the line was heavy. "Lee said Thomas just called; he's been out there all this time."

The man glanced up to see his wife standing in the doorway, hands bunching her apron. "Oh, Lord," he breathed, "what're we gonna do now."

chapter 10

The specter of bad news dangling from her like the handbag over her arm, Aunt Eva was undeterred from her plans for our next visit. Uncle Frank had not returned from Albertsville, this determined by her placing a phone call home. "We'd better go ahead and see the Hardings," she said grimly, pulling her car away from the Matthews's house. "They'll need the encouragement."

I just wanted to go home. I also wanted to tell Blair Riddum off.

She glanced at me as we stopped at the light on the corner of Minton and Main. "Lee's a good man," she said, as if I'd spoken against him. "Probably five, six years older'n you. He was livin' in Albertsville till last year, when his mama had that fall. Came back here to take care a her. Blair Riddum snapped him right up for the mill, strong as he is. And in just that short a time, he's become a real leader down there; that's what your uncle says."

I watched the post office glide by through her window. Two elderly men were sitting on the bench out front under the shade of an oak. "I don't like Uncle Frank being caught between the men and his boss."

She nodded. "I still think things'll work out somehow. We're prayin' mighty hard, you know. Have been ever since the troubles began. Besides, you know how it is here. People hash out their problems and get on with their business."

I rested my cheek against a fist and closed my eyes, hoping she was right.

Looking back on it, I'd say the die between Lee Harding and me was cast that warm June afternoon. He was wearing worn jeans and a blue short-sleeved work shirt as his oversized hand held open his screen door. Seeing me behind my aunt, he remolded his expression from distraction to pleasure. "Come in," he said as a phone began to ring.

Giving no recognition to the auspicious timing of our arrival, Aunt Eva waved him to answer it and leaned over to peck his mother on the cheek. "Now don't get up," she clucked, inquiring with forced cheerfulness about Wilma Harding's hip and insisting that the woman soon would be running around the block. Miss Wilma was tall and stocky, iron gray hair pulled to the nape of her neck. Her eyes were dark, like Lee's. A black metal cane leaned against her chair. She had a no-nonsense air about her, a radiating strength that made her seem larger than life. When I was younger, I'd found her intimidating.

Lee's sister, Connie, waddled in, one hand self-consciously resting on her huge abdomen. She, too, was big-built, with long black hair and brown eyes. Her skin was tanned, her cheeks rouged with heat. I had not seen her in a few years and had known her only nominally in high school. "Hi, Connie," I said, taking her hand. "It's so good to see you again. I brought you a little something for the baby."

"Oh," she exclaimed, her eyes moistening. "You shouldn't have."

I glanced meaningfully at her stomach with a grin. "Looks like it's about time you were gathering things."

"Guess you're right." Her gaze fell to the floor. I stood before her awkwardly, wondering if I'd offended her.

"Come, Connie," her mother prompted. "Sit down and open your gift."

With a shy glance at me, Connie huffed to the couch and fell into it gracelessly. We all watched as she opened the present, being careful to save the paper. I could hear Lee's low voice from around the corner.

"Thank you so much," she said softly, holding up the sleeper for her mother to see. "It's so cute—" Her words cut off abruptly, and she gazed at the sleeper, rubbing it with a thumb. We all waited for her to continue. When she didn't, Aunt Eva, Miss Wilma, and I exchanged glances and stilted smiles.

Fortunately, Aunt Eva found something to say. As she and Miss Wilma chatted, I listened half-heartedly. Looking around the simply furnished Harding house, I felt a twinge of guilt at my self-preoccupation in regard to the problems at the sawmill. The morning's disappointment merely threatened my quiet summer, but their livelihood depended on Lee's paycheck. Both Miss Wilma and Connie could barely move. What's more, they both were alone in their own way, one widowed, one abandoned. Given the circumstances, I thought, the bundle of unborn life sending a flush to Connie's pudgy cheeks could be more a source of fear than joy.

Lee had snatched up the phone and carried it into the kitchen, its long cord trailing to an outlet beside the chair in which I sat. His muffled voice continued to drone through the wall. "He's been on that phone ever since Thomas called," his mother was saying to Aunt Eva. "Phones ringin', tongues flyin' all over town. Somehow he's got hisself smack in the middle. But that was always Lee. Tryin' to fix everything, you know." She looked pointedly at me. "Speakin' a fixin', he'll have to show you out yonder. Another month or so and he'll have the addition for Connie and the baby done. We kept tellin' him, 'you don't got to do that,' but he insisted, sayin' a child's got to have room to grow."

I glanced at Aunt Eva, but she was the picture of innocence. All the same, I saw right through their none-too-subtle scheming. When Lee reappeared with the phone cradled in his palm, his mother flicked a casual hand in my direction. "Our guest would like to see your handiwork; why don't ya show her."

"Uh, sure," he said. His mother's intentions were equally obvious to him, and, sensing his embarrassment, I hesitated.

Aunt Eva shot me a look. "Well, go on, you two." Then, with purpose, she turned her back on me, asking Miss Wilma about the neighbor's gall bladder operation, and what would that woman and her husband do if things went poorly at the mill. Smiling weakly at Lee, I allowed myself to be ushered out of the room.

Holding my elbows, I walked with him through Connie's small bedroom, feeling awkward at the ambient intimacy. The room was cluttered with clothes, cloth diapers, and a few bright toys, awaiting small hands. "Crowded, huh." Lee pointed to an unpainted door, still smelling of freshly cut wood. "I'm addin' on here." I muttered my approval. "It'll lead to a nursery and a play-room. I got the frame up but it's not Sheetrocked yet." He opened the door and we stepped into sunlight, Aunt Eva's chatter fading away. "Mama's excited 'bout a grandbaby," he smiled, "but like most older folk, she needs her quiet. This should keep both her and Connie happy."

"I'm sure it will." I leaned against the bare frame and looked around, searching for something else to say. Lee found a hammer on the floor and tossed it into a cardboard box.

"How long you stayin' in town?"

"Till the first of August."

"What then?"

I told him my plans.

He scooted the box with his foot, kicking up dust. "I'll bet you're sorry you came back to Bradleyville."

His perception surprised me. "No. Not sorry for me. Just . . . sorry for all the trouble people are facing."

"Yeah. Well." In the distance, I heard the phone ring. Lee dragged a hand across his forehead and smiled at me ruefully. The barest of dimples shadowed his right cheek. "I'll let Mom get that."

"My uncle doesn't even know how the meeting turned out. He's still not home yet."

"Yeah, he is. That was him callin' when you arrived. I told him y'all were here."

"Oh! What does he say? What do *you* say?"

He watched a robin land on a nearby phone wire, cocking its head at us with curiosity. "I say 'no' doesn't mean forever. We got to keep dialogue open with Riddum and at the same time keep tempers in check. Includin' mine. It's not just the money anymore; it's the way he treats us. If he showed us more respect, maybe we could handle the lack of a raise. For the second time."

"And if he doesn't?"

"Things could get ugly."

"Is that what you want?"

Irritation flitted across his face. "'Course it's not what I want. It's not what anyone wants. But I got a lot to think about. My mother and sister on one hand and a bunch a angry men on the other."

A protectiveness for my own family rose within me. "What about my uncle caught in the middle? He's your manager, but he's friends with you all. He doesn't need to be dragged into trouble. In five years he could be retiring, and he'll need his pension."

Lee's gaze was steady. "I'll do everything I can," he said in measured tone, "to keep from *draggin'* Frank into trouble. Okay?"

I started to apologize for my unaccountable rudeness, but the words wouldn't come. Fact was, Uncle Frank *did* have more to lose than Lee. At his age, he'd have a much harder time finding another job. "Okay then." My voice was not as contrite as I would have hoped.

The phone rang again. I pictured his mother answering while exchanging a wink with Aunt Eva over our taking so long. Lee let out a long breath. "I suppose we oughta get back. Sounds like I got more talkin' to do."

"Good luck," I smiled. We stepped back into the house.

On the short trip home, Aunt Eva asked me no less than three times what I thought of Lee Harding.

chapter 11

The Bradleyville I knew had been so predictable. Summer's hot humidity usually descended in June, and by July it was a smothering woolen blanket. Luckier folks had an air conditioner set in one central house window that struggled to blow cooler air into back bedrooms. Most of the businesses downtown were air-conditioned except for the Laundromat, whose machines emanated heat of their own. When I was in high school, Bradleyville summers had beat a steady, torpid rhythm: old folks jawing in chairs under the Tull's Drugstore awning, kids at play, men working the sawmill, mothers choosing ice cream with their little ones at the IGA.

But the week following "Riddum's No," as it was quickly dubbed, seemed anything but predictable. On one level, life went on. The Baptist church had their first summer potluck. The hardware store announced a sale on small tools. Mothers changed their babies' diapers on the Laundromat's long folding table as clothes rumbled dry. Thomas and his two cronies, Jake Lewellyn and Hank Jenkins, lounged daily in their respective chairs outside Tull's, sipping on shakes. Women still canned vegetables and fruits; and children, oblivious to the heat, still played kickball on the school playground. Yet beneath the rhythm of everyday life beat a steady, vague dread, like the sound of distant warning drums. I was deeply affected and skittish. If I had known then what was to come, I never would have stayed.

Aunt Eva and Uncle Frank continued to pray for a quick resolution. Sometimes I prayed also—to my guardian angel. Since my dream, I had come to think of my mother as my special intercessor to God.

To keep my mind off the mill situation, I prepared for my move to Cincinnati with dogged intent. Twice, I drove to Albertsville's large fabric store to choose patterns and fabric for my career dresses. As I sewed, I mentally arranged my mother's old bedroom furniture, which was now mine, in my new apartment. Her bedroom had been a light blue. I'd already asked the manager for permission to paint mine the same color. I also wrote Brenda Todd at the Center, telling her details of my graduation and how I looked forward to seeing her. She wrote back, exclaiming over the huge, gleaming kitchen stove that had recently been donated. "You won't believe how much soup we can cook at once!" she added. She told me of two new families in particular who were there— the Westons, whose little boy was crippled with spina bifida, and the Hedingers, who had four children and no skills for employment. My heart went out to them all.

I also talked a couple of times on the phone with Edna Slate, the social worker I was to replace on September first. She was leaving the department to have her baby and did not plan to return. "Be prepared to work hard," she warned me. "You're starting August fifteenth; that only gives me two weeks to get you up to speed. I'm carrying a huge case load, and you'll have to become familiar with them all in that space of time." I knew that meant becoming acquainted with more misery. Children without parents, children abused, families in crisis. Sometimes my mind reeled, just thinking about it all. There was so much misery in the world. I knew I was to follow in my mother's footsteps and do my part, but whatever I could do seemed so minute. I'd find myself thinking in such terms, then try to shake myself out of it. I hadn't even started working or volunteering yet, and already I felt overwhelmed. No wonder my mother had said she could never do enough. I was beginning to understand the look of despair that had crossed her face as she drove away from me that Saturday.

As I busily planned my life "after Bradleyville," I tried not to think too much about the sawmill. That problem was too close to home, too frightening, and I didn't want to be caught up in it. Through Hope Center or my job, I was ready to deal with the hopelessness of men who'd lost their employment. But I couldn't begin to imagine half the families in Bradleyville facing the same terrible issue.

Meanwhile, all around me, the town rumbled.

A course-changing event in one's life, as I well knew, could happen in the space of minutes. Or it could form slowly, a primitive webbing splaying into fingers of discontent, a minuscule trail hardening into the sinewed spine of resentment. So it was with the mill workers as the heat-soaked days after "Riddum's No" marched on. Blair Riddum had added insult to injury by telling Thomas that his employees were lazy and were to blame for the "poor annual earnings." Each day when Uncle Frank dragged home, reeking of sawdust and the malcontent of men, Aunt Eva and I heard the latest. At first the men vowed to work harder, hoping still to win Riddum over. But when teeth-gritting labor gave way to further unsafe practices and no softening of Riddum's ways, the men's resolve dwindled.

Like the rest of the town, I couldn't help slowing down on my way to Albertsville for a narrow-eyed glance down the long driveway leading to Blair Riddum's newly remodeled house.

Midway through June, mill employees, cleaned up and suppered, began to gather at our home to vent their frustrations. Lee Harding was always among them. Uncle Frank, with his widebrowed face that radiated honesty and good sense, would listen attentively, displaying concern while calming bubbling reactions. Lee, too, I was pleased to hear, advocated constraint. There was a sense among the men—and the whole town, for that matter—that *something* would give, for like soup simmering in a too-small pot, a boil-over was inevitable. Everyone still prayed that Blair Riddum would back off his criticism and sanction a raise. Even a token one would soothe many ruffled feathers.

During those meetings Aunt Eva would serve cake or cookies and iced tea. Bustling about refilling glasses and plates afforded her presence the perfect *raison d'être*. I selfishly sat in my bedroom, telling myself I didn't want to hear it, but with the door wide open. Like it or not, for Uncle Frank's sake I wanted to make sure Lee kept his promise. A few times I'd answered the door when he had arrived, and we'd eyed each other until he nodded in response to my unspoken reminder.

Things became more heated once Al Bledger started showing up. And about that time Aunt Eva asked me to help her serve.

Mr. Bledger was short and wiry, with his hair shaved almost Marine-style. His eyes were steel gray, and his full lips turned down. What he lacked in size, he made up for in mouth.

"I don't know 'bout the rest of y'all," he declared one Thursday evening, "but I ain't takin' much more a this. And neither am I leavin'. I been at that mill since high school, some twenty years, long afore Riddum come along. He don't scare me none. And there's a good four or five other men I know feel the same way. I say we all band together and tell him to put out or we *git* out."

"So he says take a hike," Lee challenged. "Then what?"

"Then we take one."

"And who's gonna put food on our tables?" someone asked.

"We won't be outta work that long," Bledger insisted. "What's Riddum gonna do? He don't meet our demands, he'll be losing a lot more money than we will."

"He can probably afford it longer than we can," Uncle Frank commented.

Numerous voices spoke at once, increasing in volume until Lee shouted them down. "Wait a minute! I been sayin' again and again we cain't make a move like that without bein' willin' to face the worst. 'Cause once we're in it, we ain't gonna want to back down. So, Al, are you willin' to stay outta work for weeks if Riddum digs in his heels?"

"If I have to. But I still think he'll come around right quick."

"What if he brings in new workers?"

"He ain't gonna get three hundred workers overnight."

"There's plenty a unemployed men in Albertsville who'd be happy to drive down here to work," Ned Finks said. "My brother-in-law's out of a job. Said he'd take mine in a minute. 'Course I'd strangle him first."

"Albertsville would laugh itself silly," Tom Elkin said disgustedly. "They been thumbin' their noses at us for years. They know our mill dies, so does Bradleyville. They'd probably quit their jobs just to take ours."

"Oh, that ain't true," the man sitting next to Mr. Elkin declared, and voices rose again as neighbor argued with neighbor.

"You gotta be ready for the *worst!*" Lee hit a fist into his palm. "Who's willin' to fight to keep the mill shut down? Talk about disruptin' the town—we'd have *state police* down here. Who's willin' to take that?" He glanced around, arms extended. "'Cause if you ain't, you better not make the first move."

"Ah, you think too much," Bledger said in disgust. "That ain't gonna happen. What *is* gonna happen if we do nothin' is we keep on just like this, with Riddum treatin' us like dirt for little pay. Is that what *you* want?"

"Thomas is still tryin' to negotiate," Lee said. "Riddum knows we're havin' these meetin's; he's bound to be gittin' anxious."

"What's he got to be anxious about; we ain't *doin'* nothin'!"

As arguments popped up again, I watched Uncle Frank. He could have dominated the meeting. Instead he stood away from the crowd, arms crossed, watching—looking so tired. His lips moved silently, and I knew he was praying. Aunt Eva was fanning her face with a napkin and shook her head at me when our eyes met. Six weeks, I thought, and I'll be away from all this.

After the other men finally drifted home, still arguing, Lee lingered to talk with Uncle Frank. As Aunt Eva ran hot water in the kitchen sink, I collected plates and forks.

"We can't keep a lid on this thing for much longer," Uncle Frank sighed. "Maybe you and I need to join Thomas for another talk with Riddum."

"You worried what that might do to your job?"

"No. But I do wonder what I'd do if things came to a head. He ain't treatin' me all that poorly, and I ain't got that many years left at the mill. Personally, I could ride things out and be okay financially."

Lee and I exchanged a look. He made no comment. "I think you're right 'bout us seein' Riddum," he said finally. "Let's talk to him tomorrow after work. I don't know how much more Thomas can do anyway."

"Let's do it."

A fork slid from a plate I was holding, scattering white crumbs on the carpet. I frowned at it, my hands already full. "I'll get it." Lee stooped at my feet, picking up the fork and carefully plucking crumbs into his huge palm. He brushed them onto the stack of plates in my hand.

"Thank you," I said stiffly, feeling his closeness.

"Here, Jessie, I'll take 'em on in." Before I knew it, Uncle Frank had emptied my hands, leaving them with nothing to do. I clasped them in front of me.

"Well." Lee hesitated. "Better get goin'."

"I'll walk you out." It was the polite thing to do.

The night air met us with moist warmth. A moth was fluttering around the overhead light as I stepped onto the porch behind him, fingers on the door, not quite shut. "Thanks for trying so hard, Lee." It was the first time I'd called him by name, and he shrugged to cover his awareness.

"Well, I promised a young lady."

I couldn't help but smile. "I suppose you'll all be back tomorrow night. Which means I'll have to bake another cake."

"I guess," he sighed. "I got to start stayin' home, though; I'm not gettin' any work done on the house and Connie's due the end a July." He gazed absentmindedly down the street. "Maybe your uncle and I can get somethin' outta Riddum tomorrow."

"Maybe," I replied doubtfully. Pulling the door shut, I crossed my arms and leaned against it. "But exactly what do you expect? I mean, you should have a clear goal. Don't just give him more complaints or vague threats that the men are 'going to do something.'"

"I don't expect to walk outta there with a raise for everybody, if that's what you mean."

"That's not what I mean. It's just. . . . Look. You and all the other employees need a 'yes,' even if it's a small one. Just to turn the heat down for a while."

He raised his eyebrows, half amused. "And I suppose you have a suggestion?"

Absently, I watched the moth, thinking. I could feel Lee's eyes on me. "Maybe I do. How about this: why don't you tell him the men are talking about walking off their jobs if they don't get a raise. Ask him to reconsider over the next—six weeks—and to meet with you again August first. If he says no to that, he's an idiot, 'cause all he'd be doing is buying time."

"Uh-huh. And if he says no on August first?"

"Then you'll have to deal with it. But meantime, my uncle's had a rest and you've finished your house. And the workers have had time to really consider the consequences of a strike. And I can quit baking cakes."

He lifted his chin. "Pretty good. Smart fighter, you are."

I winced. "That's not exactly the word I would use."

"Which one? *Smart* or *fighter?*"

Annoyance flitted through me. "I don't believe in fighting, Lee. *Ever.* Okay?"

"Hey, I'm sorry; I was just givin' you a bad time." He held up a hand in contrition. "Anyway, I'll talk to your uncle about it tomorrow; sounds like a good idea to me. You'd still have to bake for at least tomorrow night. But wouldn't it be great if we had some good news to report."

I lingered on the porch as he walked to his truck. Climbing in, he flashed me a grin. "For your information," he called, "I'm partial to apple pie."

chapter 12

I baked all day, peeling apples and rolling out pie crusts. Taking one look at her wreck of a kitchen when she came home for lunch, Aunt Eva raised an eyebrow.

"Cakes or cookies are so much quicker. What you goin' to all this trouble for?"

Truth was, I couldn't answer, because I wasn't sure myself. Why on earth did I care what Lee Harding liked? I'd had only two conversations with the man, and both of them had ended somewhat testily. His cautious approach to the sawmill situation was encouraging, and he'd kept his promise to me concerning my uncle. All the same, there was something about Lee Harding that was almost frightening. Maybe it was just the fact that he loomed over me, or maybe it was those dark eyes under even darker eyebrows. But the aura of power he exuded was more than just physical; it was also the strength of an iron will. I could see why the men respected him. However, it seemed to me he was a man with a temper—if you hit him in the right spot. I sure wouldn't want to tangle with him.

"No big reason, Aunt Eva," I replied, mixing cinnamon and sugar. "Just that I've been sitting and sewing a lot, and I thought a few hours on my feet in the kitchen would be a nice change." The explanation sounded lame, even to my own ears.

"Hmm," she breathed, spreading mayonnaise on bread. "Must be nice to be young."

I stood at the counter, working pats of butter into flour with a pastry cutter. The white powder poofed out of the large glass bowl, making my nose itch. I turned my head and sneezed.

"Bless you."

"Thanks." I pressed the pastry cutter harder, working until my arm grew tired. Making pie crust was such a pain in the neck; I wished I'd never started. Aunt Eva was strangely silent, which only meant her thoughts were running a mile a minute. Without looking around, I felt her eyes boring into my back.

"You had a real good idea last night," she said. "Frank and Lee're gonna present it to Riddum after work today. Frank called the post office during his break and said don't pick him up after work; Lee'll bring him home."

My arm slowed for a second, then resumed its pace. For some reason, I didn't want to show my surprise at her knowledge. "Who told you it was my idea?"

"Lee told Frank," she replied, her mouth full of sandwich.

I pondered the piece of information. Lee could just as easily have taken the credit.

"You two must have had time to talk last night."

Her light tone spoke volumes. So that's what was on her mind. I pictured my conversation with Lee, wondering if Aunt Eva had heard his parting shot about apple pie through the kitchen window. One look at her face, and I'd know the answer. Surreptitiously, I glanced over my shoulder. In an expression only my aunt could attain, she managed to chew, grin, raise her eyebrows, and presume innocence all at the same time.

She'd heard it, all right.

I turned back to my flour mixture with a dignified sniff.

We were both on edge by the time Uncle Frank got home that evening. My pies lined the kitchen counter, the whole house smelling warmly of apples and cinnamon. I'd managed to get off my throbbing feet for half an hour, fanning my face as I lay upon the couch. Aunt Eva had begun pacing the minute she hit the door from work, every once in a while disappearing around the corner to stir her leftover homemade soup on the stove.

"Aunt Eva, you're making me crazy," I protested, laying an arm over my eyes.

"Can't help it." She picked up a magazine and thumbed through it, seeing nothing. "Word's gotten out they're seein' Riddum; you knew it would. So now the men're dyin' to know the answer, just like Thomas's meetin' a couple weeks ago. They'll be here in droves tonight."

"I made plenty of pies."

She tossed away the magazine. "For heaven's sake, Jessie, it's not that. Don't you understand? The men hear another 'no,' they'll be more upset than ever. With all the talk filterin' into the post office this afternoon, I almost called Frank back and said don't do it. It's too risky."

My arm fell away. I raised my head to look at her with alarm. "I never thought they'd be any the worse off for trying, even if the answer's 'no.'"

"Wake up, Jessie; where've you been every night? You've heard Al Bledger and Ken Beecham and the rest of that gang talk. They're stirrin' up the pot, and more men're joinin' 'em, pushin' for a strike. They're lookin' for any excuse."

I swung my feet to the floor, a prickle of fear rolling up my spine. How had my "good idea" soured so in one afternoon? The fickleness of hope and hopelessness roiling through the town bespoke an angst much deeper than I'd allowed myself to realize. I'd had my head in the clouds. So busy planning my life of service to others, I couldn't see my own family's—and town's—needs. I dropped my head in my hands, staring at the carpet. And this "idea" of mine—I had to admit it had been more for me than for the town. Six weeks would be just enough time to see me on my way to Cincinnati. Even if things fell apart then, I'd be long gone. It wouldn't be *my* concern.

Suddenly I was utterly sick with myself.

When we heard Lee Harding's truck pull up out front, we both trotted for the door. I made it to the porch first, frantically searching my uncle's face for a clue as he climbed out of the truck. Slamming the door shut, he caught sight of us both watching him like hawks. "Well, that's quite a welcome!" He grinned, and I realized I'd hardly seen him smile since I'd returned to Bradleyville. Relief washed over me like a clean spring rain.

"Riddum said 'yes,'" Aunt Eva uttered, leaning against the porch post for support. Uncle Frank strode up the steps.

"That he did. Thank God. Lee did all the talkin', and he was mighty persuasive. Riddum promised he'd look over the books and give us an answer August first. I hope things'll keep quiet until then. Evidently, even Riddum, stubborn mule that he is, saw the sense in givin' everyone time to cool off."

"Jessie!" Lee's voice rolled up the sidewalk over the chugging of his truck engine. He was leaning over the seat to look out the passenger window, his muscular left arm curved around the steering wheel. "Good goin'!"

Surprise flicked across my face. He'd done all the work; why should he congratulate me? "Good going to *you*," I called back.

"And to your uncle." He flashed me a smile. "Anyway, I gotta get home for supper. See y'all in an hour or so."

"Thanks for the ride, Lee," Uncle Frank waved.

"Well!" Aunt Eva sighed with satisfaction as Lee drove off. "Let's go have some soup before the hordes descend."

❖

And descend they did. Almost double the number of men had crowded into our living room by 7:30, eager to hear details of the good news, which had whipped through Bradleyville in record time. They squeezed themselves into every chair we could find in the house, with many left standing. The atmosphere was vastly different from the night before, the imminence of calamity greatly diminished.

I was glad I'd made six pies and that we'd decided to switch to paper plates. I'd run to the store for them after supper, quelling Aunt Eva's panic about not having enough dishes. Busily cutting the pies into eight pieces each, I listened to the boisterous voices in the next room, smiling to myself. All my baking had been worth it; Lee certainly deserved his apple pie. I was so grateful for the relief that was already smoothing the lines on my uncle's forehead. Suspending my knife before cutting the last piece, I calculated the number of servings, biting my lip. The knife went into the sink. Lee would get a double portion.

Aunt Eva bustled in, two empty pitchers in her hand. "My, how those men go through iced tea! It's a good thing this'll be the last meetin', I don't think I could take much more a this." She banged the plastic pitchers on the counter and pushed loose hair off her flushed cheek. "Those pies ready? You buy enough plates and forks? Where's the napkins? We'd better hurry; they'll be callin' the meetin' to order soon."

I suppressed a laugh. She could get herself in such a dither. "Yes to both questions, and the napkins are right here. Help me serve." I pushed the plate with Lee's piece into the corner. "I'll take that one in; it's for Lee."

"Oh!" She threw me a pleased-as-punch grin. "How *nice* to see you two gettin' along so well!"

I was sorry I'd said anything. "It's just a piece of pie, Aunt Eva."

"Sure, sweetie." She patted my arm. "I know." Sweeping up two plates of pie, she trotted out of the kitchen, humming under her breath. I made a face at her back.

As I turned to reach for Lee's serving, a sudden awareness of what I was about to do stayed my arm. Shyness crept over me as I imagined handing him his plate. Was he going to read implications into that dessert as Aunt Eva had? Implications that I certainly never intended? My eyes roved over all those pieces of pie covering the counter. Well, if he did, it was just too bad. I certainly didn't have time to bake something else now. Firmly, I picked up his piece and another plate. I would serve him and whoever sat next to him at the same time saying absolutely nothing—that's what I'd do. Lee was so distracted, he'd probably forgotten last night's comment, anyway.

I exited the kitchen, my head held high, scooting aside to avoid being mowed down by Aunt Eva on her way back in. My eyes swept the living room. Fortunately, I didn't have to weave through too many men to get to Lee. He was perched on a metal folding chair in animated discussion with Al Bledger, who was shaking his head in disgust. The cynicism twisting Al Bledger's mouth sent unexpected pinpricks of anxiety up my arms. My heart sank as I realized from his expression how tenuous the promised six weeks of peace would be, despite all that Lee had done.

"Excuse me," I mumbled, ducking through other conversations as I approached the two men.

"Okay, okay, we ain't gonna cause no trouble," Al Bledger was saying in response to Lee's black look. "But if it don't go well after that, don't expect us to wait any longer."

"Mr. Bledger, would you like some dessert?" I shoved the plate toward him none too ceremoniously. He accepted it in silence, barely noticing me.

"Lee?" I held out his huge piece, attempting an unassuming expression. His eyes flicked over the plate, stopped in surprise, then lifted to my face. Our gaze met and held. The barest hint of a smile curved his lips as he took the plate from my hand, his fingers grazing mine. "Thank you."

I gave a slight shrug. "Sure."

Unable to think of anything else to say, I turned and walked away, feeling his eyes burning into my back.

chapter 13

W hat's new? I ain't been in town since Monday. I hear the mill a-grindin' as usual. Oh, I also need two pound a them nails, by the way."

"Yep, the men're still workin'. Still grumblin' too. But they're tellin' each other to hold calm, waitin' it out till August." Dozens of nails hissed, metal against metal as they were sight-measured and weighed. The hardware store clerk poured them into a paper bag. "Tell you what, though, business is already down, what with folks savin' in case there's rainy days ahead. And I ain't the only one; the IGA and dime store say the same thing, so does Tull's."

"That so." His customer gazed unseeing at the worn wooden counter.

"What're you thinkin'?"

"That I'm glad I'm a farmer 'bout now."

"I hear ya." The clerk leaned over the counter, lowering his voice. "Tell ya somethin' else, though."

"Uh-huh."

"Even though those meetin's at the Bellinghams is done for now, Lee Harding's still beatin' a path to Frank's door." He raised his eyebrows.

"Why's that?"

"He's sweet on young Jessie. Took her home from church, I heared; plus they went out on a date Tuesday."

"Well now, ain't that a couple." The man reached into his pocket. "How much I owe ya?"

The clerk worked his register. "Ten dollars and eighty-six cents."

Roughened hands counted out bills and change. "That Lee's a busy man. Keepin' things peaceful at the mill, fixin' up his mama's house, his poor sister havin' a baby, and now he's courtin' a girl. Lord a mercy, that's some load."

They both laughed.

chapter 14

Sometimes I wonder what would have happened had I not baked those apple pies.

I went to bed that Friday night with Lee's dark eyes still burning in my head. As I drove to Albertsville again that weekend to buy more fabric and thread, vacuumed Aunt Eva's house, rescued two packing boxes at the IGA before they were flattened, and sewed in earnest, I thought about those eyes. At church on Sunday Aunt Eva led me and Uncle Frank like baby ducks to file into the pew that Lee and his family occupied, even though we usually sat farther down front with the Matthewses. Halfway in, she realized she'd be between Lee and me, and even Aunt Eva couldn't find a solution graceful enough for the house of God. Yet even with her between us, I still *felt* him, was aware of his every move. And I knew he was aware of mine. After the service he asked if he could drive me home. I opened my mouth, ready with an excuse, but heard myself say "yes."

That short drive led to an invitation for our first date on Tuesday evening—dessert and coffee at Barbara's Café in Albertsville, a cheery little place with red vinyl booths and a pink rosebud at each table. Aunt Eva was ecstatic when she heard of our plans and couldn't stop extolling Lee's virtues. Listening to her rattle on at supper Monday night, I realized she and Miss Wilma must have begun their scheming long before I'd returned home. The whole town had probably already heard the efficacy of her matchmaking. Give it another week, I thought, and no-nonsense Bradleyville would be planning a wedding.

I didn't care. Let the town think what it would. No matter how much Aunt Eva schemed, I was on a direct road out of Bradleyville at the beginning of August. And nothing, certainly not a few dates with a man, however attractive, could turn me aside. But then, sitting across from Lee at Barbara's, I could not possibly have guessed where that first date would lead. I only knew that his presence sparked something within me, like a flickering filament.

As it would happen, after all the tumult, I would indeed drive away from Bradleyville on a hot August morning. But at such a cost.

Had I not been so naïve, perhaps I would have guarded my heart more carefully. I was hopelessly inexperienced with men. I'd rarely dated in college—hadn't found time between classes and working and volunteering. And during high school in Bradleyville, I'd been too wrapped up in my grief.

At the end of our first evening together, Lee and I lingered in his truck, still talking. He asked to take me to Barbara's again on Thursday. It would mean losing another evening's work on his house, but he shrugged it away. I said yes without a second thought. Sleep eluded me that night, my mind filled with him. The next two days seemed to drag by, even though I kept myself busy sewing. Finally, Thursday evening arrived. As we drove into Albertsville, the very air around us tingled. Looking at him across the café table, I was tongue-tied.

"Won't you miss your family when you move?" he ventured.

"Sure. But Cincinnati is where I want to be."

"To me, where anybody would want to be is near family. I rented a place here in Albertsville when I started workin' at the textile factory, but when Mama broke her hip, I went back to Bradleyville.

Didn't like Albertsville anyway. Luckily, the mill job came through, so I didn't have to drive back and forth to work very long. Connie ended up movin' back too. Who'd a guessed that."

I was curious about Connie's ex-husband, but seeing Lee's expression, I didn't dare ask. "Is she doing okay?"

"Gettin' awful big. And she's scared, thinkin' a raisin' a baby herself. Wonderin' who's gonna want her, with someone else's child."

"I should visit her again."

"She'd welcome that. So would Mama. They both like you a lot."

Self-consciously, I swirled the coffee in my cup.

"So, who do you know in Cincinnati?"

"Not too many people. I suppose some of our old neighbors are still around. My apartment's not too far from where we used to live. But most of the friends I had in high school have scattered. I do know Brenda Todd, the director at Hope Center. She's anxious to have me back, and I can't wait to see her again. And, of course, I've met my boss at work. As far as friends, though, I'll just have to meet new people."

"Sounds pretty lonely to me."

"No." I wanted him to understand. "Well, maybe at first, but it's okay, because I know it's what I'm supposed to do with my life. My mother spent a lot of her time volunteering at the Center, and I'm following in her footsteps. Plus, even my career will involve helping people."

"Sounds like a good plan for your life." Absently, he fingered the pink rosebud on our table. I watched his strong hand, imagining the sensation of its touch. Something in his tone bespoke a disappointment with my unflinching desire to leave Bradleyville.

"Mm-hmm. My aunt and uncle sure don't want me to go, though. Especially Aunt Eva. And you know how well she keeps her feelings hidden."

He laughed. "Can't say as I blame her. If I had you that close, I wouldn't want you to go either."

The words flowed lightly enough, but I sensed an undercurrent. I glanced at him, not knowing how to respond, then looked away. The rest of the evening we avoided the subject of my leaving. We talked about the sawmill, about Bradleyville and its people. Things were still testy at the mill, Lee responded when I asked. Riddum wasn't doing much to change the men's feelings about him. But, Lee added, he'd promised himself we wouldn't discuss it. He got enough of that at work. Somehow, from that subject we springboarded to a discussion about politics and the Vietnam War. I told him how my mother would have hated the war, how she was against all violence and had instilled the same passion within me. He looked thoughtful at my pronouncement.

"She told you, 'don't lift your hand to *anyone?*' What if you were in danger? What if your *family* was threatened?"

The bitter memory of crimson fingerprints against my mother's cheek flashed through my head ... the stinging words of my grandfather—*you'll never be good enough!* I looked at Lee squarely, feeling my jaw set. "Even then. There's always another way. Violence is just ... unchecked temper. And it doesn't do anybody any good."

He nodded, taking a slow drink of coffee.

"I guess you don't agree with me."

He set the coffee mug on the table with great care. "I don't think violence is ever 'good,' Jessie. But sometimes a country needs to go to war. Right now, our leaders say we need to be in Vietnam. I'm glad I haven't had to go fight, but if I was called, I'd go. As for my own life right here, I like peace as well as the next guy. I certainly don't go 'round pickin' fights. And you know I've tried to keep peace at the sawmill. But I'll tell you this right now, if somebody came against my own, I'd do whatever I needed to protect 'em. I'm all my mother and sister've got right now, and they're both doin' poorly. No way would I stand back and watch 'em get hurt." He smiled, trying to lighten the conversation. "You'd probably do the same thing if it came right down to it."

His smile was so warming, I almost shrugged the comment away. But I wasn't about to let the discussion end there. "No, I wouldn't," I replied. "It's wrong, and that's all there is to it. I'm supposed to help people in this world, not hurt them."

A second, then two, ticked by as we locked eyes. Somehow, that initial testiness between us had crept its way over the table. I couldn't quite place its origin, sensing only that there were depths to Lee Harding comparable to his massive frame. He seemed to be gauging his response, deciding whether to argue or let it go. Suddenly, he grinned, the faint dimple in his cheek showing.

"You're a mighty tough one to be so pretty, Jessie Callum."

The warmth returned, seeping through me like butter on toast. "*I'm* tough. What about *you?* You started it."

"I ain't started a one of our little 'discussions.' *You* always have."

My lips pressed together. "Are we gonna argue about this too, Lee Harding?"

He leaned forward, spontaneously taking my hands in his and lifting them, lacing our fingers. A tingle ran up my arms and down my spine. "*No.*"

And that was the end of that.

I don't remember much of the conversation that followed. Only that my last bite of cake remained uneaten because I didn't want to withdraw my hands from his. By the time we finally left the restaurant, Barbara's was closing. Lee leaned against the cab of his truck and drew me close.

"You really are beautiful, you know," he whispered, lifting a strand of my hair. I couldn't think of a thing to say. Tilting my chin up, he bent down to kiss me. I had to stand on tiptoe, my head at such an angle that I nearly got a crick in my neck. But his lips were warm and surprisingly soft, and I didn't want to let go. Something sounded in my throat. He sank his fingers into my hair, kissing me until I pulled away, breathless. "Ooh," I winced, rubbing my neck, "we should have done that sitting down."

We got in his truck. He pulled me over to the middle and kissed me again. Even sitting, he was still much taller, and my neck began to throb. I didn't care; I felt as though I were floating, quite separate from my body. We drove all the way back to Bradleyville with his arm draped around me, my head on his shoulder. A mile outside of town, he withdrew his arm without explanation, and I scooted over toward the door. No need to stoke Bradleyville's fire.

We made plans for Saturday night. I volunteered to make a picnic; he said he'd bring a blanket. He knew just the place, on a tree-lined hill about ten miles out Route 347. We'd watch the stars come out, the lights of Bradleyville come on.

Somehow on Friday, I managed to finish a second dress, reminding myself of the reason I needed a new wardrobe. No matter how exciting the next few weeks in quiet little Bradleyville might be, my life was on its own course. That was where I needed to focus my thoughts. But twice as I found myself daydreaming about Saturday night, I nearly sent the sewing machine needle through my finger.

chapter 15

*Y*ou don't look good; what happened?" *The shirt she was folding stilled in her hands, anxiety lining her face.*

Her husband exhaled angrily as he sank onto the bed, its springs squeaking in protest. He pulled off a boot. Sawdust flecked onto the thin blue carpet. "I had a run-in with Riddum."

She sucked in air.

"We was pullin' in logs from the river. We'd had a big shipment—'bout twice the normal—and they were backin' up. There was the four a us down there, and finally it got to be such a jam I sent Harlan up to ask for more help, else we'd never untangle it." The second boot dropped onto the carpet. "I couldn't hardly believe it when I looked up and saw Riddum hisself standin' there. He may a promised to treat us better, but it seems he's everywhere, lookin' over our shoulders. You'd swear he's countin' every piece a wood." His head disappeared as he pulled off a grimy brown shirt. "Harlan's standin' behind him lookin' scared to death, just a young kid, he is. Then Riddum says, 'Who sent this boy up for more help?' and I says I did. And right in front a the other men, he lit into me like a house afire. Said who did I think I was, reallocatin'

where men worked, and there weren't no reason why the four a us couldn't handle the job, and if we didn't handle it, we might as well go on home and stay there."

"Oh, dear Lord," his wife's knees weakened. "You didn't get fired."

"No, I didn't," he snapped. "But almost. 'Cause I just about took Riddum by that scrawny neck a his and wrang it. I was so mad my fingers was twitchin'. Only the thought a you and the kids stopped me." He jerked down his jeans, wadding them into the corner.

"What did the other men do?"

"Harlan's eyes were near buggin' out, dartin' from Riddum to me. Billy laid a hand on my arm; he knew what I was thinkin'. Pete wasn't havin' none of it. He jumped in and said, 'That's too big a load out there, Mr. Riddum. We don't get it taken care of properly, it'll cause a snag down the line.' Riddum glared back like a drenched cat and said, 'Then get to it, Mr. Souter, or get off my property.'"

His wife reacted with disgust.

"So now we got three men mad as heck, Riddum on one side and Pete and me on the other. My arm musta started to rise, 'cause I felt Billy's fingers tighten. And then I took a mighty deep breath and looked at Pete, and he took a mighty deep breath and looked at me, and we turned around and got back to work without another word. Riddum watched us for a minute, then stalked off."

The woman dropped wordlessly onto the bed next to her husband, a fright she had not felt in five years seizing her chest.

He rubbed a hand across his forehead. "I'm tellin' you, baby, we cain't keep workin' for a man that unfair. August first seems like a long ways away. You'd think he was the Pharaoh a Egypt, tellin' us to make more bricks with less straw. Well, one a these days it'll be the last straw. I think that, and then I remember almost losin' our house five years ago, not havin' money for food. Only the kindness a neighbors and Thomas hirin' me when he didn't need to saved us. I don't wanna put you through that again."

Wearily, he put an arm around his wife's shoulders and pulled her close. Ignoring the smell of sweat and fresh-cut wood, she buried her face in his neck.

chapter 16

Well, Miss Jessie, sounds like you been a might busy."
Thomas Bradley's voice over the phone Saturday morning
held a mixture of challenge and tease. "Don't believe everything
you hear," I replied airily.

"You gonna tell me about it?"

"A girl's got to have some secrets."

He grunted. "Matter a fact, that's just what I called about. This
town's been right down-in-the-mouth lately and could use some
perkin' up. How 'bout you and me raisin' a little ruckus."

I had to laugh, imagining the animation on his face, the hitched
eyebrows. "What are you up to, Thomas Bradley?"

"I got me a little job to do and thought you might like to
help. One rule though. We ain't gonna say one word 'bout the
mill business."

"Fine with me. But what's the 'little job'?"

"Well, now, Miss Jessie, if I tol' you that, I'd take half the fun
outta it."

"I'm supposed to visit Connie this afternoon. Will we be done
by then?"

"I wouldn't think a keepin' a young lady like you from her social life. Now come on, you're either in or you're out. Which'll it be?"

I shook my head at his fluid charm. "I'm in."

An hour later, Thomas was climbing into my car after carefully placing a brown grocery bag on the backseat floor. Yep, Bradleyville needed cheering, he declared again, and naturally, there was no one better qualified to fix whatever ailed the town than himself. Following his command to drive out Main, I tried to imagine Bradleyville without him and could not. I knew if I were to ask, he'd say that his life had been full here in this tiny metropolis, even though he'd been overseas in two different wars and had certainly seen what other places had to offer. "Bradleyville was built independent—strong," he'd say, "and it's stayed that way. That's just how I like it."

He leaned a tanned arm out the window, chuckling to himself, right leg jiggling. A hot breeze was blowing hair across my face, and I tried vainly to tuck it behind my ears. I couldn't guess what he was up to. Being chosen as his coconspirator was quite an honor, but then ours was that kind of friendship. We could talk about almost anything. Except for war. Currently, of course, that meant Vietnam. The previous Christmas Thomas had made the mistake of asking me if I'd witnessed "any a those crazy kids" protesting the war on the university campus. I'd bristled. "Afraid so, Thomas," I'd replied, keeping my voice steady. "Matter of fact, I've been in peaceful sit-ins once or twice myself." I'd stared at him, daring him to say more, but he'd wisely changed the subject.

I'd gotten used to hearing about the times he won his three medals in the wars, however. You couldn't live in Bradleyville and not appreciate those stories, for they certainly were drilled into you, if not by proud residents, most certainly by Thomas himself. Far as I knew, most of the town denizens could recite every detail.

I hadn't been in Bradleyville but a few months when Thomas told me his favorite story—about his crossing the Volturno River in Italy under full moonlight. He'd volunteered for the task in order to scout out a German camp, swimming underwater on his side while breathing through a long reed stuck in his mouth. Had he surfaced just once, he'd certainly have been shot. He accomplished his mission so well that he not only returned with news of how to infiltrate the camp but he brought back a German canteen as a souvenir.

I sat in his living room that day as he related the story, cautiously fingering the worn brown canteen, thinking of the enemy mouths it had quenched, the shoulders it had chafed. They had been young men who'd wanted to live too—those soldiers— with parents and wives and children. Thomas's own wife, Adele, was busy in the kitchen making us supper as he told his tale. When he finished, eyes bright and mouth pitched in a grin, I'd remained silent. "See that medal there." He pointed to one of three open blue velvet boxes lined up on the coffee table. Each displayed a bronze star medal attached to a patriotically striped ribbon. "That's for the Volturno."

I thought of the blood and carnage of war, then of my mother, peacefully doling out plates of mashed potatoes and baked chicken to hungry children at Hope Center. Pain and resentment flashed through me. If only they gave out medals for caring.

"Now, Jessie, where has that mind a yours taken you?" Thomas had asked.

I looked away at nothing, not wanting to offend. "I guess war's just not my favorite subject."

His face clouded. "Because of your cousin, Henry, you mean. A course. I don't talk 'bout it 'round your aunt and uncle; I shoulda known you'd be sensitive too."

I flinched inwardly at my own self-centeredness. I hadn't even thought of Henry. "No, it's not that. It's that ... my mother was against all violence. Especially war. She taught me that from an early age."

"Why do you suppose that was?" he asked quietly.

Once again, I remembered the *slap* of roughened fingers on a smooth cheek, their crimson mark on Mama's white skin, the pain in her eyes. I wondered how much Thomas knew of Mama's and Aunt Eva's upbringing; I didn't want to say more than I should. "Her father," I replied tersely.

Thomas had seen through my reticence. "I know. Your mama must have been a wounded child, just like your aunt." He reached for the boxes holding his medals and began to close them one by one. "Eva still bore the emotional scars when she came here as Frank's new bride. I think that's one reason why she's loved this town so much. It was far removed from her folks, and it's peaceful. I believe she thought she could hide here forever from violence. Then the war reached out and took her own son. He volunteered, you know; he wanted to go so badly." Thomas gazed through the front window, his eyes growing distant before he blinked them back to regard me intently. "No one likes violence, Jessie. Especially those of us who've seen it firsthand. But there are times when you got to fight."

I shook my head. "I don't know about that. Mom always said, 'Raise your hand to no one.' She worked all her life doing the opposite of violence. No matter how hard life became for her, she gave more and more. She cared for others until she was so tired, she could hardly stand."

Thomas thought that over for a moment, compressing his lips. "Did it make her happy?"

His voice had been gentle, but the words were like a punch in the stomach. I stared at him, dismayed that his ridiculous question would remind me of the brief look of despair that had crossed my mother's face moments before she drove to her death. "Of course she was happy," I responded with a measure of indignance. "Nobody was *making* her do it; she *chose* to. She could have done lots of other things, you know. There's a lot more fun things in life than serving the poor."

"Well," Thomas inhaled deeply, "you're right about that."

I hadn't been quite sure what "that" referred to, or what was left for me to be wrong about. At any rate, I hadn't wished to pursue it. Something told me Aunt Eva had talked to Thomas in a less-than-positive manner about my mother's pursuit of giving.

"Jessie. *Jessie!*" Thomas nudged me in the shoulder, bringing me back to the present. "Where's your mind at? Are you listenin'?"

"Yes, Thomas," I blinked. "Of course I'm listening."

"All right then. Now, here's the thing." His voice dropped, as if eavesdroppers ghosted the backseat. "We got to be real stealthy, like soldiers on a raid. In other words, we cain't be seen. Somebody's gonna notice soon enough, and if my aim is right, that somebody'll be ol' Jake. He'll come gunnin' for me in a hurry, tell you what." He slapped his leg with glee, forgetting to be quiet. "Whooee! It's gonna be somethin'."

Jake Lewellyn was the same age as Thomas, and depending upon the day, they were either lifelong friends or avowed enemies. As the Bradleyville legend went, when they were both nine years old, Thomas tricked Jake into trading his favorite marble for a toadstool, and Jake had been scheming to get it back ever since. Their resulting "bestin' feud" had carried them through the years, affording the town some of its most beloved stories. Usually the stories were at Mr. Lewellyn's expense, Thomas's cunning far outwitting his somewhat slower and decidedly pudgier friend.

"Poor Mr. Lewellyn," I put in, stopping at the light at the corner of Minton and Main. "He just can't seem to keep up with you, can he?"

"Hah!" Thomas snorted, "poor Mr. Lewellyn, nothin'. Man's been a thorn in my side for over sixty years now; you think he'd take a rest."

I swallowed a smile. "He idolizes you. And of course, you do nothing to provoke him."

"'Course not!" Thomas was indignant. "Just live my life, that's all." He rolled his shoulders. "Cain't help it if I'm smarter'n he is."

"That's just it. You've always been smarter, and he can't accept that. He works like crazy to be you."

"You're right," he grinned. "Poor Jake Lewellyn."

A short distance out of town, Thomas told me to slow down, then turn around. "Now here's what we're gonna do," he said, leaning around to fetch the grocery bag. "And remember, it's got to be stealthy, like savin' the French on D-Day."

Like a good soldier, I kept a lookout while he performed his task.

chapter 17

By the time I arrived at Lee's house that afternoon after helping Thomas, the temperature had hit eighty-five, with equal percent humidity. All the windows in my Ford were down, and still it felt like an oven. Lee was waiting for me under a shade tree on the front lawn, a phone call having alerted him that I was on my way. His white T-shirt and old jeans were clean, his hair wet. I knew he planned to continue working on the house as I visited with Connie and his mother, and wondered how they viewed his showering midjob for my benefit. I could just picture the gleam in his mother's eye.

"Hey there," he smiled, looking wonderful. I wanted to touch him but dared not. The eyes of Bradleyville were ever-watchful. *Tonight*, I thought, *tonight*. "I noticed this as you were drivin' up." He squatted down to run a finger over my right front tire. "Looks pretty bald. You should get it replaced. Before you leave."

His last sentence pulsed. I bent over him, my hair brushing his shoulder. "Okay."

Lee's house was not air-conditioned, and I noticed his mother's discomfort as she huffed over to hug me in the doorway, her good hip rolling with the strain of hauling the other. My heart went out even more to Connie as she panted with the effort of greeting me, her stomach huge under a tent dress, cheeks mottled with heat. Her hands and feet were swollen. "It's hard to breathe," she apologized. "No room for my lungs."

I urged her back onto the couch, lifting up her feet. Miss Wilma took her cane in hand and struggled toward the kitchen until Lee and I insisted on fetching the iced tea and sugar cookies. Gratefully, she fell into her arm chair.

Once out of sight, Lee pulled me into his arms and kissed me. I melted into him. When we pulled apart, I couldn't hide the concern on my face. "What?" he whispered.

"They look so uncomfortable in this heat."

Defensiveness flecked his forehead. "I been wantin' to buy an air conditioner. But with all the money goin' into the addition...."

"I didn't mean—"

"We'd a had it by now if I'd gotten a raise."

"I know." Once again I saw the reality of Blair Riddum's greed. My own household was comfortable enough with its two incomes. How sheltered my outlook had been.

I turned toward the table, keeping my voice light. "Here." I handed him the plate of cookies. "You take these and one glass. I'll bring the rest."

Back in the living room, Lee sat with us for a few minutes, then reluctantly announced he had to get back to work. "Come say good-bye before you leave?"

I nodded.

"Would you help me up, Lee?" Miss Wilma held out a hand, smiling at me in apology. "I just need to make a quick trip down the hall."

Connie breathed heavily in the silence after they left. She looked so forlorn and lost. "Here, eat something, Connie," I offered, handing her a cookie. I pushed her iced tea glass closer so she could reach it easily, then regarded her with helplessness. "I wish I could do something for you—take the heat away, the discomfort."

Her smile was rueful. "Not much anybody can do right now. Even me. All I can do is wait."

The "wait" seemed to refer to more than her delivery. I wondered if she hoped her ex-husband would return. "Your baby's going to be beautiful, Connie. It'll bring you so much joy."

"I know. I know it will." Her brow furrowed. "This is all just hard for me right now. Thank goodness I've got Mama and Lee—especially Mama. She's here all day for me. We've talked a lot."

This was the most Connie had ever said to me. I wanted to keep the conversation going. "What have you talked about?"

Her shoulders lifted. "Life. Babies. Men." She paused. "Most of all, God."

I couldn't suppress a smile. "Aunt Eva talks to me about God a lot too. Sometimes I think she should have been the preacher, rather than Pastor Frasier."

Connie nodded. "Yep. She and Mama are a lot alike. They're praying women, and lots of times when your aunt comes to visit, they talk about Christ in their lives. I know they both have been praying for me."

On cue, my guard came up. I reached for a cookie and bit into it.

"Anyway, I did what they have been praying for," she ventured almost hesitantly. "Asked Christ into my life, I mean. And ever since then, things have been easier to handle." She raised her eyes to mine with self-consciousness. I admired her fortitude in stating her beliefs, especially given the fact that we'd not mentioned religion during my prior visit. My own reticence at the subject lifted; the last thing I wanted to do was make her uncomfortable.

"That's good. I'm ... glad you have something that helps you."

She gazed at me intently, gauging my personal understanding of her words. I pinned an encouraging expression on my face.

"Now Mama's praying for Lee," she added.

"Because of the sawmill, you mean?"

"That too. But mostly that he'll understand he needs Christ in his life. 'Cause bein' a Christian is more than just goin' to church and believin' in God, isn't it?"

I smiled a polite agreement, taking another bite of cookie.

"He's crazy about you, you know."

A crumb caught in my windpipe, and I coughed. "Who, God?"

She laughed throatily. "No. Well, I mean, sure. But I meant Lee."

"Oh." I took a purposeful drink of iced tea.

"He talks about you all the time. And when he's not talkin', he's got this dreamy look. I've never seen him like that before."

"Maybe he's just thinking about all the work on the house."

"No." She wiped sweat from her forehead. "It's you."

Her candor was embarrassing. "Hasn't he had girlfriends?"

"Plenty. At least, that's what the girls thought they were. My friends used to go nuts over him. But he was never interested in very many. And not anybody like you."

"Well, I think he's . . . very nice also."

A sudden grimace rolled across Connie's face. Her hand went involuntarily to her belly.

"Are you okay?"

She closed her eyes, holding her breath. I grew alarmed and started to rise. "I'll call Lee."

"No, no." She held up a hand. "It's all right." Exhaling slowly, she carefully shifted her position. "I been gettin' these pains lately. Used to think I was goin' into labor, but Mama says they're just puttin' me in practice for the real thing. She had 'em with both her kids."

"How will you know when they're real?"

Her eyes fell on me, and in them I saw her vulnerability. "Cain't rightly say. Since this is my first time."

Half a cookie was still in my hand. I put it on a napkin. "You're right; I'm glad your mom's here for you."

"Yeah. She's been such a help. And Lee too; he takes care a us both. He's a good provider."

Connie had a gracious subtlety that her mother and my Aunt Eva lacked. No expression gave her away, no particular tone of voice. All the same, I saw a flash into her soul. It was not the "selling" of her brother to me that was surprising. It was the fact that she did it so unselfishly in her own time of need.

"I'm sure he is," I mumbled.

Fortunately for me, Miss Wilma shuffled back into the room about that time.

The three of us talked for more than an hour, fanning our sweating faces with napkins. I found myself admiring Miss Wilma more and more. She was so down-to-earth in her outlook and even joyful amid the hip pain she tried to hide. Unlike Connie, she showed no self-consciousness in mentioning Jesus. His name seemed to slip into her sentences whatever the subject—her healing hip, struggles at the sawmill, Connie's future, Lee's talents. The depth of her devotion to her faith left me wondering and somewhat envious. The closest God had ever seemed to me was during my dream about my mother, and that had been more than seven years ago. A tiny voice inside whispered that Miss Wilma seemed to know something I didn't. It was an uncomfortable thought, and I pushed it away.

I'd stayed long enough. "I'm sorry I have to go," I said, rising, "but I'd like to get in a couple hours' sewing. Before my date tonight." I added the last sentence with a knowing smile, just to see their faces light up.

Before leaving, I threaded my way through the addition and found where Lee was working. He was on his knees, multicolored electrical wiring in his hands. "Hi," I said, stopping to lean in the doorway. He smiled at me as he searched my face. "I love them— your sister and mom. They're wonderful, wonderful women, Lee. They deserve you."

He put down the wires, dusted both knees, and rose. Silently, he took me in his arms.

chapter 18

W hat happened to Connie's husband?" I asked Lee that evening. We were sitting on his blanket, spread buttercup-yellow upon deep green grass on a hill overlooking Bradleyville. Leaves from a gnarled oak shaded us from the setting sun. Pushed off the blanket were the remains of our sandwiches, tea, and dessert along with an old wicker basket of Aunt Eva's. A slight breeze tickled my arms as I wrapped them around my legs, gazing at lights twinkling on in the town. Drifting on the wind were the smells of honeysuckle, apple pie, and Lee's lime aftershave.

"Ex-husband, you mean." He watched the hills across the valley. "Not sure. But he won't be comin' back."

"How do you know?"

"I just know."

"Sounds like there's more to it."

"There is." He flexed his jaw. "But somethin' tells me you wouldn't approve."

"Oh, come on, am I that judgmental? Tell me."

He turned toward me, his expression almost challenging. "All right, I'll tell you. The reason I know is because I told him if I ever saw his face 'round here again, I'd bash it in. And I'm a lot bigger'n he is."

"Oh." Immediate disapproval swirled within me. "Why would you do that?"

Flickering leaves danced shadows across his profile. "It's a long story. There was this girl named Tammy who lived next door to Connie and Bart in Albertsville. She was still in high school. Bart took up with her. Connie was too ashamed to tell us what was goin' on till I heard the whisperin' around town. She near had a breakdown. I coulda killed the man. I told him he'd better stop or he'd have me to deal with. But he didn't stop at all. Then what was I gonna do. I'd shot off my mouth, with no way a backin' it up without gettin' myself in trouble. Then Connie found out she was pregnant." He shook his head. "She was thrilled, thinkin' that would stop Bart. By then he wasn't even tryin' to hide it. But the news didn't change a thing. So I went to see him again. And I gave him the surprise a his life—five hundred dollars, all my savings. Told him to take Tammy and hit the road and don't dare come back. If he wasn't gonna change, at least he wasn't gonna flaunt it in front a my pregnant sister. About that time I came back to Bradleyville to live. I brought Connie with me."

Oh, boy. My notions about the complexity of Lee's personality were proving true. It was hard to imagine the hothead he'd just spoken of being the same man I'd watched calm the mill workers at our house night after night. He'd certainly meant what he'd said about protecting his own.

"Does Connie know?"

"Yeah."

"Was she mad at you for what you did?"

"It was over, Jessie; she'd lost him. She just didn't have the strength to leave him."

"So you did it *for* her." I couldn't keep the accusing tone from my voice. Why should the end of his sister's marriage have been *his* decision?

"I protected her," he replied levelly. "I did what she was incapable of doing."

Maybe she didn't want your protection, I started to say, but thought better of it. My toes dug into the blanket as I tried to assimilate this side of Lee.

He nudged my arm. "Still like me?"

I managed an unconvincing smile.

We sat in strained silence.

"I knew I shouldn't tell you," he said finally.

I thought of poor Connie then, and my heart twinged. She was so sweet and unassuming. I'd be furious too if I saw someone treating her so badly. At least Lee hadn't given in to his inclinations and beat the guy up. He'd never laid a finger on the man. He'd simply found a way to rid his sister of a bad husband—at his own expense.

"It doesn't matter," I heard myself saying. "I don't like what you said to him, but you ended up doing the right thing, bringing Connie home. *Without* fighting. I'm sure she's better off here. Imagine her going through this pregnancy in Albertsville, knowing her husband was sneaking off to be with someone else." Scooting closer, I put my hand on his arm. "I think you're a wonderful big brother. She thinks so too. You should hear her bragging on you."

Relief washed over his face. His eyes told me he understood my risk in stretching beyond familiar bounds. When he wrapped his arms around me, I laid my head against his chest. *I don't care*, I told myself. *So what if he has a bit of a temper.* I even sent a little prayer heavenward, asking my guardian angel to understand. It was inexplicable, really, this sudden willingness to blur the boundaries of my mother's teaching, like brazenly coloring outside the lines. But I didn't have time to pursue that thought.

"Tell me," he was saying, his lips brushing the top of my head, "tell me why you're so afraid of violence."

My breath stilled. I could hear his heartbeat through his shirt. "I told you before. It's what my mother taught me."

"I think there's more to it than that. I saw it on your face when we talked about it. Did you see someone get hurt, a person killed at that homeless center or something?"

I raised my head. "No. Nothing like that." What I'd seen had been much less—and far more—than that, for it had cut to the very core of me. I'd never told anyone the story, for words would bring renewed clarity to a scene too hurtful to dwell upon. What's more, how could I make anyone understand how the occurrence had molded me, weighting my mother's mere exhortations with the stark reality of example?

Lee brushed hair off my cheek. "Come on, Jessie. I want to know *you. Inside* your heart."

He would hear no further protestations. And so, eventually, I did tell him. Sitting beside him on his yellow blanket, my eyes focused on the twilit valley below. I told him of the November day when I was ten years old, when my mother and I had received an unexpected letter from my grandmother, inviting us to drive to their home in Columbus, Ohio, for Thanksgiving.

"Let's go!" I'd cried. I'd dreamed of meeting my grandparents, had pestered Mom about them many, many times. All my friends had at least one grandparent who sent them money for birthdays, presents for Christmas. Why couldn't I have my own; why did my mom refuse to take me to see them? We hadn't heard from them in years; now they'd asked us for Thanksgiving! Mom and I didn't have the money for a huge meal, but I was willing to bet they did. Maybe Grandma would serve those wonderful candied yams and homemade bread and lots of stuffing. Maybe they'd even give me an early Christmas present.

Mom hesitated. "I'm supposed to be at the Center that day, sweetie. Helping serve. You're needed too. You know how many extra people we'll have to feed."

"Get somebody else to work!" I'd pouted. "We *never* do anything on holidays; you're *always* volunteering. Why can't we go just this once."

I badgered Mom unmercifully, even calling Brenda Todd myself and asking if Mom could be replaced at Hope Center for the day. She'd given us her blessing. Mom had finally capitulated. If I'd been a little older and if I hadn't been so selfishly excited, perhaps I'd have paid more attention to the anxiety lining Mom's face when she said we'd go. Perhaps I'd have taken to heart her intimations over the years about her difficult childhood. Instead, I thought only of myself and my rose-colored dreams.

I dressed carefully that Thanksgiving day, wearing a pink dress, white tights, and my black dress shoes, shined to the hilt. The drive took only a couple hours, but it seemed an eternity. Full of antic-ipation, I watched cars whiz by the car window, pretending not to notice my mother's unusual quiet.

"Jessie," she said as we entered the city limits of Columbus, "you must be very, very good. Remember all the manners I've taught you. Compliment your grandmother on all her food. Speak only when spoken to, especially with your grandfather. *Don't* give him any cause to get angry."

"I won't, Mom." I looked at her impatiently, vaguely annoyed with her skittishness. This was a special day, and I wasn't about to have my exuberance quashed. "Why are you so afraid he's going to be mean?"

No answer.

"If he was mean to you, that was a long time ago. You're grown up now. Things'll be different, you'll see. You'll get along just fine, and we can keep coming back."

Her lips curved into a wan smile. "I hope you're right, Jessie. I really do."

When we arrived, my grandma hugged me and told me how much she'd missed me. She said the last time I'd been at their house I was only two years old, and look what a beautiful young lady I'd grown into. She said my dress was lovely and how pretty my hair was. She was wearing a red-and-white-checked apron over a cream blouse and brown skirt. Her hair was gray, and she wore glasses. Her appearance was very much what I expected in a grandma. My mother exchanged hugs with her, smiling, but there was a caution in the air that I couldn't fathom.

"Where's Dad?" Mom asked.

"Upstairs." Her mother turned back to the counter and began cutting out dough for the rolls. "He'll be down shortly."

It was half an hour before my grandfather appeared. Eight years' separation, and he couldn't even get downstairs to say hello. I wondered about that. My mother was setting the dining room table when he entered the kitchen, and even from where I stood, stirring gravy on the stove, I could see the tension roll across her back.

"Hi, Dad," she said through the dining room doorway, her voice unnaturally light.

"Hello, Marie." He nodded to her, as if she were a distant relative. "And who's this pretty girl?" he asked, chucking me under the chin. He eyed my face, my dress, a slight smile on his lips, as though he liked what he saw. I was glad—and relieved—that he was pleased with me.

The meal was all I'd hoped for. Turkey and dressing, thick gravy and sweet potatoes, rolls and cranberry sauce—all home-made. We were even going to have pumpkin pie afterwards, with all the whipped cream I'd want. I was on my best behavior while we ate, telling my grandmother how good everything was and being careful not to take more than I could hold. The conversation was stilted from the outset, with pauses in between. In the silence, our forks seemed to clink louder than usual against the plates, my grandfather swallowing his wine audibly. Every time he drained his glass, Grandma rose as if on cue to refill it. He drank most of the bottle.

The atmosphere around the table grew unsettling, fraught with some dismal expectancy I couldn't quite discern. My mother sat ramrod straight as she ate, her eyes sliding toward me as I sat at the end of the table on her right. Grandpa was opposite me, on her left, and Grandma was across from my mother. Just before we'd sat down to eat, Grandma had taken off her apron. I'd complimented her on the lacy blouse she wore, and she'd thanked me.

The three adults spoke of people I didn't know—longtime neighbors and friends. At first Grandpa's comments about this or that person were only mildly derogatory. But the more he ate—and drank—the more caustic he became, leering in his contempt for whomever was mentioned. My grandmother's opinions grew more scarce by the minute, until she only nodded, no matter what he said. I watched my mother's fingers tighten around her fork, her shoulders brace. She looked as though she wanted to flee. I was sorry for her obvious discomfort and began to wish we hadn't come.

My grandfather continued drinking, the corners of his mouth drawing down to his chin. His words became more vile. He uttered curses about various kids Mom had grown up with. Mom winced, upset that I had to hear such language, but said nothing. Systematically, methodically, she ate. Fork to mouth, fork to mouth. A fear stole over me as I watched her, until I had trouble swallowing. Then I was afraid of leaving food on my plate and forced myself to eat, my actions matching hers. Her father talked louder, now jeering his opinions on the governor of Ohio, the president, the nation. Mom kept her eyes on her plate.

The once-luscious smell of cooling pumpkin pies drifted in from the kitchen. I wondered if I'd be able to stomach a piece.

"Marie, you been mighty quiet," Grandpa said suddenly, picking up his wine glass. "Tell us what you been doing with yourself."

My mother forced a bite of stuffing down her throat. "I still have my job as a receptionist."

"Had that job for years, haven't you?"

"Yes. Almost ten."

He grunted in disgust. "Don't you think it's time you did something better with your life? Answering other people's phones all day, that's a slave job."

"Guess so." My mother's voice sounded almost childlike. "But it pays the bills."

"Not that well, obviously." He sniffed loudly as he speared a turkey leg. "One look at how your daughter's dressed would tell you that."

My lungs froze, my shoulders drawing inward. I felt as though I were shrinking. And dirty. My eyes raised to his face for a clue to his disdainful remark. I'd tried to look so pretty; he'd even *said* I was. What had I done to make him change his mind? And why was he being so vicious to my hardworking mother?

Mom's face pinched. She did not look at me, but I knew the hurt she felt was more for me than herself. Her eyes remained on her plate. The sickening realization hit me that she'd known something like this was coming. What's more, I realized that our presence at this hateful man's table was my fault. I'd begged her to come; I'd pestered her and heaped guilt about our lack of relatives on her head. Now she was paying for my selfishness.

"So what else do you do?"

"No, Mom," I wanted to yell, *"don't tell him about the Center! Don't!"*

She hesitated—and in that second of hesitation, the pain of her childhood opened itself before me. For in that one brief moment, I saw her frailty and fear as she scrambled for the most diffusing of answers. "I still volunteer at the homeless shelter," she replied quietly. Further shadows played across her face. Then, with courage—or was it resignation?—she raised her eyes to his.

His lip curled. "Hanging around a bunch of dirty, worthless bums. That's about what I'd expect from you."

"They're not worthless, Daddy; they're just people in need." Her defense of the helpless leapt from her mouth of its own accord. She caught herself, the awareness of her mistake widening her eyes.

My grandfather's neck thickened as he recoiled, his face hardening like granite. With lightning speed, his right hand whipped out, slapping my mother's left cheek with a resounding *smack*. I gasped. Her head rebounded in my direction and hung there, tears springing to her eyes. Instantaneously, a large handprint screamed red upon her white skin.

"You think you're such a goody-two-shoes," he sneered. "Trying to make up for the rotten kid you always were. Well, hear this. You'll *never* be good enough."

Anger rose within me, so caustic, so acidic, that it burned my very lungs. I thought it would flow right out of me, sweeping me across that table so I could smack my grandfather silly. I pictured myself punching his ears and pulling his hair, screaming at him for what he'd done—just then and for years long past—to my mother. I felt my leg muscles tense to raise me from my chair, felt my face go hot. Then my mother looked at me. And I saw in her tear-filled eyes a warning, a *pleading* for me not to move.

"Oh, dear," my grandmother tut-tutted mildly, playing with the buttons on her blouse, "look how you've gone and upset your father."

I don't remember actually driving away from that detestable house. I do know that we left quickly, the odor of uncut pumpkin pies now sour to my senses. I also remember bursting into tears. Crying and crying until my mother pulled over on a city street to calm me down.

"I *hate* him!" I exploded, smashing my fist against the window. "I wanna *kill* him; I wish he was *dead!*" She tried to hold me, but in my shame I pushed her away. "I'm sorry for asking to come, Mom; I'm so sorry," I hiccuped, pulling her back. "It's all my fault! We're never going to come here again, you hear, *never!* And I don't care what he says, you're *good*; you're the *best* person I know! You're the best person on this whole *earth*, and I'll never, *ever* let anybody say you're not. Not *ever again!*"

To this day, thinking of that afternoon stabs at my chest. By the time I was through telling Lee, searching vainly for words to capture the pain, I was crying. He pulled me close, his arm protectively around my shoulder.

"And you know the amazing part?" I sniffed against his shirt. "My mother, with her face still red and surely stinging, comforted *me* in that car, even while telling me with an incredible, quiet dignity that I should not be saying those things. That no matter what my grandfather had done, I had to look to my own actions. 'Raise your hand to no one, Jessie,' she told me. 'Now you see the meaning of those words—because people giving in to violence are always at their worst.

It hurts the innocent. And when you give back the same, you've only sunk to their level.'" I pulled away from Lee, reaching for a napkin to wipe my face. "Can you believe that, Lee? Even in her own hurt, she wouldn't allow me—or herself—to be vindictive."

He nodded, his expression grave. "She must have been a wonderful woman."

"She was. She really was." My throat tightened, and I could say no more.

"Jessie," he said with intensity, cradling my face in his hands, "listen to me. I got a temper sometimes; I guess you've seen that. But I've been downright cool-headed about the sawmill problems, and you know why? Because you made me that way, through makin' me promise I wouldn't lead your uncle into trouble. You understand what I'm sayin'? I'd probably have acted a lot different if it hadn't been for you. But you're like your mother, Jessie; you bring peace. And you *do* somethin' to me; you have since the first day I met you, last Christmas in church. This week with you has been the best week a my life." His fingers ran over my cheek, smoothing away a tear. "Now that I understand you more, I'll make you another promise. I promise I'll keep on bein' cool-headed, okay? I won't let you down. For your sake. And for mine."

His words sent warm colors rolling through my head. In faint echo, reality whispered, reminding me that I was leaving in a few weeks. And the very reason I was going was to pursue the path on which my wise and gentle mother had placed me.

Lee lifted my chin and kissed me then, and all such thoughts fell away.

chapter 19

Sleep eluded me that night. I tossed and turned, caught between my growing feelings for Lee and the unshakable knowledge that my plans would take me away from him. The drive from Bradleyville to Cincinnati was almost six hours long, due to the narrow, winding roads of eastern Kentucky at the beginning of the trip. It would be too long for a normal weekend visit. Besides, I'd be at the Center every Sunday, so that would leave us no time at all. And even if we could visit, where would it lead us? Our lives were heading down very different roads. Lee's heart was in Bradleyville, his home. My heart still lay in Cincinnati, my home. For more than seven years—ever since the vision of my guardian angel mother—I'd planned and dreamed of returning, where I could literally "follow in my mother's footsteps." I'd chosen my sociology major, knowing I'd use my training to serve in that city. I had volunteered hours I didn't have at the soup kitchen in Lexington, sensing it was only a down payment on the time I would give to Hope Center when my education was finally complete.

Sighing, I rolled over in my bed. The memory of Lee's fingers, tender against my cheek, sprang into my head, followed by non sequitur thoughts of the apartment awaiting me in Cincinnati. How happy I'd been to find it, how convenient it was to my work and the Center, both of which were downtown. I'd stood in the bedroom of that apartment with the apologetic manager, ignoring the mess of its current tenant, imagining my mother's old furniture in that room. I'd pictured the bed against one wall, the tall dresser against another, the smaller dresser under the window. And in the far corner would go my sewing machine. I'd opened the closet door, envisioning newly sewn dresses hanging there, awaiting my first days at work. The manager had even said I could paint the walls a light blue, as my mother's bedroom had been. In the living room, I'd turned in a slow circle, thinking of the couch I must rent, the table and chairs, the TV and stand. The kitchen was small, which was just as well; I had need of only a few pans and dishes.

These details—my nesting—would be taken care of during my first two weeks in Cincinnati. How I'd looked forward to moving in, to making that apartment my home before launching into my career and a life that would honor my mother. I had not the slightest doubt that this was the right plan for my life—the plan my mother set in motion even while beyond the grave. Nor did I doubt that God smiled on it as well, for had he not sent her in that dream to guide me when I was most bereft?

The air was hot. I kicked back the sheet and fluffed up my pillow. Outside my window, the night was clear, star-lit. I gazed at the sky, thinking that my guardian angel was up there somewhere, watching me. Did she know why I couldn't sleep? Did she understand the tug I felt in my heart, knowing my attraction to Lee could lead no further than a few weeks' exhilaration?

Imagining the compassionate face of my mother as she smiled down on me from that night sky, I felt a twinge of remorse, worrying that my feelings for Lee—and the ease with which I chose to overlook his admitted temper—bordered on betrayal. I prayed to her then, asking for strength when it came time to leave Bradleyville. For the first time, my anticipation of that joyous day was dampened with the reality of saying good-bye to Lee. I didn't like that ambivalence. I didn't like it at all. And when I thought about it, it didn't even make sense. I had planned the launching of my new life for seven years; and now, in just seven days, I'd allowed some of its shine to slip from my fingers. No man was worth that.

I really would have to be more careful.

chapter 20

*S*he was getting too old to pray on her knees. By the time they were done, she'd probably be so stiff she couldn't get up. No matter. They didn't usually kneel when the four of them met for their weekly prayer time, but under the circumstances tonight, she'd told them they should.

They'd been talking to God for about half an hour, taking turns praying out loud. First, as always, they'd sent praises to heaven for the Lord's majesty and faithfulness, for the many answers to prayer he'd sent them during the more than seven years they'd been meeting. Now, silence reigned as they each listened to God for his leading on how to pray for the town.

"Dear Lord," the man next to her began, "our hearts are heavy because of the knowledge you have given to our sister in Christ this week. Heavy and yet light, for Lord, we expect a miracle."

"Yes," she whispered, and the others breathed their assent.

"We know, dear Jesus, that you are in charge. That you have called us to pray. You have heard our prayers as we have prayed for the town, for our churches and places of business, and for individual folks in need. And now you've sent us word that the time of your prophecy is almost upon us. We thank you, we praise you for that knowledge, Lord, so that *we can request your protection and mercy over Bradleyville when the crisis arrives."*

Her legs were beginning to numb. She shifted her weight, leaning an arm against the couch.

"Father, we pray for the employees at the mill," the man's wife continued. "We thank you for the agreement in June. That was a direct answer to our prayers. Now, Lord, with all we hear 'bout anger returnin', we ask for your peace to descend so that agreement can last till August."

"And please, Lord," she jumped in, her fingers gripping the edge of the couch cushion, "please spare the lives a our people. We know you got lots to teach us; we know that as a town we ain't let you be Lord a our lives. And we know that, like the nation a Israel, you're gonna let this crisis come to bring us back to you. But please, dear Jesus"—tears formed in her closed eyes—"have mercy on us and don't let anyone die. Send your angels, Lord, and protect us all."

The third woman of the group spoke up, asking God's "special blessin' and protection" on the person whose face had been clear in the vision. "Lord, you know how we've prayed for this dear soul over the years. We ask for you to grant your strength and comfort and pray that, through all that happens, you'll make your purpose and plans known."

The four of them fell silent once again, listening for guidance from the Holy Spirit. Her legs had gone to sleep.

"Lord," she entreated, "when the crisis comes, send someone into the very midst of it to pray. Someone who is filled with your Spirit. Protect this person physically. And grant your wisdom of what to do, what to say, and how to pray. . . ."

chapter 21

I sat between Lee and Miss Wilma in church the following morning, choosing to ignore the raised eyebrows and whispers of those around us. Connie had stayed home, too uncomfortable to sit in the hard pew. The small sanctuary was stifling hot, even with all the windows open. A few elderly ladies whisked paper fans before their shiny faces. My aunt and uncle filed into their usual pew with the Matthews, Aunt Eva catching Miss Wilma's eye and proudly slanting her head in my and Lee's direction, as if our sitting together was all her doing. Celia Matthews looked back at me with a tiny smile, trying to hide her obvious disappointment that, for the second Sunday in a row, I would not be sitting next to her. Something about her expression tugged at my heart. Even surrounded by her family, she so often seemed sad. Beside her, Thomas threw a grin over his shoulder at us. Pressing his lips together secretively, he slid his eyes across the aisle to Jake Lewellyn, then back at me. I lifted my eyebrows, acknowledging the look.

"What's that all about?" Lee whispered.

"Oh," I replied vaguely, still smiling at Thomas's back, "you know Thomas, always up to something."

Lee grunted under his breath.

After my disquieting night, the hymns we sang that morning were comforting. I'd become familiar with quite a few hymns during my Sundays in Bradleyville. Singing about God and his goodness, I felt renewed in my calling to return to Cincinnati. *Thank you for sending the dream of my mother to me*, I prayed during the silent moment of confession. *Thank you for showing me through her what I am to do.*

For his sermon, Pastor Frasier chose a text from Matthew 19. The verse numbers sounded vaguely familiar. As he began to read, I smiled. It was a story I well understood.

"And, behold," he read, starting at verse 16, "one came and said unto him, 'Good Master, what good thing shall I do, that I may have eternal life?' And he said unto him, 'Why callest thou me good? there is none good but one, that is, God....'" Pastor Frasier continued, reading how Jesus commanded the young man to keep the commandments. "'All these things have I kept from my youth up,' the young man replied; 'what lack I yet?'" Jesus' answer was the part I best remembered. It would have been my mother's verse. "'If thou wilt be perfect, go and sell that thou hast, and give to the poor, and thou shalt have treasure in heaven: and come and follow me.'"

Briefly, I wondered how Pastor Frasier would approach the verses. Their message seemed a far cry from the beliefs he'd expounded in our conversation so many years ago. I'd been to church many times since then, slowly learning to respect the man, even though we obviously didn't agree. True, my respect had been grudging at first, given the way that conversation had ended. But I'd had to admit he lived his beliefs, just as I was living mine. So who was I to judge?

Lee's roughened hands rested on his legs, fingers spread. He looked so handsome in his blue Sunday suit and tie, the lime scent of his aftershave hanging in the air. I longed to hold his hand but knew better. If we so much as touched shoulders, not a person behind us would hear a word of the sermon.

"'What good thing shall I do?'" Pastor Frasier was repeating. "What *good thing?'* Do ya see, right from the very beginnin', the wrong assumption this young man was makin'? He'd kept the commandments all his life. Leastways, that's what he claimed." The pastor drew in his mouth, widening his eyes. "Far better man than I. And so, you see, he thought what he needed was one more *good thing.*

"Now let's stop right there for a minute. Why do you suppose, if he'd always kept the commandments, this young man thought he had to do somethin' else? Anybody got a guess?" He gazed around the sanctuary. A few rows back, someone coughed. "The clue is right here in verse 20. 'What lack I yet?' he asks. Can you imagine that? A man with youth and health and wealth. Got everything goin' for him. Most of all, remember, he's *good.* Kept the commandments all his life. Even looks right at Jesus and tells him so. So *why,* brothers and sisters, should this young man, of all people, *feel he lacked anything?"*

I glanced at Lee. He was listening intently, his brow slightly furrowed. I knew the answer to the pastor's question. The man had kept all the commandments—that was for himself. But what had he done for others? That's why Jesus had told him to give what he had to the poor—in other words, to realize his riches weren't as important as a willingness to serve his fellow man.

Pastor Frasier's answer to his own question was far different than mine. "Look again at verse 17. Do ya see where Jesus said to the young man, 'why callest thou me good?' He goes on to say only God is good. In other words, young man—you who think so much of yourself, you who say you've kept all the commandments—what 'good' is your 'good' when compared to God's? Only *he* is perfect. And perfection, brothers and sisters, is what he demands. . . ."

Irritation wiggled up my spine. Pastor Frasier was going off on one of his tangents again. I should have stayed home, claimed a headache. I could be sewing right now, finishing another dress. I was behind in my sewing. I'd planned to make at least six outfits, but I'd spent so many hours baking and serving for those silly sawmill meetings. I needed to make up for lost time. If only I had a better sewing machine; my mother's was sadly outdated.

Lee shifted his weight, wiping a bead of sweat from his forehead. I smiled at him, but his attention remained riveted on the pastor. I hoped he would offer to drive me home.

"You see, folks, we're all gonna fall short. Just as this poor, rich young man did. 'Cause if you try to live your life by being 'good,' you'll never quite measure up. There'll always be somethin' more you need to do—somethin', by the way, that you *won't be willin' to do*. That's just what happened here. Jesus knew this young man's heart. And so when he asked, 'what lack I yet?' Jesus came back with the one thing he knew would be too hard. Too much. And that was to give away all he owned."

Pastor Frasier paused, placing two fingers against his chin. "But you know what? Jesus didn't stop there. 'Cause if he had, there'd be no hope for any of us. No, sir. He added four words after that. Four little words that are so big, so immense, that they mean the difference between judgment and eternal life. What are they? Look at verse 21. 'Come and follow me.' Come and follow me. That's it. That's salvation in a nutshell. Not just keepin' the commandments, although that's important. Not just comin' to church, although I hope y'all will keep on comin', lest I'm left with nobody to preach to. Not even givin' all ya own to the poor. But followin' *Jesus*, that's the key. And *that's* what was missin' from this young man's life. He wasn't willin' to give up what he, personally, needed to give up in order to make Jesus first in his life.

"Let me ask ya somethin' as I close, folks. What is it that you're not willin' to give up? What's holdin' *you* back?"

By the final hymn, I was all too ready to leave church. I did stop to give Celia a big hug, promising I'd see her sometime that week. She'd probably tag along with her beloved granddad when we went to Tull's Drugstore.

Lee's truck was an oven when we climbed in. He drove slowly out of the unpaved parking lot, trying not to kick up dust through our open windows. He was unusually quiet.

"What are you mulling about?" I asked. "Problems at the mill?"

He shot me a self-conscious smile. "No. Just 'bout pastor's sermon."

"Oh." It was the last thing I wanted to discuss.

"What'd you think about it?"

I shrugged. "Not much of anything. He and I have had our discussions. We don't see eye to eye on some things."

"Hmm," he grunted, as if he understood all too well. Which annoyed me.

"So what did *you* think about it?"

He tapped the steering wheel, then raised his fingers in a wave to someone driving by. "Well, it got me . . . considerin' a few things. Things Mama always talks to me about."

"Giving your life to Jesus Christ, you mean," I said bluntly.

He looked almost embarrassed. "Somethin' like that."

I crossed my arms and looked out the window. "Well, if that sounds good to you, maybe that's what you need to do, then." Why did I sound so petulant?

"Hmm," he grunted again. I shot him a look. We pulled up in front of the house. "Later, maybe." He put the truck in park and twisted in his seat to face me. "Right now, I'd rather be kissin' you."

The petulance fell away. I rolled my eyes. "Right here, Mr. Harding? In front of the whole town?"

He made a point of looking around. "I don't see anybody."

"That's because they're all hiding behind their windows. Look carefully, you're bound to see the curtains pinched back."

"So is that a 'no'?"

I lowered my eyes coquettishly. "Well, only for now. For right *here*."

"So you *will* go out with me again." He looked pleased with himself, like a lawyer who'd just scored a major point in court.

"Who said I wouldn't?"

"Nobody." His expression turned. "But you are leavin' in a few weeks." He paused, as if waiting to hear that I'd changed my mind.

"That's true," I replied softly. "I am, Lee. You know I have to go. Don't you?"

He took a deep breath, nodding his head once. "I know. You got your job, your plans."

"It's more than that." I'd told him so little, really. "It's . . . what I'm supposed to do. What *I* have to do to follow God."

Confusion flicked across his face. I reached for his hand. "I haven't told you about it—the dream I had of my mother after she died, and what she said. And how that dream, and the way she raised me, has pointed me in this direction."

He gazed at me with intensity, his face falling. Without knowing the details, for the first time he seemed to grasp how unfailing was my purpose in leaving Bradleyville. He withdrew his hand and turned back to the steering wheel.

"Well, we'll talk about it soon." The forced lightness of his voice did not conceal the hurt. "Right now, I gotta go; there's a lot a work left to do on the house. Plus I got some people to call 'bout the mill. Things aren't goin' well there at all." He rubbed his face wearily.

I stood on the sidewalk and watched him drive away, a tightness in my chest.

The rest of the day, I sewed on my third dress, a yellow one with a white, broad collar. I barely lifted my head from the machine, so intent was I on finishing the dress that day. Even Aunt Eva sensed I was in no mood to chat. Her imminent questions about my date with Lee the previous evening would have to wait.

Futilely, I tried to push thoughts of Lee from my head. The louder those thoughts clamored, the harder I worked, banging down the scissors and threading the machine needle with brow-tugging focus. I could not open my heart any more to him; I could *not*. I'd only had three dates with him, anyhow, so why should I even be worrying about such a thing? *Three dates.* What were they, compared to my plans, my *life*. Not to mention our incompatibilities. Now he was even talking seriously about Pastor Frasier's sermons, for heaven's sake.

Lee phoned around 3:00. When Uncle Frank appeared in my doorway with the news, I impatiently pulled my foot from the sewing machine pedal. The needle's whirring slowed to a stop. Staring at the yellow cloth spread before me until it blurred, I considered what to do. Talking to Lee would just make me feel worse. And yet I sensed his phone call was like an outstretched hand, seeking reassurance that I did feel something for him.

"Tell him I'm call him back," I replied after a moment. "I can't stop right now."

"You sure?"

"Yes." I pressed my foot against the pedal, and the whirring resumed.

Toward the end of the afternoon, when I knew Aunt Eva was out visiting, I took a break to pour a glass of iced tea in the kitchen. It had grown terribly hot in my room, and I stopped to inhale air-conditioned comfort from the unit in the living room window. The house seemed dark. I peered toward Uncle Frank's lounge chair, where he sat reading the paper. "Look at the clouds. It's gonna rain." As if in answer, thunder sounded in the distance.

"Good," he muttered. "Cool things off."

I took a drink. "Who's Aunt Eva visiting?"

"The Matthews." He lowered the paper and eyed me. "You call Lee back?"

"No."

He raised his eyebrows, the sports section rustling in his hands. "You goin' to?"

I shrugged. "Sure. Later."

Clearly, he wondered whether or not to pursue the subject. Aunt Eva would have had no such compunctions. "Did you ... have a good time last night?"

"Yeah. The picnic spot was beautiful. We could see Bradleyville."

"Good."

"Uncle Frank," I said quickly, "does your offer still stand to help me move?"

"Of course."

I walked around the rectangular coffee table and perched on the edge of the couch. "The problem is, August first is on a Thursday."

"Uh-huh." He folded the newspaper section and tossed it on the carpet. "It can wait till Saturday the third, can't it? We can load the rental truck the night before and leave early in the morning. I'll stay the night and head back Sunday."

"But if I'm not there on the first, they might rent out the apartment to someone else."

"No, they won't, Jessie," he replied, amusement tingeing his voice. "You've already paid your deposit. Just tell the manager you'll be arrivin' on the weekend."

I rested the iced tea glass on my knee, feeling its coldness. He was right, of course. But I didn't want to wait two extra days; I should leave the very first moment I could. Maybe even earlier than I'd planned. An irrational panic that my departure would never arrive filled my chest.

"Jessie, it's the only thing to do. You can't drive your car and the rental truck too. Plus you gotta have help movin' in, even if it is only bedroom furniture."

"I know." *Good grief*, I thought, *I'm going to cry*.

Uncle Frank was searching my face. "Honey, what're you worried about?"

A sheet of rain swept suddenly, darkly over my car and down the street. "Nothing. I just ... really want to go. I have lots to do there before I start work. Get the bedroom painted. Rent the rest of the furniture. I want time to drive around Cincinnati. Visit the Center...." My words died away as a picture of Mom reading to children, cross-legged at her feet, flashed before me. I blinked as I caught myself staring at the torrent outside.

"Hey." Uncle Frank leaned forward. "We don't want you to leave, you know that. I personally believe God's got a few things to teach you before you step out into the world. And I pray that when you do leave, it'll be to follow a plan centered around Christ. But, Jessie, nobody can keep you from going, if that's what you're bound and determined to do."

My throat was tightening. "I know."

"Then what is it? Is it Lee?"

Another image hit me in the chest. The image of Lee waving in the pouring rain as I drove away. "Six hours away isn't the edge of the world, you know," I said. "We could maybe see each other once in a while."

"Sure you could."

"And I'll come back for holidays and things."

"Uh-huh."

Slowly I reached for a section of the paper, put it on the table, and set down my glass. "Anyway." My smile was forced. "Saturday the third sounds fine. Thanks for taking a whole weekend to help me."

His eyes followed me as I rose.

For the rest of the day, I worked diligently on my yellow dress, far too busy to call Lee. Shortly after midnight it was finished, hanging crisply in my closet. I fell into bed and was instantly asleep.

chapter 22

The next morning I was back at it, sewing my fourth dress. I'd planned to spend the entire day working. Now, besides keeping my mind off Lee, I had another reason to occupy my brain. At breakfast, Uncle Frank had asked Aunt Eva to pray throughout the day that the temporary agreement at the mill would hold until August first. Evidently, Lee had called again in the evening, this time to tell my uncle of phone conversations he'd had with some of the employees. Tempers were rising, and things sounded tenuous. At the news, I'd prayed too—both to my guardian angel and to God himself. I worried about my uncle and Lee in the midst of the agitation. And, selfishly to be sure, I worried about getting caught up in the contention myself, through my ties to both of them. Enough had already happened since I'd come back to Bradleyville. And all I'd wanted was a little peace!

By the time my aunt and uncle left for work, I was already cutting out my pattern. The gentle *snip-snip* of the scissors sounded louder than usual in the quiet house. A niggling worry kept worming its way into my head. After Lee's conversation with Uncle Frank, why hadn't he asked to talk to me?

The phone jangled in the living room, and I jumped. Flicking the scissors from my fingers, I hopped up to answer it. Maybe Lee had found some way to call me from the mill.

"Hello?" I said, expectant.

"This is the day!" crowed a familiar voice.

I let out a disappointed breath. "Hi, Thomas." His statement sank in. "How do you know?"

"Jake's gone into Albertsville."

"Ah." *Albertsville.* I'd forgotten I might have to drive there today. I was low on the blue thread I needed for my dress. It was a depressing thought, possibly having to take that extra time.

"So, you goin' with me to Tull's, ain't ya?"

My eyes closed. "When?"

"Should be there by noon, I'd say."

"Well, I was working on a—"

"It'd be nice if you picked me up. Kinda hot to walk today; the rain just made it more humid than ever."

There was a part of Thomas that would never grow up.

"Celia'd like to come along."

"Okay, Thomas, okay. I'll be there at quarter till."

I hung up the phone with a sigh.

"Good day, Thomas. Got your girlfriend along, I see." Mr. Tull moved birdlike as he efficiently whipped up two strawberry shakes for us plus a Coke float for Celia. She tugged at my hand and grinned. Hank Jenkins, Thomas's second-oldest friend, was waiting nearby, sucking noisily on a Mountain Dew.

When he'd reached sixty, Mr. Jenkins had retired from the mill. He was tall and skinny, with big ears protruding from beneath an ever-present, sweat-stained red baseball cap. None of his seat-worn pants quite managed to cover his ankles. He was three years younger than his two best friends and got more kicks from their renowned arguments than anyone else in town. He would guffaw and slap his bony knees at their antics, head swiveling back and forth at the volley of words.

Orders filled, we stepped back into the heat.

"Where's Jake?" Mr. Jenkins asked as he eased into his chair under the awning. Thomas was already ensconced in his own. I'd drawn up another to form a loose semicircle, leaving Mr. Lewellyn's chair empty. Celia sat next to me, cross-legged on the sidewalk.

"Went to Albertsville for somethin'. He'll be along soon."

I cast Thomas a pointed look. He scratched the side of his nose, feigning innocence.

Downtown Bradleyville seemed oppressed somehow, and it wasn't the heat. Watching people come and go, I sensed a disquiet. Numerous times the snatches of conversations I heard were grumblings about husbands' woes at the mill. All ears, Mr. Jenkins pumped us for the latest news. A preoccupied Thomas answered that the men were "tryin' their best" to wait it out till August, hoping for a permanent solution then. Celia added that her mama was tired of hearing about it and got mad whenever Granddad mentioned it. "Now, Celia," Thomas responded, peering up Main, "don't be airin' your laundry on the street." She went back to spooning ice cream from the top of her float.

Fifteen minutes later, I'd finished my milk shake. Mr. Jenkins was nearly dozing, and Thomas looked dejected. Celia was playing with a ladybug on the sidewalk.

"I'll be right back," I said, placing my empty glass beside her. "I've just got to run into the dime store for a minute."

"Hurry back," Thomas put in, "you wouldn't want to miss nothin'."

"Lot to miss," Jenkins snorted, rubbing his eyes.

The dime store was out of the thread I needed. *Drat.* I did *not* relish going all the way to Albertsville for it. Shading my forehead as I recrossed the street, I caught sight of Alice Eder through the window of her sewing shop, three doors up from the drugstore. She should have the color; perhaps she'd sell me an extra spool. I veered in her direction and stepped inside, a bell above her door tinkling.

Alice's Tailoring commanded one large room of an old red-brick building that housed studio apartments on the second and third floors. Miss Alice and her husband owned the building, living frugally in a three-bedroom apartment on the fourth floor. Their collected rents and her shop were their main sources of income, Luke Eder having suffered a heart attack seven years ago that had forced his early retirement from the mill.

"Hi, Miss Alice! Looks like you're keeping busy." I gestured toward numerous pieces of clothing hanging from a portable aluminum rack. Stretched across a worktable was a length of flowered chintz, ready for cutting into curtains. I stepped over to feel the fabric. "Pretty." I could imagine them ruffled and draped, framing a large window.

"Oh, you have the eye, all right," she laughed, running her hand over the fabric. "Your Aunt Eva's tol' me how good a seamstress you are."

"Yes, I like it. I find it . . . calming." Wondering at my use of the word, I let my eyes drift to her sewing machine. "That looks like a *wonderful* machine!"

"Oh, it's the best. Fastest you can find."

I examined it with awe. "Lots of stitchings, huh."

Miss Alice sank with purpose into one of two ruby-colored chairs angled near the front window. "Sit down, won't ya, Jessie. Funny you stoppin' in here today; I been meanin' to call ya." Her wrinkled hands rested on the arm of the chair, her blue eyes dancing. Miss Alice was a petite woman, smaller than I, and had held her figure well even though I guessed she must be close to seventy. Her hair was curly and almost pure white. A pair of glasses dangled from a golden chain around her neck.

I obliged.

"See, it's like this. I been wantin' to slow down. Luke's health is fragile, you know, and besides, I been workin' all my life. Got grandbabies I'd rather be seein' and other things. Anyway, I been thinkin' a hirin' somebody to help me out maybe four, five hours a day. So I asked God to help me find somebody. I was thinkin'

I'd find a mother to come in while her kids're at school. But right now it's summer, and kids're at home. Then God reminded me a you. I know you'll be here through July. Think you could help out until then, earn yourself some extra money?" She smiled brightly.

I smiled back, hiding my fluster. It's not often someone announces you're their answer to prayer. But I couldn't imagine accepting her offer. I still had three dresses to make for myself. My hesitation dulled her expression.

"I know this is unexpected," she added hastily, "but it wouldn't be for long. Any help you could give me, I'd much appreciate."

Regardless of Miss Alice's sincerity, I sensed the specter of Aunt Eva at work.

"Miss Alice, I'm really flattered at your offer; I know this shop means a lot to you. Tell you what. Let me think about it for a day or two."

She sighed, satisfied. "All right then. You do that."

Once outside her shop I turned to wave good-bye, and she wagged her fingers at me with enthusiasm. Too late I remembered the blue thread I needed. I started to turn back, but at that precise moment I saw Jake Lewellyn's long green Buick glide down the street.

"Jessie, come on back now!" Thomas called.

I hesitated. Thomas beckoned furiously. Throwing a final smile to Miss Alice, I hurried back to my chair.

Not five seconds passed before all peace was shattered.

Mr. Jenkins was just beginning to brag about the whopping size of his brother's tomatoes when Mr. Lewellyn pulled up to the curb, heaved himself out to slam the door, and declared with a shake of his chubby finger, "I *know* it was you, Thomas Bradley!"

"Oh, gracious," Hank Jenkins breathed midsentence, "what now."

Celia clutched the remains of her Coke float to her chest, shrinking toward me. "He looks like a bulldog, doesn't he?" she whispered.

I tried not to laugh. "Never thought about it, but you're right."

"Thomas Bradley!" Mr. Lewellyn was yanking checkered pants over his round belly. "Let me tell you somethin': this time you've gone too far! As if the town ain't got enough trouble nowadays. I'm not goin' to stand for it!"

I patted Celia reassuringly on the head. Thomas was taking a long slurp from his near-empty milk shake.

"Aahh," he sighed, wiping his mouth. He smacked his lips and looked Mr. Lewellyn up and down. "Why don't you set down in your chair, Jake; take a load off. And I do mean a *load.*"

Hank Jenkins suppressed a giggle.

Mr. Lewellyn hopped around the sidewalk like water droplets on a hot griddle. "Don't give me none a your straight-faced lyin', Thomas. You know what I'm talkin' 'bout."

"You hear that, Hank?" Thomas said. "He's callin' me a liar, and all I did was invite him to set down."

"You painted a new number on our sign!" The words exploded from Mr. Lewellyn's mouth, shaking his fat, red jowls. "That's defacin' city property, ol' man, and it ain't legal. No matter *what* your last name is!"

Bradleyville's city limits sign on Route 622 was a symbol of pride for the town. Jonathan Bradley had carved the first one years ago on a glossily finished rectangle of oak, mounted on top of a tall two-by-four. Ever since then, Bradleyville had insisted on this hand-hewn display of independence, eschewing the ugly metal sign issued by the state. And every five years, the town conducted its own census, celebrated by a new sign, donated by the mill, which declared its name and current population in large black letters.

"Aw, Jake, you're actin' like a chigger in tall grass, jumpin' 'round like that." Thomas was stirring his shake. "This ain't Miss Turner's fifth grade class the day someone put a tack in your seat. Why don't you just calm down and set a spell."

Mr. Lewellyn's glare was ferocious. "I can see you won't be reasonable. If I was still a policeman, I'd haul you off to jail—"

Thomas threw back his head and laughed.

"Just like Miss Turner sent you to the principal's office."

A sour look stole over Thomas's face.

"As it is, I aim to report this immediately to Bill Scutch, and he can do the honors."

With that, Jake Lewellyn turned on his heel and stalked across the street toward the police station, nearly getting run over by a truck heading toward the sawmill.

"Tell him to bring his cuffs!" Thomas called. "I ain't goin' easy!"

"Whoo, what a show." Folding his hands across his stomach, Mr. Jenkins tipped back his chair. "I don't s'pose you know anything 'bout that sign, Thomas."

"Granddad, you aren't goin' to jail, are you!" Celia cried. The ice cream in her glass had long since melted, her Coke float resembling slushy snow.

"Don't you worry, missy," Thomas replied. I squeezed her hand.

It wasn't long before Mr. Lewellyn was headed back across the street, dragging Policeman Scutch with him. Bill Scutch was about thirty years old, a handsome blond with hazel eyes and a quick smile. I'd had a crush on him years ago, when he first became the Bradleyville policeman, but I'd been too young. He was now married, with two kids. I knew he thought Thomas walked on water, and they often went to the school basketball games together.

"Hello, Jessie, Celia." He winked at the little girl as he eased over the curb.

Thomas nodded. "Bill. Nice day. Buy you a drink?" He lifted his glass.

"No thanks." Bill cleared his throat. "Jake tells me our town sign's been painted over. Frankly, I ain't seen it myself."

"Well," Thomas shrugged, "if Jake says so, it must be true." He smiled grandly at Mr. Lewellyn.

Hank Jenkins jumped up to pull over an extra chair. "Have a seat."

Mr. Scutch settled himself reluctantly, Mr. Lewellyn pacing under the awning, sweat running off his nose. "Eight years,

Thomas," he muttered. "Eight years earlier, and I'd be comin' after you myself."

"That'll be the day, Jake," Thomas laughed, "when you *quit* comin' after me, town policeman or not."

"We're not kids anymore!" Mr. Lewellyn stormed. "When're you goin' to grow up! I had my own grandboy born three years ago, just after our last census; you don't see *me* changin' that sign. There are limits, Thomas, even for you."

Mr. Lewellyn suddenly looked exhausted. He pulled his chair forward and plopped into it, fanning his face with a beefy hand.

For a moment, no one spoke. I glanced sideways at Bill Scutch, wondering what he'd do. The slightest flicker of a smile curved his lips, then was gone. He stared at Mr. Lewellyn, rubbing his forehead, eyes narrowed.

"My stomach hurts," Celia whimpered.

I leaned over to put my arm around her shoulders.

"You're right, Jake," Bill pronounced. "It's not fair for one person to deface town property. If everybody did that, this place'd be as messy as Albertsville."

"Now hold on a second," Thomas interrupted. "This is just one a Jake's accusations, and he's been accusin' me a things since the first day a school. Nobody can prove I did anything."

Bill Scutch puckered his chin. "That's true."

"We all know you did it, Thomas!" Mr. Lewellyn jumped to his feet again. "No other baby's been born lately in this town, and certainly nobody else would think hisself so important that he'd change the sign that belongs to all of us just for his own grandboy!"

"Now hold on, Jake," Mr. Scutch held up a hand. "I think I have a solution."

"The Lord punishes sinners. Put him in jail until he pays for it; that's the only solution!" Mr. Lewellyn's scarlet cheeks were shaking again.

"Yeah, we could do that."

Thomas looked not the least bit worried. "Let's hear your solution," he said, leaning over to set his empty glass on the sidewalk.

"We could paint over the sign again."

Mr. Lewellyn slid to a halt. "Don't worry 'bout fixin' that sign back, Bill; we'll have to git a new one made. But I want *him* to pay for it—with money *and* with a night in jail."

"No, gentlemen. What I mean is . . . ," Bill Scutch leaned forward. "That last number on the sign woulda been changed from a two to a three, right?"

"S'pose so." Thomas sniffed.

"Well, then, it's simple. We'll paint over it again. Change the three to a four."

"Huh?" Hank Jenkins's jaw flopped open, and Mr. Lewellyn stared at Bill Scutch as if he'd gone mad. Even Thomas's eyebrows shot up before he caught himself. "What in the world for, Bill?" he asked.

"It's like Jake said, Thomas. It's not fair the sign changed just 'bout the time your grandboy was born. Regardless a who changed it. At any rate, the harm's already been done. So until 1970, when we git ourselves a new sign, we'll just paint over that last number one more time. This one'll be for Jake's grandboy."

Thomas slid a look at the policeman, his surprise dissolving into poker-faced perception. When he turned back to Mr. Lewellyn, his expression was one of utter betrayal. "Bill Scutch," he declared, "whatever's gotten into you? Some vandal's gone and wrecked our town sign, and now you're advocatin' wreckin' it some more?"

Bill held Jake Lewellyn's astonished gaze. "Well, Jake?"

"Uh, I don't know." He gripped the arms of his chair and slowly lowered himself into it. "I never woulda thought a that."

"Aw, forgit it, Jake." Thomas sounded disgusted. "You're just mad 'cause I still got your marble. You want me to spend a night in jail, I'll spend a night in jail, whether I done anything're not. I been in far worse places in my fightin' life; it makes no never-mind to me."

A change spread across Mr. Lewellyn's face, as if he'd sucked to the middle of sour candy and tasted sugar. "No, now wait a minute, Thomas. You don't need to be sleepin' in jail, with your old bones. And Bill's right, that sign's already ruint, so one more paintin' over's not goin' to hurt it none." He nodded his head once. Firmly. "I think it's a good solution. Let's do it."

Thomas sucked on his teeth. "I don't know, Jake."

"It's the best way. And it'll put you in your own bed tonight."

I watched Thomas's fingers drum against his chair. "And just when do you suppose we'd take care a this little assignment? I got to get my grandgirl home in time for supper."

Bill Scutch raised his eyebrows and shrugged.

"Well," Mr. Lewellyn said, "we could do it right now, I s'pose. Wouldn't take long. The hardware store's right across the street; all we need is a brush and some black paint." He stood suddenly, pushing back his chair. "In fact, I think that's the best idea—do it now and git it done." He fished in a pocket and pulled out his car keys. "I'll drive. Hank, Bill, you both come along to see it's done right." He jerked his chin toward the hardware store when Thomas failed to move. "Well, let's go, ol' man. Let's git this unpleasant business over with so you can git home."

Thomas had linked his fingers under his chin and was gazing up at his adversary.

"Git a move on, Thomas!"

He would not budge.

"Would you come on! We got a sign to paint!"

A long silence. Slowly, Thomas began to shake his head, back and forth. "I never thought I'd see the day," he said, clicking his tongue against his teeth. "Jake Lewellyn—my boyhood friend who grew up to wear the Bradleyville badge for thirty-five years. Who was honest as the day is long. And now"—he pressed his lips together—"now after retiring with honors, you're fixin'—with great excitement, I might add—to buy some black paint and a brush and vandalize the sign a the town my daddy founded. Lord help us, what *is* this world comin' to."

I pressed fingers against my mouth. Mr. Jenkins burst into laughter, then tried to cover by coughing into his fist. Bill Scutch valiantly clung to a straight face. Mr. Lewellyn's jowls were turning purple. "Now you hold on!" he yelled. "This wasn't—!"

"Jake," Thomas pronounced, "you said it yourself. You know very well our town sign's not changed every time a baby's born. We counted everyone in 1965 and we'll do it again in 1970, and until that time you're just gonna have to wait." He turned to Bill Scutch. "What sort a punishment would be appropriate for our fallen brother?"

Mr. Lewellyn's mouth was opening and closing with no sound uttered, like a fish flopping on the riverbank.

"Let me see." Bill Scutch sighed and rubbed his chin. "I guess a night in jail oughta do it."

That did it. Jake Lewellyn recovered enough to let loose a few words that Celia should not have heard. When he stomped away, I could have sworn the sidewalk shook. We all watched as he yanked open his car door, shoved himself inside, and roared away.

"And I still got your marble too!" Thomas hollered after him.

"Whoooeee!" he cackled, leaping from his seat to slap Bill Scutch on the back. "The wisdom a Solomon, I do declare; I done taught you well." Grabbing my hands, he pulled me up and jigged me around the sidewalk. "The town's needed somethin' to laugh at, Jessie Callum. Just wait till it hears this!"

chapter 23

So you were right in the midst of that brouhaha, I hear." Aunt Eva ladled peas onto her plate, pushing them together into a small mound.

It never ceased to amaze me how fast word buzzed around Bradleyville. But then, working in the post office all day, Aunt Eva did tend to sit in the center of the beehive. "I was there, all right."

"Thought you were gonna sew all day."

I sank my fork into the first bite of mouthwatering meatloaf. I'd hardly eaten anything all day, and after I'd put it in the oven to bake, its tantalizing aroma had seeped all the way into my bedroom as I sewed. "I was. But Thomas called and asked me to go to Tull's with him. Plus, I promised Celia I'd see her sometime this week, and she was there."

"Mmm." Aunt Eva eyed me with curiosity. I could practically see the wheels turning in her head. Uncle Frank was busy dressing a baked potato with butter and sour cream. His mind seemed elsewhere. "You were awful busy sewin' yesterday," my aunt pressed. "Not a minute to spare, even for a telephone call. Now today you're runnin' 'round with Thomas."

Savoring the peppery meatloaf, I remained silent. I wasn't quite sure what she was getting at—my reticence to talk to Lee or the depth of my involvement in Thomas's shenanigans. Or both.

"So did you know all that was comin'?"

Pure innocence pasted itself on my face. "How could I have known? We were already there when Mr. Lewellyn came roaring up, mad as could be."

A tiny smile played over Uncle Frank's lips. He spread the sour cream with a knife, quickly glancing at me, then back to his plate. I sniffed and took a drink of iced tea. Uncle Frank always did have the uncanny knack of seeing right through me.

Aunt Eva opened her mouth again, and by the look on her face, I knew she was going to ask me about Lee. Without thinking, I jumped in. "Guess what. I saw Alice Eder while I was downtown, and she actually offered me a job for the next few weeks." As soon as the words were uttered, I could have kicked myself. Out of the frying pan, into the fire.

"It's a *great* opportunity for you," my aunt gushed, showing no surprise at the piece of news. "Why don't you take it?"

I shrugged. "I don't know. I have a lot of sewing to do here. Three more dresses. Plus I've been looking forward to these weeks of not having to fit into anybody else's schedule."

"Sounds good to me," Uncle Frank put in. "You been workin' awful hard the past five years."

Aunt Eva glared at him.

"Well, Alice wants to retire, you know." She arched an eyebrow as she sank her fork through meatloaf. "It would be just perfect for you to take that shop over."

"What in the world would I want with that shop?"

She looked offended. "To have as your own business, of course. You could stay right here and make a very good living, particularly with your skills."

"Aunt Eva, I have a 'living' to make in Cincinnati. I've already got a job there, remember? *And* an apartment. *And* Hope Center."

"All right, all right." Her hand fluttered in the air. "It was just a thought." She bent over her meat with purpose, frustration rounding her shoulders. A strand of red hair straggled from her bun, and she pushed it from her face with impatience. In the ensuing silence, I could hear her jaw popping as she chewed. When she put her fork down on her plate with a clatter, I jumped. "Well, I don't think you should go."

"Now, Eva," my uncle said.

"Don't 'now, Eva' me," she retorted. "You know good and well you agree with me; you just won't say it to her face."

Irritation plucked my nerves. For a moment, I wished I'd never come back. I should have gone straight from my graduation to Cincinnati. Now that I was here, I kept bumping into one complication after another. The sawmill, Lee, now my aunt flagrantly trying to run my life. *Keep calm*, I told myself, *this is nothing to get upset about*. I looked from my aunt to my uncle, searching for the most benign way to deal with this particular roadblock. The subject of my moving away had been lurking over our shoulders ever since I'd come back to Bradleyville, and we might as well deal with it now so I could enjoy a few more weeks of relative peace.

Summoning a neutral expression, I looked to Uncle Frank. "Is that so?"

He set down his utensils and inhaled audibly, as if preparing himself for a long-delayed confrontation. Then he nodded.

"You told me just yesterday that nobody could stop me from going."

"That's true, Jessie." His voice was gentle. "But I also told you I want you to be followin' Christ's plans for your life, not your own."

I stared at him, a familiar defensiveness rising within me. "I *am*, okay? I'm following what God wants me to do, what my mother told me to do in my dream."

He processed that for a moment. "Remember when we talked about that dream, so many years ago? Remember how I asked you to read the Bible to better understand God's purpose for your life? You told me you were doin' that."

"And I was. I read most of it, anyway. But what's that got to do with me leaving? You trying to tell me God only lives in *Bradleyville?*"

"Of *course* not," Aunt Eva interjected.

I ignored her.

"No, Jessie." My uncle's patience sparked remorse through my chest. "Not at all. What we *are* tryin' to say, and what we've been prayin' for all these years, is that you will turn your life over to Christ fully, completely, and—with diligence—seek what *he* wants you to do." He spread his hands. "It's not that your plans are bad. They're good ones; they're laudatory in terms of helpin' other people. Here you are, a beautiful young woman, and you're not seekin' fame or fortune, but how to serve others. Understand me, there's *nothin'* wrong with those goals as far as your career goes. But that's just what they are, Jessie, they're plans for a career. They're *not* plans for salvation. The road you're going down is the same one your mama was on. And she set herself on it because of her own sorrow-filled, abusive upbringin'. You don't *need* to continue that cycle; you were raised with lots of love. You forget that your Aunt Eva had the same upbringin' as your mama, the same angry father. She's had to deal with all that hurt too. And I know she would tell you that the answer to breakin' that cycle lay in acceptin' Jesus Christ and understandin' that he could cleanse away all the horrible feelin's of worthlessness her father had instilled in her."

I looked at my plate, on the verge of tears. This was the longest speech I'd ever heard my uncle make. I trusted him, respected him greatly. And I knew he and Aunt Eva loved me and would never try to lead me astray. What's more, I had to admit that deep within my uncle I sensed a serenity that I wished I had. Even my aunt, with all her chattiness and impulsive interfering, seemed much more grounded and free of her past than my quiet mother ever had. In quick succession, two images flashed through my head—my grandfather's spite-filled pronouncement, "You'll *never* be good enough!"; followed by the brief visage of despair that had crossed my mother's features during what was to be our final moment together.

Our final moment.

My mother's time on earth had been so brief. And she'd spent it unselfishly—on me, on others. Something within me stirred at my uncle's words, and yet those words repelled all that my mother had lived for, like magnets of the same force. All that she had *died* for.

Silence suspended itself over our table. Even Aunt Eva wasn't jumping in to fill it. I raised my eyes to her, seeking a diversion. "You're awful quiet."

"I'm prayin'," came her terse reply.

Uncle Frank said nothing. I had the sense they'd sit there all evening, awaiting my response. I found a speck of lint on the tablecloth. Pinched it between finger and thumb. Let it drop onto the carpet.

Softly, I cleared my throat. "Well. You know I understand your beliefs; I really do. And I think they've . . . helped you a lot. Deal with life and all its problems, I mean. So I respect that." I nudged the handle of my fork further up my plate. "When I first came here I was really hurting too. More than anything else, that dream I had about my mom, and the course it put me on, helped me get over the pain. I've worked"—my throat clinched, and I fought to control it—"I've worked really hard to graduate and get the job I wanted. I've planned for this a long, long time. And I believe absolutely that it's the right thing to do. It *has* to be."

I stopped abruptly, blinking at the inexplicable tinge of desperation in my last sentence.

"Okay, Jessie," Uncle Frank said. "You have our blessin'. You know we love you. Maybe your plans will take you where God wants you to go. One thing I know, he can work for our good no matter *what* we do. But regardless of where you live, I still pray— and I know your aunt will too—that you will come to know

Christ personally. Because only through him are you goin' to find true meanin' for your life. *His* purpose for you is the *perfect* plan. So no matter how great your own is, you could be missin' out on the very best."

Aunt Eva started to say something, but Uncle Frank took the napkin from his lap and placed it on the table with finality. "All right, then, favorite niece." He pushed back his chair. "We promise not to preach to ya anymore. We'll just let God do his own work. Right Eva?"

Stymied, she pressed her lips together, giving her husband a look. Then, with a little huff, she wagged her head in my direction. "Right."

chapter 24

*Y*ou hear 'bout Thomas 'n' Jake yesterday?" The lid on his metal lunchbox clanked as he withdrew a sandwich. He inspected his grimy hands, wiped them half-heartedly on his sawdusted shirt, and unwound the plastic wrap.

"Whole town's heared. Wish I coulda seen it."

"Yeah," a third worker grunted, biting into a thick, home-canned pickle, "I can just see Jake's face, red as a rooster's comb. Hey, is that some a your wife's barbecued pork on that bun?"

"It is, and you keep your grubby hands off."

"My hands. Look at yours." The rest of the pickle disappeared into his mouth. "His wife makes the best barbecued pork I ever tasted. But don't tell mine I said so."

"I never thought I'd hear a Jake in jail," the second man added.

"Aw, he didn't spend the night in jail."

"Yeah, he did."

"He did not."

"That's what I heared."

"Well, you heared wrong. He roared off in his car; wouldn't have none of it. Bill Scutch didn't expect him to do that anyway; he was just playin' along with Thomas. The two a them's close as stacked crackers."

"If I know Jake Lewellyn," the first man said around a mouthful of pork, "he won't show his face for a week."

"The July Fourth parade is Thursday. He wouldn't think a lettin' Thomas lead it by hisself."

"Guess so. Hank tol' me Thomas shouted, 'I still got your marble!'" They all laughed. "That musta hurt."

"You think that marble really exists?"

"Oh, yeah. I seen it myself one time I was over to the Matthews. Real pretty, black and silver, just like the story says. Thomas has the thing settin' in a child's play teacup on his bookcase. Tol' me he polishes it ever mornin' along with his medals."

"Jake'll never git it back."

"Jake'll never quit tryin'."

"My last bite a barbecue. Wonder if I should share it?" The first man considered his coworker's anticipation. "Naw." He shoved it into his mouth.

"Some friend you—"

"Hey. There's Riddum."

"It's still lunchtime."

"No, it ain't, it's 1:00."

"But we didn't set down till 12:30."

"That's y'all's fault. He's lookin' this way."

"Too bad. I'm gonna finish my lunch."

"Me too."

"Not me. He's headin' this way and I'm goin' back to work. Y'all're crazy if you stick around. A few bites ain't worth it."

"Doggone it all! Wait, I'm comin'."

"Well, good fer the both a ya. I ain't movin' till my lunch hour's over."

chapter 25

By midmorning Tuesday I'd finished my blue dress. Luckily, I'd had all the thread I needed. Wasn't it humorous, I thought with sarcasm as I donned the dress, that I'd gone to see Alice Eder for nothing. Now I would have to find a tactful way to deny her request. Standing in front of the bedroom mirror, I admired my own handiwork, turning this way and that. The color was certainly striking against my hair. Yet I felt no joy in the dress's completion.

Sighing, I took it off and hung it with the others in my closet. What to do now? The day stretched before me. The last thing I wanted to do was start on another project. I was tired of sewing; it left my mind too open to thoughts of Lee. And, goodness knows, they'd plagued me ever since Sunday. Last night, after that strained discussion with my aunt and uncle at supper, I'd sat before my machine, tensed, waiting for the phone to ring—even while knowing the ball was in my court. I was supposed to be returning *his* call. I just couldn't do it. I really wanted to, but I couldn't. How could I explain to him my sudden avoidance? How could I make him understand the intensity of my desire to move back to Cincinnati? And why should I *have* to, anyway? I'd had enough discussions about the subject with my aunt and uncle. I was tired of explaining myself.

I sighed again loudly, my gaze drifting to my sewing machine. Compared to Alice Eder's, it seemed hopelessly antiquated. How great it would be to make my next dress in her shop. The stitchings I could create, in no time! Standing in the middle of my bedroom, hands on my hips, I stared at Mom's old machine, mulling. I wondered how much a new machine like Miss Alice's would cost. Maybe I'd just drive into Albertsville after all, look around at new models. Looking wouldn't cost me anything. And it would give me something else to think about.

I walked over to the dresser and picked up my hairbrush.

Driving out of town on 622, every window in my car rolled down, I couldn't help but smile as I passed the Bradleyville sign. What a kick it had been, watching for cars while Thomas painted over that number. A mile or so farther on the right lay the long, tree-lined driveway that belonged to the Riddums. Automatically, I slowed, gazing down the leafy path. At its end, the Riddums' new porch pillars gleamed white under the hot sun. Unexpected anger jolted me. I didn't know the man, but he sure sounded greedy and sour.

My head swiveled back to the road, my foot pressing the accelerator. I was *not* going to think about the sawmill—or any other problems—for the rest of the day.

In Albertsville, I walked into Sears expectantly, only to be informed that they didn't carry the model I was looking for. I lingered awhile, looking at other machines, but soon grew restless. The clerk sent me across town to a store that displayed every kind of machine I could imagine. As I'd guessed, Miss Alice's was the top of the line. And, of course, far too expensive for me to ever buy, given the low salary I'd be making. I left the store dejectedly and found myself back at Sears, trying on shoes, considering purses, even looking at earrings, something I never wore. By the time I drove back to Bradleyville, it was 5:00, time to start supper. I'd bought two pairs of shoes, a purse, three pairs of earrings, a blouse, and skirt. Never had I been so impulsive. What's *wrong* with me, I lamented as I rounded the curves outside town. I was almost ready to turn around and take back the items. Without a doubt, I was getting more antsy about going to Cincinnati every minute.

It was as if spending all that money on career clothes somehow cemented my plans.

After supper that evening, Connie phoned. "Can you come over?" she wheezed.

"Are you okay?"

"Just tired. But I'd love to see you."

I hesitated.

"Lee's almost done with the rooms; you should see 'em. He said he'd be paintin' by this weekend. We want the smell gone by the time the baby arrives. Could you help me pick colors?"

Connie desperately needed a friend, and I knew I should be there for her. Thinking of all the wasted time shopping, I flinched at my selfishness. I could have visited her while Lee was at work. All the same, her plea had a certain . . . timing. "What colors were you thinking of?"

"I don't know. Pale yellow maybe. Or blue. But then what if it's a girl?"

"Blue's always nice."

"I suppose. Who'd want pink walls anyway?"

We fell silent. I tried to imagine the awkwardness—and anticipation—of seeing her brother.

"Am I bothering you?" Her words were tentative.

"Of course not. And I'd love to come, really. Let me just . . . finish what I was doing and I'll be over."

"Good! Mom's baked a dessert. Apple fritter."

I pictured Miss Wilma rocking about a hot kitchen on her bad hip. Timing indeed.

Lee was in the back rooms, working, when I arrived. Well, I huffed to myself, if he couldn't even take the time to say hello to a guest, I didn't need to go see him, either. My gaze fell on Connie. She looked terrible. Her hands and feet were more swollen than before, as was her face. She could barely move from the couch. I knelt beside her on the carpet. "You look so hot."

She smiled faintly. "Heck, it's 7:30. This is cool."

"How about if I get a cold washcloth for your face?"

"I've tried that," Miss Wilma put in, "but it just gets warm so quick. It's hard for me to keep runnin' back and forth."

"Well, that's why I'm here." I fetched a clean washcloth from the bathroom, then went to the kitchen to search for a large pan, which I filled with ice cubes and water.

"Here." Kneeling again beside Connie, I dunked the cloth in the water and wrung it out. She placed it over her entire face.

"Aahh, feels good." Her lips moved under the terrycloth. A few moments later I dunked it again.

"This baby's got to come soon; this is too hard on you."

She put her hands over the washcloth and choked on a sudden sob.

"Oh, Connie." I squeezed her shoulder.

"I'm so scared," she whispered. "I don't know how I'm gonna do this by myself."

"You're not by yourself," I crooned. "You've got Lee and your Mama and me. And Christ."

Why had I said *that?* The words felt awkward on my tongue.

"But I got no husband. I *hate* Bart. And I *hate* Tammy; I *hate* her!"

Her outburst didn't last long. Just time enough for Miss Wilma to move to the end of the couch and begin patting her feet. "Oh, darlin'," she breathed. "Oh, Lord Jesus, help us."

"I'm sorry," Connie sniffed into the tissue I'd brought her. "I shouldn't have said that. You must think I'm a big silly thing."

"I don't think you're silly." I pushed my knuckles playfully into her arm. "Just big." She smiled in spite of herself. "I think you're really strong to be going through this so well. I couldn't do it."

"I don't think I'm doin' all that well. Mama's right; without Jesus' help, I couldn't do it at all."

I brushed a strand of hair off her forehead, still cool from the cloth. "I'm glad you found him."

"I didn't find him; he found me." She managed a grin. "The only thing I need to find now is a man."

Miss Wilma and I laughed, then fell silent. I gazed from mother to daughter, both with their own aloneness, then busied myself, dunking the washcloth. Miss Wilma grew interested in a bird outside the window. Connie covered her face again. From down the hall floated noises of Lee at work.

"Well, guess it's time for some apple fritter," Miss Wilma announced, disappointment in her voice.

"I'll get it." Pushing away from the couch, I rose. Then, stupidly, stared at nothing out the window. With a sigh, I swept wet hands through my hair. "Actually, could you wait a minute? I should go say hi to Lee."

Miss Wilma tried to appear nonchalant.

I found him throwing fragments of wood and wiring into a box, sweat running down his neck. For a moment he didn't know I was there, and I watched him move, shoulder blades gliding under his T-shirt, muscles flexing. The mere sight of him sent sparks through me. My heart quickened. I wanted to feel those muscles, run my hands over them. He turned, though I'd made no sound, and straightened, standing stiffly. We looked at each other, and I saw why he had not called again. He'd hung his heart out on a line, and I had turned away. His vulnerability was now palpable. His expression was guarded, almost defensive. In that moment, I knew my next words would determine the path we'd take while I remained in Bradleyville. I also knew, still, that nothing could stop my leaving. It would be so much easier on us both to cut things short right now.

"I've missed you," my mouth said.

The words unfurrowed his face. In five steps he crossed the room. When he wrapped his arms around me, I didn't mind that he smelled of sweat and dust. I held him tightly. "Connie wants me to help her with colors," I blurted into his chest. "She needs so much, and I haven't done enough for her. Let me help you paint this weekend. Also, I think I'll make her some curtains."

He looked at me with gratitude in his eyes. "You don't have to do all that."

I pulled back from him self-consciously and gazed around the bare walls. "I think pale yellow would be nice for both rooms, don't you? The curtains could be sunny and bright, with a matching blanket for the baby. I'm a good seamstress; did you know that? I could make her all kinds of—"

"Hush, chatterbox." He bent down and kissed me, his lips warm and lingering. I clung to him, barely able to breathe.

Later, over two helpings of highly cinnamoned apple fritter, a radiant Connie and I discussed decorating details, with Miss Wilma and Lee adding ideas. "Everything will be beautiful," I said to Connie before Lee walked me to my car. "And you will be fine, you'll see. Also, Connie," I took her hand, "would you promise me something? When your labor starts, would you call, even if it's the middle of the night? I'd really like to be with you."

With tears in her eyes, she promised.

That night in bed, I thought long and hard. The next morning I went to see Miss Alice. How about we strike a deal, I told her. I'd work four or five hours a day if I could use her sewing machine for myself the rest of the time. She was delighted.

chapter 26

L and sakes, what a week," Aunt Eva declared Friday at supper as she buttered a roll. "Thomas and Jake spattin', a July Fourth parade in the rain, and Blair Riddum's actin' crazier than ever, accordin' to folks. You may a been quiet, Frank, but just about everyone who comes into the post office has a tale to tell." She stirred her tea for no reason, ice cubes clicking. "You and Lee looked awful cute together at the parade," she added, feigning an afterthought.

Cute. I'd looked like a drowned rat, with one of Lee's work shirts drippingly held over my head. The heavens had burst open while I was at his house helping Connie get a pair of her mother's shoes on. She could not see her own feet. We'd all planned to watch the parade together, but Miss Wilma quailed at the rain, saying she'd seen enough Independence Day parades for one lifetime anyway. Connie would not be turned back; she felt house-bound enough to sit through a torrent. The rain soon softened to a drizzle, allowing the parade to begin only a half hour late, which was near-record time. But I was already soaked, having stopped to help an overwhelmed third-grade teacher mold her amorphous class into marching formation.

Everyone always came to the annual parade, which began downtown and made a beeline up Main toward Route 622. Folks from the country drove in, their cars lining side streets and the two church parking lots. The parade was the same every year, but no one cared. After all, kids were a year older and, one hoped, the town band a year better. A filly too young to show off last year would now be a full-grown mare, with patriotic ribbons braided into her mane, and two previous high school juniors would now wear the senior king and queen crowns.

Despite their latest feuding—which had given the edgy town something to laugh about, just as he had hoped—Thomas and Jake led the parade, waving side by side from one of the town's two wailing fire engines. Bill Scutch and his family followed in the police car, and behind them fanned a cacophony of sounds and sights, from toddlers to retired school teachers, all decked out in red, white, and blue. A popular favorite was a large group of mill workers wearing wigs and housedresses while pushing IGA shopping carts and pretending to fight over groceries. Connie had to sit down on the curb, she laughed so hard.

"Why aren't you out there?" I shouted to Lee.

"Not on your life!" He hugged me, grinning.

Remembering the parade, I couldn't help but smile at Aunt Eva's remark. It had been sheer fun and a welcome relief from my own conflicts and the town's as well. I'd felt so *right* standing with Lee and Connie, seeing all the familiar faces of Bradleyville. At that moment Cincinnati seemed as far away as China. All the same, today, after five hour's work for Miss Alice, I'd started on another dress.

Aunt Eva looked pleased with herself. But when she glanced at her husband, her animation waned. "You haven't said one thing since ya came home, Frank. You have a bad day?"

My uncle ladled lima beans onto his plate and salted them down. His hair was still wet from a shower, and his shirt pocked with water droplets, as if he'd been too preoccupied to dry off carefully.

"Come on, Frank," she urged.

Memories of our discussion Monday evening slowed my chewing. Here we were at the table once more, with Uncle Frank looking mighty serious. I braced myself for another encounter.

"Well," he said slowly, cutting into a chicken breast, "it's been a long two weeks since Lee and I talked to Riddum."

That was it. Aunt Eva eyed him expectantly, eyebrows raised. The longer his silence, the farther over her plate she leaned. "And?" she burst.

"I want to eat my supper, Eva," he replied mildly. "Then we'll talk." Aunt Eva seemed taken aback, but acquiesced. She was suddenly very interested in her meal. Uncle Frank ate another bite of chicken, then looked at me. "You been workin' hard, huh."

"Yes. Lots of alterations for Miss Alice, plus I started making myself another dress. I've got to make Connie's baby stuff next. And, by the way, I called my apartment manager and told him I'll be there August third."

"That's good. You still excited about goin'?"

"Sure. Why wouldn't I be?"

Aunt Eva cut her chicken with great care, offense at my remark hovering about her like a fog. "You goin' out with Lee again tomorrow night?" she asked after a moment.

"I don't know. We've got all that painting to do. And I have to take Connie into Albertsville to choose fabric for the curtains."

"That Lee, he's worked so hard on those two rooms. One thing you can count on, he takes good care a family." She looked at me pointedly.

Supper finished and the dishes cleared, Aunt Eva decided she'd waited long enough to hear from her husband. "All right," she declared, setting a piece of carrot cake before him. "You've had your supper."

Uncle Frank took his time tasting the dessert. Then he put down the fork, splayed his fingers on the table. "Eva, I don't want my words repeated around town, you hear? I work closest to

Riddum, and my opinion might carry too much weight. I don't want to be the one to start an out-and-out fight."

I slid a look at Aunt Eva. "Heaven's sake, Frank," she huffed, one hand against her neck. "'Course I'll keep quiet."

He held her gaze for a moment to show he meant business, fingers drumming silently. "All right then." He shifted in his chair and looked upward as if searching for words.

A warning bell sounded in my head at his trepidation. Only then did I notice that Uncle Frank's smile lines cut more deeply into his face, that his forehead was more furrowed. Where had I been the last two weeks? Self-absorbed, that's where, and then I'd begun to spend my spare time helping Connie. It was all well and good to help a friend in need, but Uncle Frank was *family*. How difficult it must be for him, I thought, caught between his boss and the men. My problems paled beside his.

Rising, I slipped my arms around his shoulders. "It'll be okay, Uncle Frank. If anybody can do what needs to be done, you can." After a moment he pulled away with a mixture of surprise and gratitude. "Thank you, Jessie," he said gruffly.

We exchanged a smile. I pulled my chair close to his and sat down, a hand on his arm. Aunt Eva looked on in consternation, fingers rubbing her neck.

Uncle Frank absentmindedly pushed his dessert plate away. "Blair Riddum is a power-hungry man," he began. "I think his ego was mightily stroked by becomin' owner of the most important business in town. Everybody looked up to him, all knees bowed, so to speak. Now that power is being threatened by his own employees. And nobody likes him anymore, with good reason. Mentally, that man has broken with Bradleyville and its people. My feelin' is, I don't think he'll change a thing come August."

I leaned back in my chair, a slow dread creeping through my veins. Everything was supposed to work out. I didn't want to drive away from Bradleyville afraid for my uncle and the town. And Lee. Thinking of him in the midst of an angry mob scared me to death.

As if reading my mind, Uncle Frank turned to me. "Lee's right in the thick a this, you know."

I locked eyes with him, a silent knowledge flowing between us, both revelation and warning. In that moment I realized he knew more about my feelings for Lee than I'd known myself. And I felt the suction of an impending storm.

I squeezed his arm. "It'll be okay," I whispered, feeling no reassurance.

chapter 27

Sweat dripped between her shoulder blades as she busily polished a pew in the sanctuary. Her knees were sore and her arm ached, but hers was an important task. She and her covolunteer had been at it for two hours, sprucing up the Baptist church for its midsummer cleaning. Too many sweaty thighs had dulled the wood. Another hour and the place should be shining.

"You heared anything yet 'bout a weddin' at the Methodist church?"

"If you're talkin' 'bout Jessie and Lee, you best forgit it. Eva says the gal's still plannin' on leavin'."

She rewaxed her cloth. "I cain't understand it. Lee Harding is such a good-lookin' man, so tall and strong. And all that black hair. How could any girl turn her back on that?"

"Listen to you, talkin' like a shameless harlot!"

"Well, jus' 'cause I'm old don't mean I'm dead."

"Huh." She rubbed her forehead with the back of her hand. "Anyway, Eva's mighty discouraged. Says Jessie can be awful determined when she puts her mind to somethin'. The devil himself couldn't stop her."

"Don't mention the devil in the house a God! He hears and sees all, you know."

She flicked a gray wisp from her flushed cheek. "If he sees all, he'll see that grimy print you missed."

"Oh, hush yourself. I was gittin' it."

They worked in silence.

"Did you hear that Patsy Walling saw Esther Riddum the other day in Albertsville?"

"Huh uh."

"It was at the K-Mart. Patsy said hello to Esther and mentioned she and Blair hadn't been seen around Bradleyville lately. Esther kinda fumbled with her bags and said she had to git to her car. Gave some lame excuse 'bout how they hadn't needed to drive into town lately."

"So they drive all the way to Albertsville?" She was disgusted.

"Yep. Don't sound good, does it?" She plopped down on a pew, exhausted. "Whew! I gotta rest a minute."

Her friend sank down beside her. "Sounds like things ain't lookin' good for the mill."

"'Fraid not." Sighing, she gazed around the church. "Tell you what is lookin' good, though, and that's this sanctuary. I'll bet the Methodists' ain't half as shiny."

"Amen to that."

chapter 28

The next three weeks were a blur. I worked in Miss Alice's shop until supper, either on her projects or my own. Six new dresses now hung in a multicolored row in my closet. Combined with the items I'd bought, they constituted an impressive wardrobe. Time and again before I fell into bed I tried on the yellow dress and slipped into my new shoes, gazing at the mature woman before me in the mirror. How like Mom she looked. I could almost feel my mother watching me from heaven, smiling proudly. I also finished Connie's curtains and matching baby blanket. She and I had chosen the fabric together during a scorching trip to Albertsville that had left her exhausted. I was glad that the excitement over room decorating had lifted her morose spirits. And when I wasn't sewing, I was at the Hardings, helping Lee paint Connie's new rooms. I even helped nail down carpet.

When that work was finally done, I hosted a baby shower for Connie, borrowing folding chairs from the church to set around the finished nursery. Lots of women came, from friends her age to widows, lugging presents and baby furniture. The sunny rooms filled with lively chatter and a mounting pile of baby clothes, torn wrapping paper, and curled ribbon. By the time the last guest left, I was giddily happy and enlisted Lee's help in pushing the furniture where Connie directed. Then she and I put away the clothes in drawers, marveling anew at the tiny sleeves and footed sleepers. "I can almost see my baby in them," she breathed, eyes sparkling. When we were through, we stood in the nursery doorway, gazing around. Everything was in readiness and looked so lovely. "I can't wait," she said, grasping my hand, "I just can't wait." Fleetingly, I thought of the nursery I'd have some day, picturing baby furniture in a house somewhere in Cincinnati.

With all the time we spent together, Lee and I only wanted to be with each other more. As we knelt side by side to unroll carpet and doused paint-flecked hands with turpentine; as he hung curtain rods while I signaled up or down—we basked in the aura of each other. Even when I could not see him in the adjoining room I was aware of his exact location and what he was doing. Darkness did not fall until after 9:00, and by that time we were tired, but we still went for a drive most evenings, parking on an old dirt road about five miles outside town. As soon as his truck rolled to a stop, I'd slide next to him, snuggling against his strong shoulder. Time and time again I thought, *How can I leave him?*

One night, I told Lee about my dream and everything it had meant to me. I thought it would help him understand my determination to be in Cincinnati near Hope Center, my anticipation of helping others through my job. Little good it did. After that, through tacit agreement, we did not discuss my leaving anymore. What was left to say? I knew Lee dreaded it. And sometimes, so did I.

Nor did we discuss issues at the mill, even though I saw the constant worry on his face. I knew things were not going well; Uncle Frank related the stories every night. I would listen attentively and encourage him, but as soon as I rose from the supper table the subject was pushed from my head. I simply would not consider their striking in August. It could so easily lead to violence, and I couldn't bear to think of Lee or Uncle Frank in danger.

Then, before I knew it, August first was nearly upon us. I had only seven days left in Bradleyville, and time slowed its jig into a gliding dance. My dresses were done; Connie's rooms were ready. All I had to do was work for Miss Alice, and that took only half a day. Lee and I had more opportunity to be alone together. And those moments began to spin themselves out, subjects previously avoided now pendant between us.

"We have to talk about this," he said Saturday night over supper at The Roastery, a splurge for us in Albertsville. I had taken nearly an hour deciding what to wear. All those new dresses, yet I couldn't bring myself to don one for Lee. They represented my life apart from him. I'd finally chosen something older—a blue skirt and cream-colored blouse that set off my hair and eyes. "I can't understand why you're still so determined to leave me."

I touched his hand. "I don't want to leave *you*; it's just that I want to *be* in Cincinnati."

"But you have to leave me to do it."

"It's only a six-hour drive. You can visit. And I'll be back here for holidays."

"Jessie, you know I'll never visit."

I started to protest, but the look in his eyes told me this was no time for games. We were beyond that, and that's exactly why he would never make the trip.

"If you leave," he said quietly, "you'll have chosen a life without me. What good would visitin' do?"

"Lee, I don't want to hurt you."

"Then don't."

I couldn't reply.

His voice tinged with frustration. "You have everything here—your family, me. Now you even have a job. And I know you love Bradleyville more than you realize. Yet you want to live in a big city where you'll be alone."

"It's the city I grew up in, Lee. It's the city where my memories with Mom are stored."

"They're just memories. Good ones, sure. Important ones. But you got new memories to make."

I smarted at the word *just*. Food lost its appeal, and I pushed my plate away. "My 'new memories' will be built on my old ones. You can't understand, Lee. You haven't been through what I have. You don't know what it's like to yearn for your mother. Look at you; you moved back to Bradleyville just to take care of your mom. I can't be near mine anymore. The most I can do is follow in her footsteps."

He looked away for a moment. "And you say this is what God wants you to do?"

"Yes."

"Mm. Then how come I think God wants you to stay here?"

I gazed at him with uncertainty, unsure whether he was serious or teasing. I preferred the latter. "Good grief," I replied, "you sound like Aunt Eva."

"That bad, huh."

We both managed a smile.

Neither of us wanted to spoil the evening. Taking up the subject again would only lead to argument, so we said no more. Lee's eyes flicked around the table as he seemed to wrestle with another issue. "Speakin' a God, I been meanin' to talk to you 'bout some-thin'. You remember that sermon a month or so ago? About the rich man and Jesus?"

This subject did not thrill me either. I nodded once.

He toyed with his fork on his plate. "I still think there's some-thin' to that. Followin' Christ I mean. Mama and I have talked about it a lot since then. She says all I have to do is pray and tell Christ that I'll let him lead my life." He wouldn't look at me. "I don't know, though. I think a doin' that, but then I think I wouldn't want to do it unless I was serious 'bout it. It's not some-thin' to play 'round with, you know? And I can be a hard man sometimes; got a bit a temper. I don't show it 'round you, but it's been difficult keepin' it at the mill lately, what with things the way they are. I'm beginnin' to feel like Riddum's nastiness is aimed straight at my family, since if I lose paychecks, that's who's gonna be hurt the most. And I don't take kindly to anyone threatenin' my family. Anyway, thinkin' the thoughts I do sometimes, I question if I'm the sort a person Jesus would want."

I searched for a response, wondering which troublesome issue to pursue. His allusions to the seriousness of problems at the mill sprayed me with fear. As for "following Christ," that subject had long ago become one that instantly raised hackles of defense within me. But I was most struck by his last sentence. He sounded almost childlike, questioning his worth in God's eyes. I felt a stab of pain for him.

"But, Lee," I said, reaching for his hand, "you're wonderful. Who *wouldn't* want you?"

Swiftly, his eyes rose to mine and locked. Too late, I realized the irony of my statement. My throat tightened. "Oh, Lee. I *do* want you. You must know that."

He leaned forward, cupping my chin in his other hand. "I love you, Jessie," he said thickly. The unexpected words shimmered between us. He looked almost surprised at himself. "There, I finally said it."

His face blurred. "I love you, too," I whispered.

So much for an expensive meal. Neither of us touched another bite.

On the way home we took a detour to the hill where we'd had our picnic. Lee pulled the yellow blanket from the back of his truck and spread it over the grass. We sat side by side, arms around each others' waists, and watched the stars birth in an inking sky.

"Jessie," Lee's words were weighted, "we got one week. We need to talk more about everything, okay? Figure out what we're gonna do. Maybe we can visit each other after all. We have to do *something*. I can't just let you out of my life when you move. Maybe we should even pray 'bout it together. That's what Mama's been sayin' we should do."

His mama was also in cahoots with my Aunt Eva to get me to stay in Bradleyville. I saw right through Miss Wilma's pious plan.

"Sure, Lee," I said, meaning not a word of it. "We'll do that."

chapter 29

The march of time is an inexplicable thing—relentless and inevitable, while life plays out in a multitude of paces. I sat in a seemingly never-ending church service next to Lee the following morning, listening with closed ears. Monday, I bent a languid head over Miss Alice's magic sewing machine, yet my thoughts were as swirling as the gathering winds in the streets of Bradleyville.

I tried not to hear the talk as folks poked their heads in the shop to gab with Miss Alice. The more I tried not to listen, the louder their voices grew. Blair Riddum had engineered half a dozen run-ins with various employees Monday, telling them all in one way or another that they weren't fit for their jobs. By Tuesday afternoon word had already filtered into town about an argument that morning between him and Al Bledger, who'd refused to back down when informed his cuts were ragged.

"Well, Al always did have a bit of a temper," Miss Alice commented as she huddled with Elsie Mae Waller. Miss Elsie Mae's husband worked at the IGA, and he'd heard the news from the Clangerlees, who'd heard it from Laura Princeley herself. Miss

Laura had taken her husband's forgotten lunchbox to him at noon only to emerge shaken by the ominous atmosphere at the mill.

"Maybe so, but Al's been at the mill for years. He oughta know how to cut wood."

"True, true."

Miss Alice's clothes rustled as she turned to look at me. "Better not say anymore," she whispered theatrically to Miss Elsie, as if I couldn't hear. "She's been quiet all week. Worried 'bout Lee, you know."

She was half right. I was worried about Lee. I was worried about Uncle Frank too, and the town. And Aunt Eva was clinging to me in near apoplexy in her own fear. "What if they strike and there's fightin'!" she'd wailed to me more than once. "I can't lose Frank; I already lost my only son." Shoring her up only frightened me more. I'd become so worried and so afraid of what might happen, I just wanted to run away and hide. And I began to dread saying good-bye to Lee so much that I longed to have it over with. The ambivalence was driving me crazy. I almost wished I could leave *that day*. August first was Thursday; I wished I didn't have to wait until Saturday for Uncle Frank's help. Who knew what would happen by then? How could I leave Lee in the midst of chaos?

I'd visited his house Monday evening to check on Connie. Her false labor pains had increased, but every time she thought the time had come, the pains stopped. "I want so much to have the baby before you leave," she breathed, her eyes begging me not to go. "I need you there with me."

The more I was needed, the more selfish I felt. And angry. I tried to pray to my guardian angel, but it did no good. Then I railed at God as I packed books Monday night. I was *mad* I'd fallen in love with a man I had to leave. Everybody seemed to be turning to me, as if I had undying strength. And because of my mother's pacifist teaching, I'd advocated patience with a selfish mill employer who now just made me want to spit. I'd never even seen Blair Riddum, but I hated him for what he was doing to me and the ones I loved. I ranted on in my head, only by sheer will slowing the arm that wanted to throw my books, stilling the foot that wanted to kick a box. After a long exhale, I stacked the books carefully and pushed the boxes into a corner.

Tuesday night, Lee and I went for a drive after supper and couldn't decide whether to hold each other or fight. I couldn't blame him for his testiness. Within a few days he would lose me and perhaps his job while his unwed sister was having a baby whom he must support. By the time we reached our knoll and had spread out the blanket, I was close to tears. Three nights ago we'd held each other; now our impending futures hulked between us like monsters in the night.

We ended up fighting. He told me bitterly that the whole thing was silly. No one was making me go. My obstinacy was costing us both dearly, and for what. He said I was selfish and unkind, and he wished he'd never met me. We stormed across that hill and that blanket, throwing frustrated hands to the heavens. I knew everything he said was true. I also knew I had to go, that years of planning could not be cast aside—even for the whims of love.

"A *whim!* Is that what you call this?" His voice was tight.

"No, Lee." I sank dejectedly onto the blanket, head hung. "I said *love.*"

He held my face with both hands. "I say *love* too. And let me tell you what love does. Love stays where it's returned. Love seeks to make the other person happy. Stay in Bradleyville, Jessie. Marry me. I'll build us a big house. My mother will love you like her own daughter. Connie already loves you like a sister. You'll be an aunt to her baby. As for work, Miss Alice wants to retire; you could buy out her shop. Work when you want to. Work around havin' your own babies. You'll be near your aunt and uncle, near Thomas. You can watch little Celia grow. And we can be together."

"You've got it all figured out, haven't you," I replied with an edge.

He held my gaze.

"And what about my dreams, my life? What about the city I long to return to? What if I get restless here as your wife, resentful that I had to give up all my plans? If you love me so much, come to Cincinnati with me."

"I *can't*, Jessie. I got family here to take care of."

"And what if you didn't? Would you go then?"

He withdrew his hand, rubbed his forehead.

"See. You wouldn't. Because it's not *you*. Your way of life is here, and you know it. But imagine losing both your parents by sixteen. Imagine having to go live in a place that's just the opposite of what you're used to. You didn't even make it past Albertsville, for heaven's sake. You would always want to come back, and as soon as you grew up, you'd do just that. So don't judge me. Don't say you don't understand, because you do."

"All *right*, Jessie!" He threw out his arms. "You win! I can't talk 'bout this anymore, because I just want to get up right now and *hit* somethin'!" He swiveled his head away, jaw set. We sat in silence, his shoulders carved against the sunset like stone. I picked blades of grass and let them fall on the blanket, green on yellow.

"We better get back," he said finally, his words ragged. "Connie might need us."

I couldn't stand his being angry with me. "You worried about work tomorrow?" I asked softly.

He snorted. "Thought you were doin' your best not to notice."

"Oh, Lee."

"Since you asked, yes. I'm worried. Your idea of puttin' things off till August bought you the time you wanted. Now that you're about to go, I got to think 'bout facin' a strike. And you don't have to tell me again you don't approve a such things."

Tears bit my eyes. "I don't want you to get hurt."

"You won't be around to see it."

"Lee, *don't*."

He ran a weary hand over his face. "I'm not gonna get hurt, Jessie. Things could get real tense, and if we're outta work long, I don't know how half the town'll eat. But my gut says it won't last long. If we don't work, Riddum'll lose a lot more money than if he'd givin' us a raise."

"But it's not just a raise, is it." I pushed hair away from his forehead. "It's the way he treats you."

"Yeah," he replied, looking at me pointedly. "He's *selfish.*"

My fingers stilled. I pulled them away. "Well, let's go check on Connie." I gazed into the distance, watching the twinkle of Bradleyville. "But let's promise no matter what happens before Saturday to come back here one more time."

"Sure. One more time."

It was a promise we would not keep.

chapter 30

A professor at college once told me of her mother's lingering, painful death from cancer. She'd thought she was prepared to see her mother's final breath, had even planned songs to be sung at the memorial service. Yet when the moment of death occurred, she was shocked to the very core of her being. It may have been imminent, but it wasn't supposed to happen *then*. Not in *that* moment, on *that* day.

In the same way, I was unprepared for worse news from the mill—but then it happened a day early. Even with talk running rampant, I told myself we need not really worry until August first. Until then, there was hope. It was my way of dealing with the anxiety.

Suddenly six weeks of immersion in self-concerns, of denial, came to a screeching halt on that Wednesday afternoon. And after that, nothing was the same.

According to plan, Lee and Uncle Frank were supposed to meet with Blair Riddum after work Thursday. The two of them discussed the meeting at length, planning how to negotiate. Thomas was to be on standby; one phone call and he'd beat it double time to the mill. I'd agreed to drive him. But as it happened, Blair

Riddum called the two men into his office Wednesday and told them he'd made his decision. He'd watched the men for six weeks, he said. He'd tried to find a way to be generous. But they simply weren't pulling their weight. A solemn-faced Uncle Frank told Aunt Eva and me at supper that he'd felt his heart sink to his toes.

"Let me tell you two somethin'," Riddum had continued, pacing his cluttered office. Accounting books were strewn across his heavy, pocked desk. Outside the grimy window, Uncle Frank could see men waiting, tense and silent. Word had spread quickly about the impromptu meeting. "I was raised up yonder in Appalachia." Riddum jerked a thumb over his shoulder. "Didn't have nothin' 'cept an old carcass-lookin' dog as starved as us kids. Slept on a pile a blankets in the corner; hunted for our supper. My daddy was steel-eyed mean, and that's when he was sober. I left that godforsaken place when I was fourteen without lookin' back, and I've pulled my own way up ever since. And that's why," he pointed a finger at Lee, "that's why I won't be pushed into doin' somethin' I don't wanna do. This is *my* mill. *I* sweat to save the money for it, and *I* work longer hours here than anybody. I stay in this hole of an office long after everybody else's gone. So I'll run it the way I please. I wasn't scared a my daddy, and I ain't scared a y'all. If you don't like it here, y'all can work someplace else, the whole bunch a ya. And that's all I got to say."

When Uncle Frank finished his retelling, even Aunt Eva was silent. If my uncle's heart had been in his toes, mine had just drained out my feet. I knew Lee must be furious. I wondered what he would do.

"So," Uncle Frank said grimly, "there's a meetin' tonight at the school gymnasium. We're gonna talk about what to do. I imagine the whole town'll be there, since it'll affect everybody. I heard Bill Clangerlee's even closin' the IGA early."

Aunt Eva's hand was at her throat. With trembling fingers she reached to squeeze Uncle Frank's wrist. "I'll be right there with you, Frank."

I looked at my plate. My beef pot pie was barely touched. "I have some packing to do," I said quietly. "Picked up all the extra boxes I need today. So I guess I . . . better do that." Glancing up, I tried to smile. Uncle Frank nodded solemnly.

"Aren't you goin' to be with Lee?" Aunt Eva's voice held more than a tinge of disapproval.

I lifted a shoulder. "What would I do?"

"*Be* with him. Stand by him durin' this hard time. He's got important decisions to make."

"Those decisions won't affect me, Aunt Eva," I replied levelly. "I'll be gone in a few days. And besides, I can't make up Lee's mind for him; he's gonna do what he's gonna do."

"I can't make up your uncle's mind for him either, but I'll still be there."

"Now, Eva—"

"Now, Eva, nothin', Frank, not this time; I got a right to talk too, you know." Her voice rose. "And I can't keep quiet any longer. I've watched her come home night after night from bein' with Lee and go right to her room to pack. And Jessie, I love you like my own. But I don't like to see you playin' with people's lives."

I stared at her, bristling. "I am *not* 'playing with people's lives.'"

"Yes, you are. Lee's in love with you; you know that. And you've also known from the beginning you wouldn't be turned away from leavin'. So you shoulda let him be. You shoulda let Connie and Wilma be too. Instead, you got 'em all lovin' you and needin' you in their own way, especially now. But you don't care 'cause you're leavin' in three days."

"*You* put us together; you *pushed* me to be with Lee!"

"I thought you'd end up stayin'! I *know* that's what you should do, and you're just too stubborn to see it! Jessie, *think* about the people who love you. This town's given you a lot. And right now it's facin' the worst trouble it's ever faced. Lee needs you. Your uncle needs you. And all you're thinkin' 'bout is yourself."

"Come on, hon," Uncle Frank grasped her arm, "don't get all worked up now."

"I have a job to go to," I retorted, gripping the seat of my chair. "I have an apartment I've already paid the first month for. I can't just back out of all that."

"Of course you can't," Uncle Frank soothed.

"Then why didn't you just *go!*" Aunt Eva's face crumpled. "Why did you come back here in June only to leave us *again!*"

I searched her face, only then beginning to understand. "Aunt Eva, I didn't—"

"Oh, never *mind!*" She jumped up, driving her chair back across the linoleum. "I've prayed and prayed for you! I've told you time and time again you need to become a Christian, so you can find the *peace* that I have! But never mind all that, Jessie; just do what you have to do. Don't worry about *us!*" And before either Uncle Frank or I could stop her, she fled the room.

We sat in embarrassed silence. "It's been hard for her," my uncle said finally, "ever since Henry was killed. You know that. And she's been under a lot a stress lately, worried about me and all the people she knows at the mill. She's got a big heart, you know. Plus, facin' an empty nest—this time for good—is a difficult thing for her."

I felt about a foot high. "Should I go in to her?"

"No." He rose. "I'll go. Can you do the dishes? That meetin's in half an hour."

"Sure."

On automatic, I cleaned the kitchen, pushing away unwanted thoughts. Everything was fine, I told myself; *I* was fine. I was so very, very fine, I felt nothing at all. By the time my aunt and uncle left for the meeting, I was in my room, door closed. I had not even called Lee.

chapter 31

*S*he was stirring soup on the stove when the phone rang. "Ah!" she cried in anxious surprise, dropping the large spoon to spatter red-brown broth, vegetables, and bits of meat on the floor. From the backyard filtered sounds of her three children playing. Their daddy had sent them outside before telling her the news. She took a deep breath; let the spoon lie. "Hello? Yeah, I heared. I'm scared to death. No, I cain't go; I got to stay with the kids. Oh, that's right nice a you; your oldest is a mighty sweet girl. You sure she can manage your kids and mine too? Well, good; I'll take you up on that. I really wanna be there. . . ."

Across town, a woman was unhooking a load of wash from the line, angrily throwing clothespins into the laundry basket. "You bet I'm mad," she said loudly to her neighbor across the fence. "I don't want my husband puttin' up with this anymore. All our men at the mill have had the patience a Job, but enough's enough. We been real careful with our money the past month, so I hope the men just tell Riddum where he can go. And it ain't the IGA! . . ."

The hardware store clerk had found an old piece of cardboard and was writing with a black marker in large block letters. CLOSED FOR MEETING. His cash register would just have to be balanced tomorrow....

"Please, God." She paced the bedroom, raking hands through her graying hair. Stay calm, she told herself, stay calm. "After all these years, what're we gonna do? Who's gonna hire him three years from retirement?..."

The young woman held up her half-finished wedding dress, sniffling at her reflection. The dress was so beautiful. For the hundredth time she berated herself for not marrying in June. Why had they insisted on saving for two more months? Now what if he lost his job? What then?...

chapter 32

I really didn't have much to do.

There were my new dresses to pack and a few personal things to put into boxes. But all the clothes in my dresser could stay right where they were. And of course some final items, such as my pillows and bed comforter, couldn't be packed until the morning of my trip. I'd reserved a small rental truck from Albertsville. Uncle Frank would drive me there early Friday morning to pick it up, and we would pack it Friday evening. I didn't have a lot of furniture anyway, just two chests of drawers, a nightstand, my bed, a bookcase, and my desk and chair. And my antiquated sewing machine. Thursday was to be my last day at Miss Alice's. That left me time Friday midmorning for my appointment at Ed Tam's gas station to change the front tires on my car.

I stared at my new dresses, thoughts elsewhere. Finally I decided not to pack them yet; the longer they sat in a box, the more wrinkled they would become. Wandering around the room, I found myself standing at my desk, looking at a diagram I'd made for placing furniture in my new apartment. I pictured myself walking through the finished rooms, car keys in hand, home from a day at work. Stacked on the table would be files I needed to go over, each one representing a family I was helping. My boss would be pleased at the wonderful job I was doing. My heart would be full, knowing my abilities and training were finally being used as my mother had wanted. Maybe, if I wasn't going to the Center, I'd be heading to take a bath, change clothes, and go out with friends. Maybe a date.

Lee's face shimmered in my mind.

A sigh escaped me. I flicked the diagram out of my hand, and it landed askew on the desk. Staring blankly at the wall, I asked my guardian angel to lead me in what to do. Mom had taught me to be a caring person. She'd also taught me to eschew conflict, but that was a laugh now. Lately, my plans had brought me nothing *but* conflict.

With resolve, I picked up an empty box and set it on the edge of my bed. Went to my closet for a couple pair of shoes. Tossed them in from a few feet away. Went back to the closet for more. Tried to throw them into the box without crossing the room. Hit it twice, missed twice. I marched over to grab the shoes from the floor and managed to bang my hip into the box, overturning it onto the carpet. I stared at it stupidly. Then, suddenly, I turned on my heel and yanked open my bedroom door. I didn't bother to turn out the light.

The school gymnasium was standing-room-only when I arrived, every window and door open for muggy ventilation. The parking lot had been full; I'd walked from down the street. I could hear the sounds from where I'd parked: the roar of voices, the calls of children blithely engaged in tag on the playground, an occasional screech from the old P.A. system. Slipping through the main door, I pressed against a back wall, nodding to a few acquaintances. Uncle Frank had been right; practically the whole town was there.

I could not see Lee or Aunt Eva. My uncle was on the platform, calling for the crowd's attention.

The atmosphere was both suffocating and surreal. Was it only three weeks ago that these same people pressed against one another to cheer the July Fourth parade? Now anxiety glowed wanly throughout the crowd, reflected in a lined forehead, a handkerchief clutched, the nervous swinging of a crossed leg. The metal folding chairs usually occupied by parents proudly watching children in a school play now were filled with mamas nervously hushing babies, fathers grumbling amongst themselves. My uncle seemed so small on the stage as he called again for order. And then, like a final settling of rocks after a landslide, the room grew dustily quiet.

I saw Lee standing near the stage steps, wearing jeans and a red knit shirt. His large hands were up, fingers spread, as if frozen after hushing people to silence. His expression was dark. My insides turned over. Before I knew it, I was on my way to him, trying my best to be unobtrusive, ducking under ranges of view, winding through knots of people. My uncle began to speak, relating exactly what Riddum had said that day, so "everyone could have the straight story." I barely heard the words as my feet scuffed across the old wooden floor, eyes fixed on Lee's back. He had not seen me, the gymnasium stretching between us. For no reason at all my heart began to beat harder, as if some terrible thing would happen if I did not reach him. And then, when I was only five feet away, I vaguely heard my uncle ask Lee to join him. I trotted the last three steps and reached out to empty air. Lee was already up the stairs and striding across the stage. I closed my eyes, feeling like a fool, and wilted back against the wall.

"Everyone who wants to, will get a chance to talk." Lee's voice boomed across the gymnasium. From the tone of his voice, I knew he was suppressing his anger. "But we'll each have to keep it short. And we got to keep things orderly."

With that invitation began a stream of caustic words against Blair Riddum as one man after another aired his grievances. For weeks they'd bottled up their frustrations; now they came tumbling out to ricochet off corners and ceiling and the bobbing of mill workers' heads. "I say we strike, and we do it *tomorrow!*" shouted Zach Bulder, whose son was a few years younger than I. "He said it himself; he ain't gonna change!"

"Strikin' ain't the answer," Lester Maddock extolled a few minutes later. "Maybe a walk-out for an afternoon, somethin' to show Riddum our not workin' could cost him far more than a raise."

"Then what?" Al Bledger shouted from the crowd. "We go back to workin' and he still don't do nothin'!"

"But what if we strike and he goes to Albertsville for more men?" Mr. Maddock shot back.

"We form a line and nobody'll get through it!"

"We'll stop 'em!" someone else cried.

"That ain't God's way!" a third voice yelled.

"Yeah, well what if I strike and you don't?" hurled a fourth. "You gonna take bread from my table?!"

The crowd roared to life, a buzz like angry bees flying toward the rafters. Men were out of their seats, shouting, wives beside them, while Lee and Uncle Frank screamed for quiet. My stomach churned, goose pimples prickling my arms. I wanted to put hands over my ears, run through a side door and escape. I wanted my rented truck at that moment, wanted to drive away from Bradleyville as fast as I could. I turned to thread my way out of the gymnasium and saw Thomas hastening toward the stage steps, face gray. "Thomas!" I wove through bodies to his side, grasping him by the arm.

"I got to git up there!" he yelled.

"Okay!" I helped clear him a path until we reached the stairs. As he hurried up them I dropped back, glancing toward Lee. He caught sight of Thomas and left the podium to greet him. He saw me on the bottom step. For a split second our eyes locked. Then he caught Thomas's elbow and turned away.

My heart sank. Clutching my arms, I eased off the step and toward a window, hungry for fresh air.

The crowd's momentum surged, then waned as folks noticed Thomas standing quietly before the microphone, arms at his sides. Neighbor elbowed neighbor, voices lowered, heads tossed into muffled words. Across the room I saw Jake Lewellyn sitting in an aisle seat next to Hank Jenkins and Mr. Tull. Aunt Eva was there too, perched nervously two rows back, shushing the woman beside her.

Facing the mass, Thomas looked frail. Yet his mere presence seemed to shame the whole gymnasium into silence. The hurt on his face was palpable. My eyes filled with tears.

Thomas ran a hand through his whitened hair and cleared his throat. "Folks," he began, then faltered. Jake Lewellyn lumbered to his feet and began a purposeful walk toward the stairs at the far side of the stage. "Folks," Thomas tried again, "I lived here all my life, y'all know that. This is the town my daddy built. And never did I think I'd see the day when the whole a Bradleyville would be yellin' at one another, neighbor against neighbor." Mr. Lewellyn had reached the stairs and was beginning to climb. "But we ain't never faced nothin' like this before neither. So here we are. And how we gonna act? Like the rest a the world? Or are we gonna stick together, like we always done?" Jake Lewellyn was crossing the stage. Thomas saw him and waited. Mr. Lewellyn reached him, put a supportive, beefy hand on his shoulder. "See who we got here?" Thomas said. "My old friend Jake. Sure, we fight and carry on like a couple a cats in spilt milk. But y'all know that's just show. You know we love each other like brothers. Right, ol' man?" Mr. Lewellyn puckered his chin, pretending to think it over. Subdued laughter undulated through the room.

"The both of us span more years in Bradleyville than four or five a y'all put together," Thomas continued. "We're united by a love fer this town. Just as y'all are. So here's what I'm tellin' ya—beggin' ya. Let's face this thing with one mind—together. I say the mill workers take a vote. We'll do it on paper, if ya like. Y'all got to vote on whether or not to strike; there's really no in-between. Either you tell Riddum you need your jobs more than his respect, or you cain't work without it. And only each a you, with your wives, can decide that for yourself. But here's the hard part. In stickin' together, we got to abide by the majority vote, whether we like it or not. Otherwise we got brother against brother, neighbor against neighbor. 'A house divided against itself falls,' so the Bible says. And so it goes for our town."

His words drained away, and Thomas looked tired.

"Let's do it!" someone cried from the crowd.

"We got to talk things over more first!" another voice answered.

Uncle Frank shook Thomas's hand and nodded to Mr. Lewellyn. Together, the two elderly men left the podium. "I think he's right," my uncle's voice rang through the microphone. "If you want to have your say, come on up. Then we'll vote."

Men began to line up, Lee first. His muscles flexed as he laid both hands on the podium. He had to lean down to speak. He looked at me then; I know he did, even though he pretended to scan the crowd. The ache I felt for him at that moment weighted my feet to the floor. "I been tryin' real hard to be patient with all this," he began, his voice tight. "For my family's sake, I needed a paycheck. And I know I'm not the only one with worries at home. I've done the best I can to work with a man that just won't be worked with. Now he tells us we're not 'pulling our weight.'" Disgust dripped from him. "So now what're we gonna do? Seems to me it comes down to this question: Can we continue with things bein' this way? A covered pot ain't gonna just simmer forever. As for me, I'm already close to boilin' over. And seein' the way Riddum was today, I don't doubt he's gonna turn up the heat."

He paused as numerous men shouted their agreement. *Lee*, I thought, *look at me*.

"So I'm ready to strike. Now the question is, what would I do if things don't go peacefully. Well, I don't know for sure. Right now I can only say if things go that route, we'll deal with it then. Personally I don't think it'll get that far. Yeah, Riddum's mean as a snake, but one day's shut-down's gonna cost him hundreds a dollars. He's also a good business man, and I'm bettin' his greed'll get the better a his stubbornness."

Applause erupted when Lee was finished. He walked off stage on the far side and remained standing by the wall, arms folded. He would not look at me, but through the remaining speeches, I know he felt me, and I felt him.

Not everyone wanted to strike. Men closer to retirement were less willing to take the chance. I wasn't sure what Uncle Frank wanted. And not all who took the podium worked at the mill. Mr. and Mrs. Clangerlee declared they'd keep grocery prices as low as possible. Neighbors said they'd share food if money got tight, and the Baptist and Methodist pastors both said their churches' offerings would go to a common fund. The sincerity of folks was both heartwarming and chilling, for it assumed not only a strike, but a drawn-out one.

It was as though Bradleyville were preparing for a siege.

By the time votes were taken, written on torn slips of paper provided by a teacher from her classroom, the atmosphere was funereal. Women exchanged consoling whispers, absentmindedly rocking sleeping children. Aunt Eva was crying quietly in her seat. Lee collected votes on his side of the room. I found my way to Thomas and hugged him, seeking solace when I should have been giving it. He gripped me tightly, then looked into my soul with over-bright eyes. "Sometimes," he said, "you got to fight."

The results were three to one for a strike.

With grim determination the mill workers gathered down front to count off one through five for "sit-down duty" one day a week. There was no need for signs or picketing, only a silent watch in case new workers began to show. Uncle Frank and Lee announced they'd be there the next morning to tell Riddum and would stay throughout the days. Pastor Frasier said a fervent prayer for the town, and we all went home to wait.

chapter 33

The next morning, Uncle Frank was out of the house by eight o'clock as usual, but it was only to sit with the "1s" at the mill and wait for Riddum's reaction. By noon we'd heard little, other than Riddum had been furious, which anyone could have predicted. Around 3:00, I was finishing my final working hour with Miss Alice. I hugged her good-bye and gave her sewing machine a final pat.

"You saved the day for me," she declared, clinging to my hand. "You decide anytime to come back here, you just let me know. I can't keep this shop goin' much longer myself, ya know."

Her unsurprising offer held not the slightest temptation. I was on the straight and narrow to leave. I couldn't wait till Saturday. My plans were still on schedule, strike or no. Meanwhile, the atmosphere around town was nothing but gloom and doom. No one was downtown making purchases; folks were already clutching their life savings like Midases. And I vacillated between hurting over Lee's snubs at the meeting and feeling almost relieved by them. Maybe there'd be no need for long good-byes. I was on my road and he was clearly on his, and they would not converge. Fine then; if he wanted to lead a strike, whatever the cost—let him. But I'd had a good talk with Uncle Frank after we'd arrived home Wednesday night. A terrified Aunt Eva and I had made him swear on his life that if violence erupted, he'd stay far away from it.

I was supposed to have a final visit with Connie after work. Driving to the Hardings' house, I steadied myself, even though I knew Lee would be at the mill site. Just seeing his house wove bands around my chest. I drove up Maple, praying his truck would not be there. Wanting it to be there.

It wasn't.

Connie and Miss Wilma wore the same furrowed brow. Connie looked miserable, as usual. "Oh, I want to show you something," she said, hoisting herself off the couch despite my protestations. "Martha Plott came over this mornin'—that sweet ol' lady—and gave me the cutest lamp. Said she was sorry she was sick for my shower. I got the lamp on that little table in the nursery."

Martha Plott was one of the most generous, loving women in Bradleyville. As far as the Methodist congregation was concerned, the Baptists had no one to match her. She was the first to set up for potluck dinners, the last to leave after clean-up. She seemed to be always taking food to the sick or running their errands or cleaning their houses. Her husband had died young, and she'd often declared that Christ had called her to help others instead of feeling sorry for herself.

"Yes, she is sweet. I'll go look at the lamp; you stay here."

"No, no." Her smile was firm. "I want to show you everything for one last time."

"Goodness, Connie," I laughed self-consciously, "you'd think I was moving to another planet." I took her arm.

"Might as well be."

The lightness in her voice was heavy as a hammer. Maybe it was only my imagination, but it seemed she was still trying to change my mind. It seemed *everyone* was still trying. Why couldn't they see that I was beyond that? That I always had been?

We lumbered through her bedroom and past the open door into the small nursery. Beyond lay the playroom through an arched doorway. My yellow curtains over white sheers fluttered expectantly from a slight, humid breeze. On a table by the window sat Connie's new cut-glass lamp with a diaphanous white shade blessed with the figures of hovering angels watching over a newborn child. Something about the expression of the largest angel struck me, and then I realized what it was. Her smile looked just like my mother's. "Oh," I gasped, a catch in my throat. "It's *beautiful.*"

"Turn it on. See what happens."

For a moment I could only gaze with awe at that angel. She was bent over the baby, feathery wings enfolding it, and on her face was the look of heaven's love. Not taking my eyes off the lamp, I glided to the table and flicked it on. I drew in a breath as the angels shimmered to life. Running a wondering finger over the wings, now golden-tinged, I exclaimed, "It really is beautiful."

"I thought so too." Connie leaned against the wall, admiring it. "It has another switch for a little nightlight."

I turned off the main bulb and flicked the smaller switch. The angels glimmered down to the palest of yellow. "They look almost transparent now," I breathed. "Like angels only the baby can see." As if in agreement, the curtains ruffled, brushing against the shade.

We left the small light on, the cut glass sparkling tiny rainbows. Turning finally with reluctance, I gazed around the room and sighed with satisfaction. "I'm proud to say I helped, Connie. It's all so pretty."

"I know. Thank you." She started to say more, but turned away as tears filled her eyes. I let her be, walking to the crib to finger the baby blanket I'd made.

"Whew," Connie exclaimed after a prolonged moment, forcing a smile. "Guess I'm just gettin' tired. Better get back on the couch."

I took her arm to go, looking over my shoulder one last time at that magical angel lamp.

By the time I had Connie settled once more, Miss Wilma had already informed me, "You still got time to change your mind, you know." I didn't want to hear it. I searched for a way to cut my visit short, but found none. And so I filled iced tea glasses and visited, patiently explaining how my apartment and job that I'd wanted for years were waiting for me. And had I mentioned I would be volunteering at Hope Center, as my mother had done? And the city, how much I'd missed it? I sat in an arm chair, legs crossed, fingers around my cold glass, tone pleasant. Smiling. Telling myself it was wrong to be irritated; that they wanted me not just for themselves, but for Lee. When it was finally time to leave, I hugged them both, Connie bursting into tears.

"Oh, Connie, please don't cry," I begged, my own eyes filling. "I'll see you again before you know it, at Thanksgiving."

"That's so long away," she sobbed into my shoulder. "The baby'll be so big by then; you'll never get to see it in those cute newborn sleepers. And besides," she pulled back from me, trying to control her quivering mouth, "I'm not cryin' for myself; I'm cryin' for Lee, 'cause he jus' don't know what he'll do when you're gone. He don't say it, but I know."

I thought my heart would break in two, both for Lee and his sister. They had major problems of their own, yet each was thinking about the other. "He'll be fine, Connie; he'll be okay," I soothed. It was such a trite, lame response.

I had to get out of there.

"I'm gonna pray for you before you go, all right." It was not a question. Miss Wilma placed her large hand on my shoulder and tipped her head heavenward. "Connie, you lay hands on her too." Breathing heavily, Connie gently grasped my upper arm. They closed their eyes. I looked at my feet.

"Dear Lord Jesus," Miss Wilma prayed, "watch over this child. I know she's yours, Lord; you've called her to be your own, even if she don't know that yet. And you know all the trials she'll have to go through. Please be a shield about her, protectin' her. Work through those trials for your glory, dear Jesus. Bring her to salvation. And bring her back to us safely."

"And thank you, Jesus," Connie put in, "for bringin' Jessie into our lives. For the wonderful friend she's been, and for all the talents you've given her. Amen."

"Amen." Miss Wilma did her best to smile as I raised my eyes. "You take care a yourself now, you hear." She gripped my hand, puffing as she and Connie ushered me toward the door.

"Sorry, I'm moving too fast," I said, waiting for her to catch her breath. "You don't have to walk me all the way out to the porch."

"Well," she grunted, casting me a penetrating look. "Steppin' through the door don't take long. It's the gettin' to the threshold that's hard."

I gazed back, brows furrowing, then smiled briefly. Days would pass before I understood her meaning.

I promised again that I'd be back for Thanksgiving and made Connie promise to call me if she went into labor in the next twenty-four hours. They stood awkwardly on their small white porch, swayhipped and swaybacked, waving as I drove away.

"One more day," I breathed aloud, wiping my face as I turned off Maple. I told myself that after my tires were fixed the following morning, I would not show my face to *anyone* else in Bradleyville. Including Lee. *Especially* Lee. Parting with my Aunt Eva would be emotional enough. I did not need any more tear-drenched good-byes.

chapter 34

*T*wilight fell and the lightning bugs magically appeared.
"*I got the first one; I'm lucky!*" the little girl cried as she clapped a lid punched with holes over one of her mother's canning jars. The bug flicked against his smooth-glassed prison, flashing yellow under black wings.

"*I already got three!*" her friend retorted.

Gleefully, they ran barefoot through the cooling grass, careful not to stub a toe as they chased bugs across the sidewalk. When the jars were full, they set them down to glow eerily against the cement. Swishing long hair off their sweaty foreheads, they plopped onto the bottom stair of the front porch, gazing idly at their catch.

"*Want a push-up?*"

"*Sure.*"

As the first little girl disappeared into her house, the second scratched her cheek, stopping to sniff her bug-scented hand. Tilting back her head, she spied the first star and made a wish.

"*It's orange flavor,*" her hostess announced as the screen door banged shut. They sat side by side, peeling off the top of their ice creams and pushing them up by their wooden sticks.

"I wished on the star." She pointed with a sticky chin.

"Whatdja wish for?"

"Not supposed to tell."

"It's okay if you're best friends."

"Oh. Well then, I wished the strike would end tomorrow so Daddy could go back to work."

Her friend smacked her lips. "Better pick another one; the whole town's wishin' that."

"Well, I could pick Mama's. She said she wished Blair Riddum'd drop dead."

"Maybe he will." The little girl's voice lowered with private knowledge. "I heard my daddy say Mr. Riddum was awful mad this mornin'. Stomped off from the mill and didn't come back all day. He's mean, ya know, and Mama says God strikes the wicked."

She was silent for a moment, savoring orange coolness on her tongue. "Well, then, I wish he'd strike tonight."

chapter 35

I sensed it even before waking.

Usually I emerge from sleep fully alert, as a child pops from water after holding her breath. But that night my sleep waters were murky and thick, and I strained against them as I fought my way to the surface. During those last few seconds of sleep, a sluggish mind can play an amazing array of tricks, swirling vague fears into a watercolor of horrors, only then to taunt that you are just dreaming. In the final horrible instant I saw my mother's face, bloodied and begging me not to leave her.

I broke the surface of sleep, shaking, but could not open my eyes. Danger sparked my nerves.

All was silent.

My eyes flicked open. Dim moonlight filtered through my slanted blinds, spilling onto the small brass clock upon my bedside table. 2:15. I took a deep breath, my heart slowing. I looked out the window again, focusing on a faint glimmer of stars through milky haze. How long did I gaze at it before realizing the haze was thickening? I frowned as I raised my head from the pillow, squinting. Somewhere deep within me an electricity began to hum, a phantasm of unknown evil puddling in my chest. As I watched, the cloudiness slowly darkened. Congealed. The stars flickered off, lowest ones first, then the moon. My room went black.

I could not move, could only listen to the staccato of my shallow breathing. Then from the living room, shrilly pealing through the still night, the phone rang. Its echo rebounded down the hallway, through the walls of my bedroom, my head. It rang again.

With a jerk I was in motion, throwing back the light covers and raking fingers over the carpet for my robe. I flicked on the lamp beside my bed, eyes squinting in affront, feet hastening across the floor. As I opened my door, I saw Uncle Frank yank open the master bedroom's door as well, jerking on a pair of pants. Our eyes met briefly, mirroring each other's fear. I followed him soundlessly down the hall, pulled up beside him as he answered the phone with a gruff "Frank Bellingham," watched sickened knowledge spread over his face. His shoulders slumped.

In the next instant, he was a caricature of purposeful motion, banging down the phone and picking it up again. I knew by then what was happening but was afraid to know where. Fingers spinning, he dialed the volunteer fireman he was assigned to inform.

"Lee Harding's house," he barked. "Maple Street."

My insides fell away. "Oh, *God.*"

Images of Connie and Miss Wilma and Lee trapped inside trampled through my head. "I'm going with you!" I cried to Uncle Frank as he raced past me to fetch shoes and socks. I ran to my bedroom, snatching pants and a shirt from my closet, fingers trembling over buttons.

"Where is it, where is it?" Aunt Eva shrilled as she bustled out of her room. In the distance a siren wailed, then another.

"The Hardings', and I'm going!" I yelled, trying to shoot past her. Horrified, she grabbed me by the shoulders.

"No, Jessie! You can't fight a fire."

"I've got to help Connie and Miss Wilma. They can't move fast enough."

"You'll not get there in time! Lee's surely gotten them out."

"Aunt Eva," I pushed away, "I *have* to go!"

"Let her be, Eva," my uncle commanded, shoving into his second shoe.

I cut around her, banged through the back door to the driveway. Uncle Frank gunned the Buick's motor and squealed onto pavement as I perched on the edge of my seat, gripping the dashboard. We ignored stop signs, glancing from street to sky, now black with curling smoke. As soon as we skidded onto Maple, we could see the yellow-orange greed of the fire, four blocks away. The house was burning like a torch.

"Lord Almighty," Uncle Frank breathed, "we're too late."

Chaos ruled. Neighbors ran down the sidewalk, barefoot, shirt flaps untucked. Cars of volunteer firemen were parked haphazardly two blocks down, the fire trucks blocking the street. We jerked to a stop as close as we could and spilled out of the car.

The noise was terrifying. The fire was a splintering roar above men's shouts and pummeling columns of water. Two hoses, held by rigid-muscled men, sprayed back and forth, up and down, a bare spit against the flames. Other hoses were aimed at rooftops on either side of the Hardings' house. Some of the volunteers were clearly tiring, and Uncle Frank hurried to help.

"Stay back, Jessie; you can't do anything!" he yelled as a breeze blew squalid heat across my face.

I stared at the crackling house in utter disbelief. "Did they get out? Did they get out?" I begged of anyone who could hear. Horror-filled, questioning eyes met my own. Through welling tears I turned back to watch the fire fatten, blur. An entire wall collapsed into black ashes that floated eerily through the night. At the sight of that collapse, panic struck me, as pure and coating as at the instant of my mother's wreck. The flames, the heat, the crowd crushed me with collective, smothering arms, and my knees turned to jelly. My own weakness infuriated me. I *had* to see if they were still alive.

Staggering off the street, I flailed over the curb and into the soft grass of a neighbor's yard, irrationally thinking to duck through shadowed backyards. But as the cloying heat fell away in sudden darkness, I dropped like a stone to the ground, frozen in fear. I couldn't bear to see them dead, I *couldn't*. Memories of stumbling to my mother's car, banging helplessly on smashed doors, screaming at the carnage inside, raced jagged-edged through my brain. I could not *live* through such a thing again. Tears squeezing out of my eyes, I rolled over, hugging my knees to my chest. After a moment, self-disgust sucked again through my veins, and I clenched my teeth, willing myself to get up.

A wailing in the distance. I registered it slowly. Another fire truck, I thought, raising my head to listen. Then something moved in the backyard of the house next door. The silhouetted figure of a man. I froze—watching—the cords of my neck straining. At the keening of the siren the man turned, a wan porch light falling across his features. Later, I would question what I'd seen. Had his expression truly been smug? Had his hair really been a grayed yellow, cut bushlike above his ears? Had his nose been too large for his face, his open lips thin, cheeks hollowed? Within a split-second he was gone, tucking down his head and fading into the darkness.

The siren grew louder and my breath caught once more. Bradleyville only had two fire trucks. And the sound was different. *Ambulance.*

A tap inside my body turned on, and I pushed from the ground, running through shadowed backyards. When a picket fence emerged before me, I veered back toward the street, jumping off the curb in time to see an ambulance from Albertsville Memorial ease around the fire trucks. Its wail died away like that of a fallen animal. Ignoring the torrid heat, I raced up the street, darting around stricken onlookers and the mania of volunteer firemen. From the corner of my eye I saw Uncle Frank, face shiny from blaze and sweat, feet firmly planted as he gripped a shooting hose with two other men. I heard Thomas shouting orders. The back doors of the ambulance flew open, a gurney was slid out and hurried toward a neighboring lawn. Upon that lawn a woman lay very still, her belly swollen against a thin blue nightgown. Lee was kneeling, shirtless, by her side.

"*Connie!*"

At my scream Lee's head jerked. His face was streaked with soot, his thick black hair matted with sweat and grime. A large bruise purpled one shoulder. He pulled to his feet as I reached him, encircling me with his arms. For a moment we clung to each other, trembling. Then he pulled away. I couldn't speak.

"She breathed a lot a smoke, but she's not burned."

I swallowed. "Miss Wilma?"

"They took her over there." He pointed to the porch next door. "She wouldn't leave Connie, but she near collapsed a minute ago."

His mother's face reflected the fire like a paste-covered orange. She swooned forward as if to erase the distance between her and her daughter. Women stood around her, holding her shoulders firmly. "She'll be all right, she's all right," I heard them insist. "Just let 'em work on her."

"God, help her," I prayed. I leaned back into Lee, wishing it all away. Then we were kneeling by Connie's feet, looking on helplessly as the medics administered oxygen and checked vital signs. I adjusted her nightgown modestly over her knees. Found her hand and squeezed. "It's me, Connie."

She squeezed back, faintly.

"What about the baby?" Lee asked thickly.

The medics kept working. "We've done what we can here, sir," one finally replied. "She's stabilized enough to take her in."

"What about the baby?"

"We have a heartbeat."

"But is it okay?"

"It's alive, sir."

Quick as lightning, Lee grabbed the startled medic by his shirt and held on. "But is it *okay?*"

I reached for his arm with both hands. "Lee, don't, the baby's fine, calm down." He swiveled toward me, furious. "Come on, Lee." Gently I loosened his fingers from the fabric. "Please." He glared at me, breathing shallowly, until the anger slid from his face like ice from a windowpane. Letting go of the shirt, he pushed back on his haunches. "I'm goin' with you," he informed the medic.

"There's not much room—"

"I'm goin' *with* you!"

"I want to go too," I protested.

"No. Stay with Mama." He caught himself at his harshness, laid hands against my cheeks. "She'll need you. Make sure she's okay, then bring her to the hospital."

I nodded, throat tightening.

He kissed me, quickly and hard.

Connie's gurney disappeared into the ambulance. Lee climbed in after her. Twin doors slammed. I backed up as the ambulance's engine roared, its taillights glowing demon red, siren rising to a keen. As it wailed up the street, I turned away to see about Miss Wilma. At that moment a loud *crack* tore through my ears, and I spun around to see the back of the Hardings' house tear apart to crash in flames against the red brick chimney.

It was the only part left standing.

chapter 36

The brown-orange chair upon which I slumped needed new cushioning. After four hours my lower back ached something awful. I leaned my head against the wall, trying to focus gritty eyes on the door of room 347, barely in view before the hall turned a corner to pass the nurses' station. Miss Wilma was sitting on a small couch to my left, staring blankly at a piece of white lint on the floor. Intermittent whispered prayers spilled from her grim lips. Every now and then she'd push at the lint with one foot, ill-shod in a neighbor's shoe. She wore a yellow housedress, also borrowed, and insanely bright for the gloom clustered above us like a raincloud. Her hair was pulled back in a scraggly low ponytail, a stray wisp against one pale cheek. Lee was next to me on my right. The green shirt I'd brought him was a size too small, pulling tight across his chest and arms. Fortunately, he'd been able to slip into his own shoes before half-carrying Miss Wilma and Connie out of their burning, smoke-choked house. He'd not said a thing to me in more than two hours. I tried to convince myself his mind was so full that words couldn't empty it. But I knew his anger at me had returned.

Lee had been here the longest. After the ambulance had screamed away into the night, it had taken me almost an hour to calm Miss Wilma, find some clothes to replace her nightgown, and get my car and purse. I'd tried to put her in bed at Elsa Brock's, who lived just a few doors down. Doc Richardson had lent a hand, pleading with her to take a sedative, but she'd have none of it. By the time we reached the hospital, she looked exhausted, and she'd barely changed positions after collapsing onto the couch.

I watched the clock. The last time we'd heard from Doctor Brights, who'd been Wilma Harding's doctor for years, was around 6 A.M. Connie was nearly asleep, stabilized by oxygen, he'd told us, when a labor pain had aroused her. She was dilated one to two centimeters. "She might as well have the baby while she's here," he soothed at our stricken expressions. "She's stable enough to handle it, and the fetal heart rate is still normal. But let her rest a while; she can doze between contractions."

The hands of the clock clicked past 9:15. I wondered if the town had gone back to bed after the fire. I wondered if Aunt Eva was at the post office as usual, if Uncle Frank was with strikers at the mill. The IGA must be open, and Tull's and the hardware store and dime store. Life went on. My life, however, would have to be put on hold for a few days. There was no way to leave tomorrow morning, not in the midst of this. I'd at least have to help Miss Wilma and Connie get settled somewhere. And Connie would be returning with a newborn to no crib, no clothes, no blankets. I pictured her beautiful nursery and playroom, and wanted to weep. The image of it all in ashes—especially the lamp of golden-winged angels—left me weak and hollow-lunged. And there was Lee, who sat beside me like a stone, edging his arm away should I happen to brush it, rubbing his palms when I reached for his hand. Sighing, I placed a finger between my eyebrows and rubbed.

At 9:45 the doctor finally reappeared, his rubber-soled feet lightly squeaking down the hall. Doctor Brights's head was half bald and shiny, black-framed glasses enlarging kind eyes. His hands were in the pockets of his white coat. When Lee pushed to his feet, he towered over the doctor, who tilted back his head with a reassuring smile. "She's definitely in the beginning stages of labor," he said. "We'll be moving her to the obstetrics ward, and I'll inform Doctor Richardson. He'll come in to take over. I'll check in on her from time to time, but she'll be in good hands with him and really shouldn't need me anymore."

"Do you know anything more about the baby?" Miss Wilma's voice was a tremor.

"Unfortunately, no. We won't know until it's born if there is any lasting damage, but we don't think there will be. Wilma," he walked over and took her hand, "I know you've been through a lot and you've gotten no sleep. This being a first baby, labor's likely to take all day. I suggest you go to a neighbor's and rest. When the pains get close, we'll call and someone can bring you back."

"No."

"Now, Wilma—"

"I said no!" she declared, gathering herself. "That's my baby girl in there. I'm *not* leavin' her!"

"Mama, maybe the doc's right."

"Hush, Lee! Doctor Brights, help me up." She scooted forward, extending her arm. He gripped it and pulled, anchoring her as she reached for her cane. The folds of her dress wafted around her knees like wilted daisy petals. "There." Straightening as best she could, she glanced purposefully at each of us. "Now let me tell y'all somethin'. I'm no spring chicken, and I been through a lot in my life, even worse than last night. Now I got a job to do and y'all best leave me to it. My mama coached me havin' my babies just like her mother done for her. There's jus' some things a doctor cain't do." She took a deep breath. "I'm goin' into Connie's room now, Doc, and when they move her, I'll follow along. Jessie, I hope you'll stay. Connie loves you, and I could use your help. Lee, there's not much for you to do here. You could go on back to town and see about findin' us a place to stay and collect some things for the baby. The churches'll help. And git Will Abrams movin' on the insurance. That done, you come on back and check on your sister. And son"—she walked a few steps to stand before him, her gaze intent—"be patient. Don't let that temper a yours get the best a you. Maybe we'll find the cause a the fire and maybe we won't. Don't go blamin' yourself. Findin' the cause don't matter much anyway; the house'll still be burned."

That said, Miss Wilma urged the doctor aside and crossed the waiting room carpet, her cane clicking tinnily when it hit tile. "Jessie," she added, half turning, "I'd appreciate a few minutes with Connie first, if you don't mind. You and Lee look like you've got a few things to settle anyway."

As she worked her way down the hall—a woman on a mission— Doctor Brights shrugged at us good-naturedly. "I guess that's that. I'll go call Doctor Richardson."

Lee heaved back into his chair and wearily put his head in his hands.

chapter 37

*T*he phone jangled impatiently on the kitchen wall, jangled and jangled until he woke from a restless sleep, rolled out of bed to answer its summons. "Hello." He swallowed thickness as the caller identified himself. "Yeah."

"It's near ten," the voice said, "don't tell me I got you up."

"'Course you got me up; couldn't go back to sleep till almost dawn. I held that hose so long my arms feel like they's busted." He blinked swollen eyes. "Any news?"

"The Hardings're still at the hospital. I heared Connie's havin' her baby."

"Oh, no. When it rains, it pours."

"Yeah. And somethin' else. There's already a couple a inspectors from Albertsville pawin' through the wreckage. Got the place all roped off. Bill Scutch and Thomas're with 'em. Bill asked for their help to figure out what started the fire. Or who."

The last two words rang in his head. "What're you sayin'?"

"Well now, don't you think the timin's a mite suspicious?"

"Are you thinkin' a Riddum?"

"Yup."

"No. Riddum may be selfish, but he ain't no idiot."

"Not in his eyes, maybe."

"Why would he do it?"

"To warn us. Strike at a leader. And because he thinks he can git away with it, just like he thought he could git away with his greediness."

He pulled a chair out from the table, sank into it. "You better be careful. We'd have to be sure."

"I know. Word's out to wait for the inspectors. 'Course Bledger's rarin' to go."

"God help us." He put a hand around his jaw. "What're we gonna do?"

The caller blew out air. "It ain't gonna be sleepin', that's for sure."

chapter 38

Lee and I sat in the waiting room, examining the walls. "You going home like your mom said?" I finally asked.

His arms were crossed. "I ain't got a home."

"You know what I mean."

"Why? You tryin' to get rid a me?"

"Lee, please."

"I don't know if I'm goin' 'home,' Jessie. I don't know *what* I'm gonna do. I got so much to do, I don't know where to start. Besides, you're the one's goin' 'home.' In fact, ain't you supposed to be packin' 'bout now?"

I steadied myself. He had a right to be upset. "I'm gonna stick around a few more days. Luckily, I don't start work till the fifteenth, so it'll be okay."

He tipped his head back to stare at the ceiling. "Don't stay around on my account."

A hot ball rolled up my throat, and I pushed it back down. "All right then. I'll stay for Connie and your mother."

No reply.

"You don't have to worry about finding a place for your sister and mother. Elsa Brock has already offered her two bedrooms, and says she can fit a crib in the bigger one. And Bill Hensley up the street said you could have his daughter's old room now that she's married. So you won't be far from each other. And I can call the church; by the time Connie goes home those ladies will have gathered everything she needs." I thought of the baby clothes we had so lovingly folded and put into drawers. The yellow walls and matching blanket. Tears singed my eyes. "It was all so beautiful, Lee. You did such a wonderful job on those rooms."

When he finally spoke, his voice was flat. Dead. "It's my fault. The fire."

I searched his face, unable to reply. How well his mother knew him.

"It started in those rooms. That's why Connie breathed more smoke than Mama or me. I've gone over and over it, sittin' here. What did I do wrong; what wires did I cross. Somethin' must a shorted, but I cain't figure out what for the life a me. But I do know I almost killed my sister. And her baby."

"No, Lee. I don't believe that."

"It's true." He nodded slowly, up and down, up and down, eyes fixed on the carpet. "I should know. I was there."

I despaired for convincing words. And then a coldness free-fell through my body. I turned to him, face blanching white. "Which room?"

He lifted a shoulder. "I don't know. I think the nursery, not the playroom. The first thing I heard was Connie screamin' it was on fire."

"Oh, no." My eyes traveled the floor. "It wasn't you, Lee," I rasped. "It was my curtains. I saw them blowing against that lamp. I *saw* it! I should have *known!*"

The knowledge pushed me to my feet, propelled me across the waiting room and back again. I stood before him, breathing hard, wanting to hit something, wanting him to hit me. Anything but that empty, black hole that was his face. I watched shadows shifting across it, blown by new perceptions, new realities. And then it collapsed as his eyes found mine. "Ah, Jessie," he rose to drape weary arms around me, "you didn't do this. Even if it did start there, it's not your fault."

I gripped his shirt and leaned against him, releasing my tiredness and fear into hot tears that soaked through the green cotton. He stroked my back, uttering soothing words. Then a silent sob jerked his chest. Instantly, I felt selfish. He was the one who needed comforting. I let go of the shirt, put my arms around his neck. "No, no, Lee, it's okay, it's all right."

We hugged until we'd cried it out. When I stepped back, his cheeks were hollow, circles under his eyes. He looked as if he'd been through a war zone. I probably looked a sight myself. "Gee," I muttered, "what're the nurses gonna think."

He managed a droopy smile. "They're used to it."

I spied a box of tissues on the coffee table and brought it over. We sat down and wiped our faces, inhaling noisily.

"Well, it's just as well you're leavin'," he said eventually, rubbing his nose. "'Cause if we was gettin' married, we'd have to put it off anyhow. I'd have to rebuild Mama's house before I built one for us. And in the meantime, you'd probably get tired a me and run off with Hank Jenkins."

"Hank Jenkins is over sixty years old."

"Yeah, well. At least he's got a house."

I thought of my hard-earned savings, squirreled away in the Bradleyville bank. How much Lee could use that money right now. He could at least rent a bulldozer and clear the wreckage from his mother's property. Maybe the funds would buy enough lumber to begin rebuilding immediately, without waiting for insurance money. And then I thought of my own needs. What about the furniture I needed to rent? Plus plates, pans, and food? What about the new tires for my car? What if I decided to buy a new sewing machine on credit and needed a down payment? A month would pass before I saw a paycheck from my new job. Then I vacillated again, remembering the money from Miss Alice's I'd not expected to earn. I could at least lend that to Lee. But how little it amounted to, in the face of his needs.

Why this petty selfishness when a family so close to me faced such tragedy? I could at *least* buy some new baby clothes for Connie. Why should I expect the ladies of the church to sacrifice when I wasn't willing to do the same? Who was I to be planning to help strangers through social work and volunteering if I couldn't even help the Hardings? I was amazed and disgusted with myself. My sense of service, the very calling through my dream, did not seem to be enough to summon my generosity at the moment. I berated myself until I remembered the most important thing. The money I'd saved for years would enable me to begin the very plans I'd made, the plans my dream had called me to.

That was the reason I'd needed. Of course I could not lend my money to Lee. My fingers bunched, crumpling my tissue. I wanted to, really, but I just couldn't.

Suddenly I had to get out of that waiting room.

"I'm gonna go to the bathroom," I said, rising. Not looking at him.

"You okay?"

"Fine. I just ... need to wash my face, get a drink. And I need to make some calls." I hurried down the hall to find a pay phone.

chapter 39

fternoon." The air hung hot and muggy, blanketed with depression. His voice remained low as he and his wife sidled to join the
grim-faced onlookers. A few nodded return greetings. He watched for a
moment, a hand on his wife's shoulder. It was hard to believe that twenty-
four hours ago a neat house had occupied those blackened ruins. "Anything new?" he asked of the man standing closest to him.

"No. They ain't talkin'."

"They must a found somethin' by now," his wife put in.

"They got a growin' pile a evidence," the neighbor pointed with his
chin. "But like I said, they won't answer any questions. Jus' keep sayin'
they want to be sure."

"I'll bet it's Thomas keepin' 'em quiet. What do those inspectors know,
from Albertsville. But Thomas there, look at how he's watchin' us out the
side a his eyes. He been here all mornin'?"

"Yep. Jake too, but he ain't been allowed inside the rope. And this
crowd's been here. People come and go; all the same, it's been growin'.
See Al Bledger and his pals over there? Man's a keg 'bout to explode."

"When're we gonna find out?"

"They say it could take all day. Maybe not till Monday. We may not last that long. You're right 'bout Thomas. It's his presence keepin' the heat down."

Keen-eyed, they watched an inspector sift through soot to lift an object for examination. After a moment, he added it to the pile of items in the corner of the roped-off area.

"I was at the mill this mornin'," the newcomer said. "Frank's there with all the '2s'. They look like a bunch a refugees. Riddum ain't shown all day."

"Probably holed up in that fancy house a his. Either that're he's skipped town."

A pickup truck's engine rumbled to a stop behind them, the cab door slamming. They turned their heads in unison.

"Uh oh."

"I thought he was gonna be at the hospital all day."

Lee's hands were on his hips, features dark as he surveyed in daylight the devastation that had been his home. Thomas waved silently, carefully stepping over the thigh-high rope to greet him.

chapter 40

A aahhhh!" Connie wailed as the contraction peaked. Her face was flushed, her forehead damp from sweat and the wet rag with which I'd sponged her. Her long black hair splayed across the white pillows like strewn seaweed. Both hands clenched the bed, her head jerking from side to side.

Miss Wilma perched nearby in a chair, gently patting her daughter's corded arm. "Won't be long now, honey. You're doin' just fine."

The contraction finally over, Connie went limp as a rag, crying softly. I wiped the tears and lay an ice chip against her trembling lips. She sucked it in greedily.

She was too tired to open her eyes. I felt too numb to close mine. I was beyond sleep, beyond the problems of Bradleyville or the promises of Cincinnati, beyond the details of moving trucks and repairing car tires and gathering baby items. All that mattered now, all that had mattered for the last four hours, was birthing this baby.

Life did not end easily, that I knew. It could go out quickly or slowly, in the crash of metal or through the spreading of cancer.

What I hadn't known was how searingly, gut-wrenchingly difficult it was to begin. I had heard of the "pain of childbirth"—that formidable rite of passage for women. Had even asked Mom about it once. But whatever her answer, it could not have sufficed. It could not have begun to describe the torture I had seen Connie endure that day. I felt so helpless and inconsequential, unable to lessen her pain even a fraction. Even the drugs they'd given her didn't seem to help. Every now and then I caught Miss Wilma's eye, silently questioning. But she explained nothing, only stroked and soothed her daughter, intoning solace.

Fervently I wished for my own mother beside me, consoling me. If she were watching from heaven right now, did she know my thoughts? Was she disappointed at my selfishness with my money? I held Connie's hand and remembered my mother holding mine; when I dabbed Connie's flushed face, I thought of the times my mother had nursed me through fevers. Twenty-four years ago, she had gone through labor for me. Watching Connie's agony over her own baby, I understood for the first time the depths of my mother's love. I understood why she'd returned to me, even after death, to ease my confusion in a dream. The knowledge washed me clean, like water gushing from a spigot.

Connie stirred, legs pedaling the sheets. The door opened and Doc Richardson appeared, a man rejuvenated by lunch and fresh air. "How's our girl doing?"

Connie's neck extended, her head pulling back. Her fingers curled to grip the bed as she started to moan. I checked the clock.

"Four minutes since the last one."

Four o'clock, and Lee was still gone. Connie's contractions were almost continuous. "Where *is* he?" I demanded through clenched teeth.

"Don't know, but I sure been prayin'," Miss Wilma replied. "I hope he's jus' takin' care a business. But I got this feelin' somethin's wrong." She closed her eyes wearily. "All the same, what good would he do here?"

I didn't know what he could do. It was far too late for him to see Connie. Doc Richardson was checking her regularly, and two nurses had gathered. Still, I was furious. All this pain, all this *grief*. And we didn't even know if the baby was healthy. Connie *needed* her brother, if only to hear he was in the waiting room. I was furious at him and furious at Bart for getting her pregnant in the first place. I could have strangled them both. Yes, *strangle*, I seethed, thinking how Mom would have chided. For the first time in my life, I thought a little violence would be well deserved.

The contraction peaked, and Connie whimpered like a weak kitten. Doc Richardson pulled back the sheet. "Should be crownin' soon." A nurse nodded in agreement.

"I'll be right back," I whispered hurriedly to Miss Wilma. "I'm gonna try to find out what Lee's doing."

I scuffed down the hall, rubbing burning eyes. Hours ago—was it only this morning?—I'd cashed in bills at the cafeteria for change, and I still had some left. In a rush of clear-headedness, I'd called Ed Tam to tell him I would bring in my car on Monday, phoned the manager of my apartment to inform him I'd be a few days late—again—and hired movers for Tuesday morning. I could no longer rely on Uncle Frank. Who knew what would be happening at the mill?

At the pay phone once again, I dug nickels out of my purse and stacked them with a *click* on the shelf. The post office was the place to start. Aunt Eva probably knew minute to minute what was happening in Bradleyville; she'd about driven the nurses crazy calling about Connie. She answered quickly, grew breathless at my voice. "No, it's not born yet," I clipped, "but anytime now. Where's Lee? He's needed."

"Well," she hesitated, "I don't know."

"Would he be with Uncle Frank?"

"Your uncle's at the mill. Nothin's goin' on there."

It was her emphasis on the word "there." I tapped the phone impatiently. My aunt had apologized Wednesday night for "gettin' so upset," and I'd tiptoed around her since then. But at the moment I was just too pushed. "Aunt Eva, is there something you're not telling me?"

"Honey, you got enough on your mind."

"*What* is the *matter!*"

"Nothin' really, child. It's just that a lot a mill folk are at the fire site, waitin' to hear what the inspectors say."

"*What* inspectors?"

"The fire inspectors. From Albertsville."

Sleep deprivation and trauma had taken their toll. I tried in vain to make rational sense of her intimations.

"They think he did it!" she blurted. "They think Blair Riddum set the fire!"

A rock dropped in my stomach. "*Who* thinks that?"

"Most a the town."

"Oh, please God, no." That kind of talk, true or not, would spread even quicker than the Harding fire. Goosebumps popped down my arms. "That's ridiculous; I don't believe it for a minute."

"I don't know. I *do* know I been prayin' and prayin'. And so are others in our church." Fear sent a tremble through her voice. "I'm gettin' scared, Jessie."

"Don't be scared, Aunt Eva; just keep praying. Jesus will make everything okay." I blinked. What a strange thing for me to say. "What's happening right now?" I added hastily, feeling self-conscious.

Her split-second hesitation spoke of her own surprise at my statement. "Everybody's waitin' to see what the inspectors say. Thomas is there with 'em, by the way."

Thomas. If anyone could still roiling waters, it was he. Thomas could even keep Lee calm. Particularly with the help of Uncle Frank.

"Is that where Lee is?"

"Last I heard."

"Aunt Eva, listen to me. I've got to get back to Connie. Here's what you need to do. Send someone to fetch Uncle Frank *right now*. Tell them to have Uncle Frank find Lee and persuade him to come back to the hospital immediately. Staying at the fire site will only rile him up. Besides, he's needed *here*. By his *family*. Okay?"

"I'll try," she sighed. "I know he should be there. But Lee's awful upset—"

"Aunt Eva! Just *do* it!"

I slammed down the phone before she could protest.

The baby crowned at 5:15. All the hours of waiting, waiting; now the room bustled with activity. I was working so hard my body shook. I didn't even have time to be upset with Lee. Miss Wilma stood, gripping Connie's hand. I remained at Connie's back, straining to hold her in a half-sitting position while she pushed out the baby. Her knuckles blanched white as she gripped now-upright bed handles. "It's coming, it's coming!" Doc Richardson encouraged. "Oh, *my!* Would ya look at all that hair!"

Connie's final scream was primal, deep-throated. Her mouth opened wide, pulled back over saliva-flecked teeth. *I keened like that once, Mom*, I thought. *When I watched you die.* The place was so hot, I could hardly breathe. The scream broke apart like shattering glass, then dropped into a rattling gasp.

"It's a girl!"

Connie sucked in air and fell dead-weighted against my arms. I sank her down against the pillows. "You did it; you did it!" I cried, watching with incredulity as Doc Richardson turned the silent baby over and smacked it. "Oh, *look*, Connie, look at her." And then one of the longest seconds I've ever lived stretched out as we all waited for that baby to cry. When her hiccuped, affronted wail took flight, I laughed until the joy froze my throat and my eyes spurted tears. The doctor checked her over carefully, reassuring himself with stethoscope and probing fingers. Connie sobbed as he pronounced her little girl healthy. A nurse cleaned the baby up and wrapped her in a yellow blanket. Presented her grandly.

"Want to hold your daughter?"

That's when Miss Wilma burst into tears.

chapter 41

A couple of hours later I drove Miss Wilma back to Bradleyville. We'd taken turns holding the baby—named Katherine May— reluctant to give her up. We'd watched in awe as she learned to nurse, Connie awkwardly poking a nipple into her mouth. We'd sponged Connie off, gotten her into a clean gown, propped her on pillows. Finally, from sheer exhaustion, she fell asleep. An efficient nurse whisked the baby away and told us to beat it home—Mama needed her rest.

So did we. Miss Wilma could barely hold her cane, and my muscles felt like wilted leaves. All the same, I dreaded returning to town. I'd called Aunt Eva at home to announce the birth, and Uncle Frank had picked up the phone. He said he'd return to the fire site and tell Lee. "Why didn't he come? Did you go talk to him?" I demanded.

"Yeah. And he said he'd get back. But he was just rooted to the spot, watchin' those strangers poke around in what used to be his home. He was standing so still I thought he'd gone unconscious on his feet."

"I don't care; he should have come." My voiced throbbed with resentment.

"Jessie, go easy on him. He's been through a lot."

"*We've* been through a lot! You have no *idea!*"

"I know. You're really tired right now; everybody's tired. Why don't you just come on home and get some rest?"

"I've got to get Miss Wilma settled at Miss Elsa's first. Has anybody brought baby stuff to her house yet?"

"From what your Aunt Eva says, the room's already near full. You can sort through all that tomorrow."

Yes, I would do that. And perhaps I would face Lee tomorrow too. Perhaps not. What did it matter; I'd be gone in three days anyway. I couldn't *wait* to be away from all this. Particularly after today's events, my heart had already flown, whisked away on the wings of my guardian angel. I simply could not allow anything else to stand in the way of my plans. Including any trouble brewing in Bradleyville. Besides, with less than two hours' sleep in the past thirty-six, I was simply too spent to care. Even if Lee was involved. He'd already shown his true colors, I railed inwardly, worrying more about possible vengeance than his poor sister. Uncle Frank had promised to stay out of any trouble; that's all that mattered.

I focused droopy eyes on the road, Miss Wilma's head bobbing as she snoozed. Every once in a while, she'd snore and wake herself up. I couldn't wait to get her settled and go to bed myself. I wished I could pull the covers over my head and sleep until Tuesday morning.

Miss Elsa, God bless her, had everything ready for her guest. She took one look at us and pulled Miss Wilma inside, waving at me to "git on home and take care a yourself." Miss Wilma managed to give me a smile and a final, mouthed "thank you." I slumped back to my car, glancing up the street at Lee's red truck. I could see him talking to Thomas, gesturing with impatience. He still wore that ridiculous green shirt. If he'd seen me at all, he paid no heed. I turned my car around, memories seeping like shadows through my head. Wondering if that was the last I'd see of him. Pasted against a dusky sky, soot at his feet.

Dully, I was imagining what he'd been saying to Thomas when my right front tire blew. The noise was slow to register, my car pulling toward the curb. "Oh, *drat* it!" I should have been glad it hadn't happened outside of town, but all I could do was bump my forehead against the steering wheel in frustration. *Curse the mill! Curse the fire! Curse rubber and tiredness and hospitals and all men— most of all Lee!* Then, jaw clenching, I drove slowly back out Main, my wheel rim in clanky protest. Pulling into Ed Tam's gas station, I handed him the keys with what I hoped was a smile. After all, he was promising to get to it by tomorrow afternoon. Full of Bradleyville neighborliness, he even closed his station temporarily to drive me home, leaving a scribbled cardboard sign swinging against the dusty door.

Finally home, I managed to talk to my aunt and uncle for a while, but memories of our conversation are vague. I do remember that both of them were beyond sleep, they were so worried about the cause of the fire. And I remember Aunt Eva's moaning that the inspectors had left with a few choice items, among them a suspicious-looking window screen. They were to examine them further at the Albertsville police station and thought they'd have an answer to Bill Scutch sometime tomorrow.

"Good," I replied flatly, too exhausted to care. "I'm going to bed."

chapter 42

*D*arkness was falling as he climbed the steps to his modest home, hands balled and jiggling in his jeans pockets. Sounds from the television wafted through the air, still tinged with the acrid smell of smoke. Every once in a while a breeze would blow just right, and the thick scent would roll off oak leaves and picket fences and a kid's bike in the yard. His boys were seated Indian-style before the TV, entranced and eating popcorn. Not a care in the world.

"Why you kids still up?"

"It's Friday night, Daddy," the oldest replied indignantly.

"Don't be smart with me. Where's your mama?"

"On the phone!" his wife called from the bedroom. "Come on in here!"

Must be his nerves. Now she was sounding sassy. She handed him the phone, lines etching her forehead. "It's Bill Hensley."

Bill had just left there not ten minutes ago. Sighing, he took the receiver. "Yeah?"

"Lee went kinda crazy on me after you left."

"What now?"

"I thought Shirley'd convinced him to git some rest. But he come outta the shower lookin' like a man risen from the dead. Face battered and weary, ya know, but full a fire. And he declared, 'I ain't seen my niece yet, I gotta go right now!' I said, 'Lee, the hospital's closed up to visitors, and Connie's probably sleepin' anyway; jus' let it wait till mornin'.' He said no, he was goin' right then, and while he was in Albertsville, he was gonna bang on the door of the police station and demand some answers. I tell you the guy's goin' nuts."

"Only thing he's crazy for is waitin' for an answer. I already know it; so do you."

"We cain't be guessin'."

"Who's guessin'? That screen's been cut. Somebody sliced it and stuck a match through to set those curtains on fire. You think it was the neighbor's dog?"

The caller snorted. "Well, you ain't alone in how you're thinkin'. Anyhow, Lee's already gone. He tol' me to keep things in line here, so I'm passin' that on. If somethin' comes of all this, he wants to lead it his-self."

His wife was listening anxiously, sucking her top lip into her teeth. He turned away, lowering his voice. "That's his right. And it's the only reason some of us, includin' Bledger and his gang, ain't bangin' down Riddum's door right now. But when I get the word, I'm ready to go; I say we settle this thing. It's been comin' for two months, and there's only so much bottlin' a man can do."

chapter 43

One of the lessons I learned that summer of 1968 was that there's a line in each of us that can be crossed—a boundary that separates what we are from the monsters we can become. The frightening thing is how quickly it can be crossed when we fail to seek God's guidance. It may take years to stub your toe against that line or even see it in the distance. Some people may never get there. Maybe their lives are just easier. But once the toe is stubbed and that just-right set of circumstances is rolling like a freight train down the track, it's all too easy to be pushed over it. Before you know it, you're looking up at the world from flat on your back. Reality has gone mad, a swirling tornado sucking up the land. And in the midst of such hurt and anger, your mind rationalizes everything you do, even the vilest of choices. Everyone else is wrong or blind, it screams; only your actions are justified.

I see this now, but I could not understand it then. Nor could I understand that a person so pushed will only cross back once the enervating whirl in one's head finally slows of its own accord. And so, when it happened to Lee, I made one mistake after another— I cajoled; I cried; I yelled—as if I could reach him.

It was sometime after midnight when he banged on our door.

For a moment, groggy and disoriented, I thought time had played a cruel trick, had circled back to relive last night's fire. I stiffened in bed, hearing the jump-start of my heartbeat, the intake of my breath. Automatically, my head swiveled toward the window, but I saw only moon-lit sky. I strained for sound, not sure what had awakened me. Then I heard the banging. Not knuckles, but fist-driven. I was out of bed before realizing it, yanking on a bathrobe, flicking on the porch light as I opened the front door. Lee nearly knocked me over when he stumbled through.

"What is it?" I cried, fearing for Connie, the baby.

"I need to see Frank."

He looked through me with unfocused eyes, the smell of sweat and wrath hanging from his shoulders. His breathing was erratic; jaw set. The maroon T-shirt he'd borrowed had damp circles under the arms.

"What's happened?" My uncle barked behind me.

Lee pushed me aside. "Frank." His voice sounded thick, unnatural. "The men'll be gatherin'. I'll need you there."

"What do you mean?" Aunt Eva appeared, hair disheveled and eyes puffy, knotting her bathrobe.

"We'll be gatherin' at the mill soon as I make some calls. We're goin' out to Riddum's place."

"What for?" I demanded stupidly. Aunt Eva shrank back, fingers covering her mouth. Uncle Frank laid a hand on Lee's arm. "Just settle a minute. Tell me what's goin' on."

"No! I ain't settlin'. I'm jus' tellin' ya. And I want you to come, Frank; you're a part a this."

"No, he's not," Aunt Eva wailed. "He's not a part of anything!"

"Hush, Eva," Uncle Frank ordered. "Lee! Please stop a minute and *tell* me."

Lee passed a hand over his eyes. "I went to the police station in Albertsville. Heard they're supposed to look at that screen tomorrow. But they claimed the evidence wasn't even there; I near got in a fight with the policeman. And Thomas and Bill Scutch were no help this evenin'. They just kept sayin', 'You got to wait for the tests, you got to wait for the tests.' Well, I ain't waitin' any longer. And I don't need Albertsville's help anyway. I could see it all over that policeman's face, that smug look that said it's time Bradleyville learned it ain't so high and mighty."

"But Thomas is right, Lee," Uncle Frank cut in. "You don't know."

"Yes, I do!" Lee's eyes glistened as he tipped his face heavenward. "God as my witness! All those hours in the hospital, wonderin' what I'd done wrong. And all that time Riddum's sittin' snug in his house. It coulda been *this* house, Frank, if you'd raised your voice against him as loud as I'd raised mine. How would you feel then?"

"I don't believe it," I mumbled. "I just don't believe he'd do that."

Lee ignored me. "I come back into town, seein' lights still on up past Riddum's fancy driveway. I nearly stopped right then. I could hardly drive anyway; I was so mad my hands were shakin'. I kept thinkin' 'bout how he almost *killed* my little sister's baby. But I cain't do alone what all of us can do together. I'm goin' back to Bill's now and start makin' calls. The men'll come, they're ready; they were ready when I left."

"And then what, Lee?" I grabbed his shirt sleeve. "You gonna burn his house down? Haul him outside and beat him up? That ought to help."

He yanked away. "Stay out of it, Jessie. We all know you'd turn a cheek rather than protect your own family."

"Now, Lee—"

"Forget it, Uncle Frank," I seethed. There was no winning that argument. "Look." I pushed myself in Lee's face. "You want to do something stupid, you go right ahead. You and all your friends. But leave my uncle out of it. You *promised* me you wouldn't drag him into trouble! Or have you forgotten that?"

"Please, Frank, don't go," Aunt Eva pleaded.

"Shut *up*, Jessie!" Lee spat. "You cain't understand. You never had to fight for anything a day a your life, never had loved ones that needed protectin'. Forget *fightin'*, you cain't even handle plain ol' anger. You're so scared of it, you cain't even see it in *yourself!*"

A coldness shot through me, snow over ice. "How *dare* you." My voice shook. "How dare you say I've never had to fight for anything! At least *your* mother made it out *alive!*"

Lee's face almost softened, then reassembled itself. "This ain't about you and me, Jessie."

"Wait! Stop!" Uncle Frank grasped my elbows and hauled me backwards. "Lee, you cain't do this. Think a minute. Where's your family goin' to be if you end up in jail?"

"I ain't endin' up in jail; who's to arrest us? You think Bill Scutch's gonna take in half his own town?"

"Bill has to uphold the law, and he'll do what he has to."

"Aw, forget it!" Lee swiveled away in disgust. "Just stay here, Frank, go on back to bed. It'll be your men out there, but don't worry 'bout us."

"Lee, wait one more day," Aunt Eva said with surprising calm. "Don't move while you're mad; it'll only lead to trouble. You know this isn't the right thing to do. Wait till we find out somethin' tomorrow. And if Riddum's guilty, let *him* go to jail. Come on in now; pray with us. We'll pray for the peace a God."

Deep in my brain a memory triggered. Perhaps it was the mention of my mother's accident against the backdrop of the fire. Perhaps it was the similar pull of my facial muscles as I stared at Aunt Eva. Or the rush of weakening emotion. Maybe even Lee's hulking stance. Whatever it was, it flew me back to the scene of the fire, to stumbling across a neighbor's yard in the dark. Raising my head to see a man in half shadow. A man with short gray-yellow hair, large nose, mouth thin and smug under sunken cheeks.

"What does he look like?" I blurted.

Lee blinked, distracted. "What?"

"What does he look like?" Fear curled my fingers. I hid them in my pockets.

"Who?" Uncle Frank thought I'd gone crazy.

"Riddum!"

A light began to dawn in Lee's eyes, pale and ominous. "Why?"

I came to my senses. Straightened. "Nothing."

"*Why?*"

"Nothing!"

"Grayish blond hair," Lee rattled off, not taking his eyes from me. "Not too tall, mean-lookin' mouth, big nose. A face that's fallin' in. Now, why you askin'?"

"No reason." They were all looking at me. I could hear the panic in my denial.

"Did you see somethin'?" Lee glared down. "At the fire?"

Through my robe, my fingers dug into both legs. "I . . . No."

He clamped a heavy hand on my shoulder. "*What* did you see?"

"*Nothing*, Lee. Let go of me!"

He held on.

"Jessie." Uncle Frank's tone was gentle. I turned bewildered eyes on him. "*Did* you see something at the fire?"

He spaced the words as if talking to a frightened child. I swallowed, watching dismay ripple across his face as he saw the truth.

"She didn't see anything; she didn't see anything!" Aunt Eva shrieked ridiculously.

"You can't do this." I looked in desperation at Lee. "It's not right, no matter what happened." My voice rose. "You can't *do* this!"

Uncle Frank's shoulders slumped. He stared at the wall, unseeing, fingers shaking through his hair.

Lee's lips were pressed. "Well, then, that's it. You comin'?"

He nodded, dazed. "I'll get dressed."

"No, Frank!" Aunt Eva caught his arm and hung on. "You promised me, you *promised!* Henry went off, and he didn't come back!"

"I got to, Eva." He tried to pry her hand away. "I'm not goin' to fight, far from it. *Somebody's* got to be there to pray."

"*Please*, Uncle Frank." I pivoted to Lee. "See what you've done! You, who talked to me about 'giving your life to *Jesus!*'" The words sneered on my lips. "You think *this* is what he'd want you to do?"

Lee looked as though I'd slapped him into an awakening. Then his eyes veiled over again with determined rage.

Aunt Eva pleaded with her husband all the way down the hall and into their room. "Don't go, Frank; they'll pull you into it, no matter how hard you try! We'll pray here! You think God can't hear us right here? Please, Frank, *please!*" When he reappeared, shirttail out and half buttoned, she was wringing her hands, tears streaking her cheeks. He pulled her to him, hugging her tenderly.

"I love you, Eva. I'll be all right. Remember Jeremiah 29:11— *For I know the thoughts that I think toward you, saith the* LORD, *thoughts of peace and not of evil, to give you an expected end.*"

I had retreated to the couch and collapsed, face in my hands. As my uncle stepped onto the porch, I rose on trembling legs, clutching the back of the sofa, the worn fabric smooth beneath my fingers. "Uncle Frank." My voice was choked. "If Jesus is really Lord, he'll keep you safe—'cause that's what I'm demanding of him. And Lee . . ." His very name dripped venom. He turned a face of stone to me. "If my uncle does get hurt, I'll never forgive you. *Never.*"

He glared at me, a knight to a fool. The door slammed on his way out.

chapter 44

I paced the living room after they had gone, paced and paced, my legs unable to stop. Aunt Eva lay on the couch, crying and praying aloud with extravagance until my ears rang. "Calm down!" I finally commanded. "I can't even hear myself think!"

"You don't know, you don't know," she sobbed into her hands like an affronted little girl, "and now you're *yelling* at me."

"Oh, for heaven's *sake!*" I hit the wall with a fist. "Will everybody stop telling me what I don't know! Have you all forgotten what *I've* lost!"

On I paced, my fury mounting. I could not squelch my anger, didn't even care to try. I couldn't even say where my anger began or ended. Of course I was mad at Lee, seething over his betrayal. And at Uncle Frank for playing the martyr. And at Blair Riddum and the town and the mill for being built in the first place. I was very mad at God for letting all this happen. And I was mad at my mother, who'd taught me to eschew violence, but not what to do if I found myself unerringly embroiled in it. She may have stood before it silent and meek, but *I* certainly couldn't. I prayed to her for strength, but felt not the least bit of comfort.

I was also mad at myself. For opening my big mouth. And for still being in this town. *Why* hadn't I left Bradleyville on the first? So what if Uncle Frank would have brought the truck two days later; I could have slept on my new bedroom floor. So what if he couldn't have come at all? I'd have hired movers as I'd now done anyway. I could be there by now. I could be painting my bedroom, renting furniture, visiting the Center.

"Lord Jesus, first I lost Henry," Aunt Eva hiccuped, wisps of hair plastered to her wet fingers, "then my sister, then Jessie off to college. Now Jessie again for good, and maybe Frank. *Please* take care of Frank!"

I paced to her, sighing. Knelt down. "I'm sorry, Aunt Eva, I'm sorry. Come on." Gently I pried her hands from her face. "I didn't mean to yell at you."

She sniffed loudly, chin trembling. Her face was red, puckered, and old. "Help me pray, Jessie; what else can we do? Only Christ has the power to calm things now."

I shook my head. "I don't think *anybody* can calm things. Lee's gone crazy." I sat back on my haunches, staring at the worn carpet. He and whoever followed him deserved whatever they got. Except Uncle Frank. "I should at least call Bill Scutch. I don't know what he can do but . . . he should know what's happening."

Aunt Eva knew his home number. She probably had the whole town memorized, I thought as she recited it between sniffles. I expected a sleepy "hello," but the policeman's wife answered, wary and alert.

"It's Jessie Callum. Sorry for calling so late, but I need to talk to Bill."

"Oh." Her voice sagged with relief, then tightened again. "He's not here. What's wrong?"

"Lee left here about ten minutes ago. He's rounding up the men to go to Blair Riddum's place. Uncle Frank's with them. Only to pray, he said." I couldn't bear for her to place my uncle in the category of those men.

"Bill already knows," she breathed.

My fingers twisted and untwisted the phone cord. "How? And where is he? I *have* to tell him something."

"He's been with Thomas all evening, looking at that stuff from the fire. A few hours ago they heard from the Albertsville police that Lee had been there, and they figured this thing might not sleep through the night. And now they're already on their way to the Riddums'; Bill just called. He and Thomas saw a bunch of cars headin' toward the mill and stopped one of 'em."

Not Thomas in danger too! "But if they want to stop the men, why go to the Riddums'? Why not just go to the mill?"

"I don't *know*." She sounded scared and defensive and upset at my pressing. I backed off, telling her—unconvincingly at best—not to worry. That everything would work out somehow. That Bill and Thomas were loved and respected and no one would hurt them. She didn't seem to hear.

"I said to Bill, 'If they want to burn down that man's house, let 'em.' He just said, 'What kind a lawman would that leave me?' But they better not hurt him." Her voice turned strident, off-key. "God help anybody who takes this mess out on him, 'cause they'll have to deal with me. I swear I'll shoot the lot of 'em."

I hung up the phone, stomach turning, picturing the town collapsing like dominoes, one ill causing the next. As I stood there, overcome by the immensity of it all, similar scenes were undoubtedly replaying across town, magnified by the sudden clicks of lamps in darkness, the shadows of women begging their hastily dressing husbands. And their inevitable anger at the firm close of each door, their own declarations of reprisal if harm came to that particular man.

Too much of it would be my fault. I may not have caused the Harding's fire after all or even supported the strike, but I'd certainly opened my mouth at the wrong time.

Aunt Eva still watched me, her tear-stained face imploring. "Now what?" she quavered.

I blew out air, dug two fingers in the center of my forehead. It was hard to think straight, but one thing was clear: I had to tell

Thomas and Bill that the men now knew I'd seen Riddum at the fire. No—*believed*—not knew. Maybe it wasn't even true; maybe it hadn't been Riddum at all. It didn't matter. What mattered was that they believed it, and that belief, coupled with their months-long resentment, would render them blind and deaf to anyone who stood in their path. Thomas fancied himself still back at the town meeting, for goodness sake, expecting reasoning minds to hear reasonable argument. This would be more like a Korean battlefield.

And that's when the outcome of my mistake really hit. As I stood in bathrobe and bare feet, eyes thick from lack of sleep, I pictured—in horrific sequence—my old friend Thomas shouting appeals, being threatened, refusing to move, being knocked aside. On a rational level I could not imagine Lee or anyone else doing such things, but rationality had flown, retribution claiming its heyday. *Please, Jesus*, I breathed, *keep them all safe*.

"Do you know the Riddums' number?"

Aunt Eva's eyes grew round. "What you want to call them for?"

"*Do* you know it?" I sounded like Uncle Frank, each word precise.

Of course she did. For a fleeting moment, I wondered if she once used to gossip with Mrs. Riddum. I dialed the numbers, hearing my own heartbeat, praying that Bill or Thomas would answer. What could I possibly say to Blair Riddum?

The phone rang ten times before I hung up. I tried again. Let it ring fifteen.

"They're not answering." I slumped to the closest chair and sank into it, a weight in my chest pulling me into the cushion. My knees were oddly cold, and I drew my robe over them, absently rubbing the fabric. Part of me couldn't believe this was happening; I wanted to go back to bed, pull a sheet over my head, and in the quiet of this house deny what was taking place a mile outside of town. I also wanted to deny my anger, to let my guardian angel rock me to sleep. For a moment, sitting there, I almost believed; I could almost feel the fear ebb away. But the faces in my head would not let me be: Uncle Frank's dazed expression at the unthinkable knowledge of Riddum's act, Lee's flat-eyed determination for revenge. A force beyond me pushed me to my feet. "I have to go out there." I did not look at Aunt Eva. "I've got to tell Thomas I think I saw Riddum at the fire—and that the men know it."

"Are you *insane?*" Aunt Eva sat up straight, tears gone.

Probably.

"What do you think a little thing like you can do?"

I was already crossing the room. "All I'm going to do is tell him. Then I'll get out of there."

"And what if you get in the way a those men? They could be headin' out there soon."

"I won't." My eyes flew to the clock, sudden urgency infusing my limbs. "I'll hurry."

"Jessie, don't!" she called, but I was already in my room, slipping out of my robe, pulling on shorts and a T-shirt, tennis shoes without socks. I grabbed my purse and plunged in a hand for car keys. I felt my wallet, a hair brush and pen, some wrapped hard candies scattered in the bottom. My fingers scrambled until in irritation I dumped the contents onto my bed. No car keys. Realization slowly dawned. My car wasn't there.

"Aunt Eva!" I trotted back into the living area only to hear her answer from her bedroom. She emerged, buttoning up a house-dress. "I'm coming with you," she declared.

I shook my head impatiently. "Did Uncle Frank take your car? Or did he ride with Lee?"

She blinked at me.

"My car's at Ed's," I snapped, turning. I ran through the kitchen and banged out the back door, jumping off the porch toward the driveway. Crossing the small yard in seconds, I saw the answer in the bright moonlight—emptiness. I ran anyway, hearing the pebbles crunch beneath my feet, and looked down the driveway's length toward the street. I then ran to search in front of the house, even though Uncle Frank never parked there. My feet slowed in the front yard, and I leaned against a tall maple tree, bouncing my head against its bark. A sob rattled up my throat, hot tears stinging my eyes. This was all so *stupid*. I kicked helplessly at an exposed tree root, grass sanding the top of my foot. Stupid, stupid *stupid!*

"Jessie? Jessie!" My aunt hurried out the front door, wan-cheeked under the porch light, clasping her dress. I pushed away from the tree.

"Aunt Eva, I'll be all right."

"Jessie, come back inside."

But there was no going back. For a split second I considered it—imagined giving up and praying for the best—but knew I couldn't. Beyond that I did not think, could not consider the foolishness of what I was about to do, even as my feet began to move. "Jessie, where are you goin'!" Aunt Eva cried. I called over my shoulder, "I'll be okay!" as I jumped off the curb and onto the street, picking up speed, elbows bending. My aunt screamed after me hysterically.

I did not look back.

chapter 45

Aunt Eva's screams faded behind me. As I ran, my body took over, adrenaline rushing, exhaustion washing away. Not until I reached the first corner, heading toward Main, did I fully realize what I was doing. I remember thinking how crazy it was. A filament of rational thought dimly flickered. It was about two miles to the Riddums'. I had never run that far in my entire life. And only once had I run for all I was worth. Even in P.E., I'd only managed a time or two around the track. I doubted I could make this. And even if I could, who was to say I'd beat the men? The thoughts glimmered, faded, poofed away. For a second my mind went blank, flashing a brilliant white light that exposed empty corners.

I was already winded. I slowed a bit, fell into a rhythm. The moon shone brightly, obliterating the stars. The after-midnight air hung hot and thick. I saw no cars, heard no sounds other than the soft flap-flap of my feet and the whooshing of my breath. By the second corner I could already feel sweat beading on my forehead. One sockless heel began to throb. The third corner was Main. When I reached it, I veered right, beginning the straight shot through town that eventually would send me past the Bradleyville sign, over two long hills, and around numerous curves to the Riddums' tree-lined driveway.

The quiet was eerie, like a sleeping dragon soon to be awakened. Trees and flower beds jerked by in peripheral vision, alternately lightened and shadowed by yellowed streetlights. I wondered at the silence, guessing whether it meant the men were still gathering or were long gone. The sound of a distant engine brought my head up, and I sucked in air, listening. Without slowing, I glanced over my shoulder to see a car turn onto Main— headed toward the mill. Air rushed from my lungs.

I saw the post office in the distance, its wooden bench out front gleaming golden and desolate under the moon. Long before I passed the building I was exhausted. I was only a half-mile from home, a half-mile often traversed by Aunt Eva in good weather. "You drive yourself to work today," she'd say to Uncle Frank. "I'll walk." In time the post office clipped by, and I set my eyes on the next goal—the stoplight at Minton and Main. I watched it bouncing three blocks away, methodically changing from green to yellow to red, directing air.

My chest ached. Still, I could not think of stopping. Visions— both past and present—crowded into my head, visions I did not want to see. With conscious effort I blocked them, forcing thoughts of Cincinnati. In three days I would be gone. I longed for it, dreamed of it like a parched nomad dreams of water. With a jolt I realized I'd stopped praying to my guardian angel, so I whispered to her, seeking her strength. But I did not sense an answer, and my legs still ached. Then the visions crowded in again, tripping over themselves. I saw myself running the one other time in my life I'd covered any great distance. It had been summer then too, and hot, the midday sun without mercy. And then, as now, I ran with no other plan than to Get There, my legs pumping, my ragged breath singing a tuneless song of its own. Terror had driven me. That and a similar disbelief of what awaited.

I passed the intersection at Minton and Main, lost in a replay of that day eight years ago. At this moment on this silent and strange night, my weariness and my stumbling run—almost dreamlike—focused the memory acutely. Every jolt of my foot against pavement, every jagged breath, brought it back with numbing wholeness. I'd known then as I knew now that my running was futile, that I was an insignificant cog in a very big wheel that had spun off course.

The Bradleyville sign bounced by on my left. The sidewalk ended and I hugged the edge of the road, beginning the long climb of the first hill.

I'd climbed a long hill then too, leaving behind houses and sidewalks and life as I'd known it. Viewridge had been cliffed and winding, and my legs had turned to rubber, the hot sun's fingers spindling down to squeeze my neck. Far up ahead, on some other plane, a blinding glare skidded off glass fragments and bent metal. Strangers were there, appearing from nowhere, stopping cars, banging doors shut, calling, yelling for a doctor, an ambulance. As I neared the scene, a voice, foreign and rasping, screamed, *"Mom! Mommeee!"* I flung myself, breathless and sobbing, toward her car, strangers' arms reaching out, holding me back. "No, no, honey, you musn't." *"No, NO,"* I fought, flailing, straining, knowing my mother was dead, not *believing* she was dead. Couldn't somebody just help, couldn't somebody do *something!* Sheer obsession possessed me until I broke through their grasps and leapt for the car, which was battered and bent and horribly still. The crushed door clanked and knocked beneath my helpless beating but would not open its precious contents to me. They dragged me away again, overcoming me until the wrecker came with the fire truck and police and ambulance, dissonant sirens shrieking. Sobs wracked my body until my lungs threatened to collapse, my eyes run forever dry. I could not believe it; I *would* not believe what was happening. For days I would not believe it, could not grasp the stark reality even through the grim-faced policeman's declaration, the consolations of neighbors, the funeral, the move to Bradleyville. I would not believe it because to do so was to admit my mother had *left* me, had blithely made a fatal decision to drive away and leave me. Alone.

Why did you do it, Mom? I gasped as I neared the top of the first hill outside Bradleyville. Why did you have to go to Hope Center that day? I *told* you to stay home. *Why* didn't you stay and rest? Look at what your decision to help others has *cost* me!

I started downhill, hitting the pavement with hard, robot-like strides. Somewhere along the way I had begun crying. The symmetry of motion now and eight years ago had cycled me back to then. I couldn't be sure which crisis the tears were for. My cheeks were wet, nose dripping. I registered the sound of ragged sobs remotely, like a distant radio station fading in and out. I could hardly feel my body.

I would not have made it. I would have collapsed, for the weight of my crying dragged at what little reserve I had. The second hill loomed before me, oversized and impassable. My legs slowed. Then a crack of light split the road before me, spilling downward as a car crested the ridge behind. I jerked around, fear prickling my scalp, expecting to view a cavalcade, but I spied only one vehicle, racing toward me with abandon. I jumped into brush, awash in the car's headlights, and froze. It caught up to me. A big car. It braked suddenly and stopped. A portly figure leaned over and yanked down the window.

"Jessie Callum? What on *earth* are you doin'?"

Relief crackled up my throat. "Mr. Lewellyn! What . . . where are you going?"

He gaped at me. "I'm goin' out to Riddums'; where're *you* goin'?"

"Oh," I managed to say and then started to cry all over again, squeaky strangles of breath adding even more weirdness to this bizarre night. "Would you give me a ride?"

He unlatched the door and pushed it open. I fell inside, gasping, holding my ribs. The car surged forward.

"You run all the way out here?"

"Yeah, my car's in the garage."

"What *for?*"

"Flat tire."

He looked at me, a parent to an idiot child. "Jessie. *Why* are you out here?"

I sucked in air while trying to form an answer. How much to tell him? He wasn't Thomas; never would be. "The men are on their way there. I guess you know that."

He nodded impatiently.

"Thomas and Bill Scutch are already there. I have to tell them something."

"Must be important."

"It is."

He obviously expected me to tell him too. He drove in reckless silence that I would not fill until the tilt of his shoulders displayed his disappointment. "Good thing I came along," he said finally. "Don't think you'd a made it."

"No, Mr. Lewellyn," I reassured him. "You saved me, no doubt about it."

He braked quickly, throwing me forward, and screeched onto the Riddums' driveway. I saw house lights in the distance.

"I couldn't sleep," he rattled, hunching over the wheel. "Saw a bunch a cars go by and knew somethin' was up. Called Bill to see what I could do to help and got his wife. She said they was already out here."

"How can they *do* this, Mr. Lewellyn?" I demanded. "How *can* they?"

He shook his head, his words clipped. "If we get through this, Jessie, maybe someday we'll understand. For now, just remember one thing. God can use the worst times in life to teach us the most, if only we'll listen."

The meaning of his statement was buried under my own surprise. Even though he was in church every Sunday, I'd never heard Jake Lewellyn talk much about God. I wiped at my face with a sleeve.

"Oh, boy, look at that."

I lifted my head, arm in midair. The Riddums' long, white-columned porch sat awash in carriage lamplight. Five, no six, Albertsville police cars were parked haphazardly in front of the house and to the left. Bill Scutch's car was farther aside.

"How did they know?" I gasped.

"Bill musta called 'em for help," he muttered, snatching his keys from the ignition. "Things've got to be bad for him to do that."

He tried to hurry but his age and size slowed him down. Even in my weariness, I hit the porch before he'd clambered out of the car. "Thomas!" I shouted, banging on the door. "Thomas!"

Blair Riddum's massive oak door swung open, and Thomas appeared in the threshold, forehead creased with tension and amazement. "Lord's sake, Jessie! You cain't be here! Jake? What y'all think you're doin'?"

"I'm here to help you, ol' man," Mr. Lewellyn huffed, mounting the porch steps with indignance.

I stumbled over the entryway, fresh tears welling. "I have to tell you something, I just want to tell you something!"

"Okay, okay." Thomas caught me under a trembling elbow and held me up, Bill Scutch hurrying to my other side. Mr. Lewellyn stepped inside, head held high, and looked around as if to summon his army. Blurred faces of uniformed policemen, billy clubs and guns attached to their waist belts, stared at him, then at me. There must have been at least a dozen, prepared for battle. The sight of them infused me with dread. My mouth flopped open, throat constricting. "I . . . I have to talk to you alone."

Thomas half dragged me through the tiled hallway and onto plush blue carpet. "Sit here," he ordered, nudging me into an armchair, then turned aside. "Let us be for a minute."

I gazed up in confusion, wondering whom he was talking to. A flash of movement at the far end of the room caught my attention, and my eyes flew to its source. The man hesitated, frightened, like a deer caught in headlights, eyes boring into mine. He was about fifty-five, average height, blond hair going gray. His cheeks were sunken, shadowed, and his lips thin.

My breath rattled to a stop.

Quickly he turned and was gone.

I faced Thomas, eyes wide. "Was that Blair Riddum?"

He nodded.

I might as well have seen a ghost. It could have been Satan himself for the horror that figure instilled in me. "I *saw* him, Thomas. The night of the fire, hiding in a neighbor's backyard. It's really true; Riddum did it. And now the men know it."

Thomas's face darkened. The fear in his expression terrified me. I never thought he would be afraid of anything. "How do they know?"

The lump in my throat would not be swallowed. "I didn't mean to tell Lee. I *didn't* tell him. But he saw it on my face. He was mad enough already. And then he took Uncle Frank with him!"

"Thomas!" Bill Scutch rounded the corner in a trot, grabbing the doorjamb. Mr. Lewellyn, as best he could, was hot on his heels. "They're comin'."

"Stay here," Thomas pointed at me. He hurried to a double front window and drew aside a thick curtain. I followed close behind, peering over his shoulder. In the moonlight I could just make out a line of cars slowly cruising up the driveway, lights out. It was their slowness that was so frightening. Not rushing anger, quickly spent, but the steady, silent determination of vengeance demanded.

"God help us all," Mr. Lewellyn mumbled.

Thomas let the curtain fall and put urgent hands on my shoulders. "Jessie, forget what you saw that night and listen to me. You're not really sure who you saw anyway, are you. It was dark, right? And you saw someone. But you cain't be sure who. So hear me when I say it wasn't Riddum. He and his wife were at her aunt's house. The old lady's sick, and Esther Riddum's still there now. You understand, Jessie? You hear me?"

I searched his face. Outside, the first car door slammed. His fingers jerked.

"Do you hear?"

My lips were trembling. "I hear."

"Good." He straightened. "Now. What to do with you." I could see the wheels turning in his head. "Bates!" he hollered, and an Albertsville policeman quickly materialized. "Have one a your men take this young lady out the back door; it may not be safe in here for long. Tell him to go way out to the right side a the yard and follow it to the front, where he can watch and see if he's needed. But until he's needed he's to stay with her, out a sight. Understand?"

"Thomas, I don't need—"

"Hush, Jessie," he snapped. "Stay with your policeman and keep away from things; I got enough to worry 'bout. Now go."

"Do as he says," Mr. Lewellyn declared, his pudgy face mottling.

Bates motioned to a young stocky officer with a high forehead under a crew cut and a neck as thick as my thigh. All business, he took my arm firmly, pulling me toward the door. "No time to waste." His face was grim, alert, his eyes snapping from the window to me.

"The rest a y'all," I heard Thomas command, "stay outta sight in here until the last minute, like we talked about. Those men see the whites a your eyes, they're gonna be mad as hornets."

"There's too many of 'em," Bates insisted. "We cain't let you go out there alone."

"I'll go with him," Mr. Lewellyn interjected.

I skidded to a stop, yanking away from my escort. "Thomas, don't go out there by yourself! You can't stop them!"

He threw us an irate glance. "Get her *outta* here!" He swiveled back to Bates, ignoring his old friend. "You don't know these men like I do! I'm telling ya, you go out there right now and I guarantee you'll have a fight on your hands."

"That's right," Jake Lewellyn echoed.

My policeman reached for me again, irritated at being yelled at. "Let's *go.*"

I pivoted away. "No."

"And I'm tellin' you I have a job to do!" Bates shot back at Thomas.

The two men glared at each other.

Firm hands seized both my arms. "We're gettin' out of here *right now.*"

"Thomas!" I cried as he half dragged me toward the door. "Please! You don't know how mad Lee is. And tell them not to hurt Uncle Frank; he's not here to fight!"

But I heard no answer, for I was already outside, skimming along grass under the moonlight, propelled by a man used to being obeyed. Over the house's roof and around its corners I could hear engines rattling off, more car doors slamming, an undercurrent of men's voices. We reached the far back corner of the huge lot and turned right, following the tree-lined white wood fence down the side, keeping our heads down. When we were even with the porch, I saw a sight that made my blood run cold. The men were gathering, Lee at the forefront, many gripping two-by-fours and a few with crudely fashioned torches eager to be alight. Al Bledger carried a can of gasoline, his jaw set and shadowed in the umbra of the porch lamps.

"Lord help us," the policeman breathed. I tried to slow, but he pushed me on toward a large oak tree about fifty feet from the men, one branch pointing off-kilter toward the earth. We sank to our knees behind its massive trunk, panting.

"What's your name?" He slid his billy club from his belt and laid it on the ground.

"Jessie. What's yours?"

"Lester."

The lawn was cool beneath my legs. My tongue felt swollen, thick. I'd had nothing to drink, and my throat begged for water. I shivered, prickles skittering down my arms.

"Are you cold?"

I inhaled deeply, shaking my head. "Just . . . tired. And scared."

In truth I felt I was suffocating. The air was still so hot, humidity clinging to me. The scene before me turned surreal, like a bad dream. There was something so wrong about it all. These were the men to whom I had served cake in Aunt Eva's living room. Whom I sat across from in church. For whose wives I'd mended a dress or let out a waistline at Miss Alice's. I'd greeted these men on the street, stood beside them at the July Fourth parade. And there was my uncle, apart from the milling crowd, praying. And Lee—standing on the first of Riddum's three porch steps, palms low on his hips, back turned defiantly toward the house as if nothing in it could harm him. He was staring, hard-mouthed, at the police cars, calling to his friends down the driveway to "come on!" His shoulders were straight and his legs planted wide apart, his mouth granite. This was not the man I knew. This was not the one who'd kissed me so tenderly, who'd begged me to stay in Bradleyville and marry him. The man who'd wondered about giving his life to Christ.

I shivered again, amazed at the irrationality of anger.

chapter 46

The men were almost assembled, hitting expectant palms with two-by-fours, prowling, voices a low rumble. Their fury pulsed across the lawn, a bomb about to explode. Suddenly, as if on cue, their voices rose.

"Come on out, Riddum!"

"Think you can hide behind police?"

"Come out before we burn you out!" Al Bledger yelled, raising his can of gasoline.

I huddled behind the tree, sinking fingernails into my knees. Lester was coiled to spring, mumbling, "Keep calm, keep steady...." Over the chaos hovered an unspoken yet tangible sense of order. Lee was clearly the leader, his personal losses catapulting him into command. Everyone else's grievances together could not match his.

He turned away from the men and toward the front door. "Riddum!" he brayed hoarsely over the din. "Got some men here need to talk to you!"

Uncle Frank's hands were now tightly clasped, knuckles pressed against his mouth, his head bent.

Harsh laughter rose from the crowd and the roar swelled. When the front door opened, Lee tensed, fingers splaying. Movement behind him slowed in surprise, as if no one had expected it to be so easy. When Thomas and Jake Lewellyn eased onto the porch and latched the door behind them, the two-by-fours froze, the din fell away. For a moment, no one moved, the unexpected face-off sparking the air. Lee backed off his step onto the sidewalk. The two old men stood firmly, straight-backed. Thomas held a paper bag in one hand.

Black dots danced before my eyes. I could barely breathe.

Lee gathered himself. "Thomas, Jake, you two git off the porch afore you git hurt. This ain't about you."

"It's about me, all right," Thomas declared loudly. "It's about the mill my daddy built. And y'all are part a the town he founded. He ain't around to blame. So here I am."

"And I'm as old as he is!" Jake Lewellyn shouted breathlessly. "Been part a this town since the day it was founded. You ain't movin' me either."

Low guffaws rolled through the men, their clubs again in movement.

"This ain't about respectin' you or the town!" Lee retorted, stepping back on the stair. "I'll pick you up one at a time and move you myself. As for your backup help hidin' in there, we're a lot more than they are. Bill Scutch!" he threw back his head, shouting toward the top window of the house. "You in there with the rest of 'em, you better come on out!"

"You gonna have his blood on your hands too, Lee?" Thomas challenged.

"I ain't gonna have no innocent blood on my hands!" Lee punched the air with his fist. "We're here for *one* man and one only. The man who almost killed my *family!*"

"Blair Riddum didn't set your house on fire!"

The reaction was immediate, men shouting their disgust, weapons rising. From across the lawn I could see Jake Lewellyn's legs begin to tremble. He lowered his head to cough. Thomas raised the bag in his hand, yelling vainly until his voice broke through the noise. "I'm tellin' you the truth, Lee!"

"He was seen, Thomas!" Lee cried.

"Why're you protectin' him?" Al Bledger raged. Others echoed his disdain.

"Will you *hear* me? Will you at least hear me!"

Lester, half-crouched, took his gun out of its holder.

"What are you *doing?*" I uttered, astounded. "Nobody out there's got a gun."

He snorted softly. "You see all those men? You know how many there are of us? You should be worryin' about *me.*"

"You can't pull a gun on men who don't have any. Is that what they teach you?"

"This ain't the classroom, Jessie; this is real life. We're over-powered."

My throat tightened. "Please don't shoot it."

"We'll give 'em a chance. They put down their weapons, nobody'll get hurt."

"But you don't understand; he won't stop. The one on the step." Tears filled my eyes.

"How do you know?"

He leaned toward me, searching my expression. I thought of Miss Wilma, exhausted and destitute. Connie and her fatherless baby. My mouth went to mush, a hand flying to cover it. "He has good reason. What if *your* family was almost killed?"

Lester's jaw hardened. He turned back toward the men. "You cain't take the law in your own hands."

"What's your proof, Thomas!" Lee challenged. "We know the screen was cut! We know he lit the curtains."

I looked from Lester's gun to Lee, then gasped as Uncle Frank broke through the mob to join him. Aunt Eva had been right; no way he could stay out of it. "That's my uncle!" I choked. "He's not here to fight; he wants to calm the men down. You *can't* hurt him."

"Quiet, all a ya!" Uncle Frank commanded, waving his arms. "We're gonna listen. Give Thomas one minute."

244   cast *a* road before me

"You ain't our manager out here," one of Al Bledger's cronies threw out.

Lee stretched his fingertips wide above his head, as if blessing his friends. Their rancor quieted to a sizzle.

Thomas jumped in, voice rising in the thick night air. "Blair Riddum wasn't around the night of the fire! He and his wife were visiting her sick aunt in the next county—"

"You gonna believe that?" Zach Bulder called.

"Esther's still with her aunt. As for the fire, if you wanna blame someone for it, blame Martha Plott."

"Martha *Plott!*" Caustic echoes surged through the night. Al Bledger, disgust dripping from his shoulders, edged toward the back of the crowd, gesturing to friends.

"That's right, sweet ol' Martha Plott!" Jake Lewellyn bellowed. "Y'all wanna burn *her* house down?"

Thomas threw a shushing hand at Mr. Lewellyn and raised the paper bag above his head. "Lee! You saw us pull this piece a cut glass from the ruins a your house." He opened the bag and withdrew a large, jagged fragment, held it high between two fingers. "You told me it was from a lamp Martha gave your sister the day a the fire. It was right by the window, remember, by the curtains. Bill and I and the fire inspectors have been lookin' at that piece a screen all evenin'. It wasn't sliced clean, with a knife. The lamp caught the curtains on fire first, the glass exploded, and then a piece cut through the screen! Here." He pulled a foot-long piece of half-melted screen from the bag. "See for yourself!"

"We don't believe none of it!" someone at the edge cried, hoarse with hatred. In one fluid motion he twisted, drawing back a two-by-four like a bat. "*None!*" With two-fisted strength, he smashed the wood into a police car window.

The heavy crunch of glass reverberated through the limbs of those men, shattering any semblance of logic. They went wild then, and after that, everything happened very quickly. Their yells drowned out Thomas's pleadings. Other sticks lifted heavenward, and their rage turned on the six Albertsville police cars, quickly surrounding them to smash windows and bash in doors. Bill Scutch's car sat apart, for the moment unharmed. Uncle Frank trotted a few steps from Lee and raised his hands over his head, loudly praying. "Lord Jesus, send your calming Spirit!" his voice rose over the din. "In the name of Jesus, still the hands of these men!" Lee seemed caught between the two camps, hurling a wooden beam one moment, then jumping onto the porch to peer at the screen and glass. Even in his fury, I knew he wanted to believe. In a gesture that pierced my heart, he dug fingers into his skull as if to burst the blister of his confusion.

Something broke inside me. Anger dredged itself up my stomach, bile-ridden and acidic. It was no longer anger at Lee but at the insanity his misapplied zeal had wrought. I knew in that instant deep in my gut that someone would be hurt, and that person would be a part of Bradleyville, a part of my heart. Even more frightening, a part of me suddenly understood the men's foolish violence. For anger as deep as theirs, as rising as mine, demanded a target, and finding none, would create it.

"Stay here," Lester commanded, springing to his feet as his colleagues began to spill through the Riddums' front door, washing Thomas and Mr. Lewellyn aside. Lee cast out his arms, calling for them to stop.

"No!" Without thinking I leapt up, catching the policeman by his shirt and pulling him backward. He uttered a surprised curse, shoving me away. "You can't shoot them," I begged, "they don't have guns!"

"Stay *back*," he whispered vehemently, punching a finger at my face, "or I swear I'll handcuff you to that tree."

I grabbed for him again but he sprinted away, angling his gun upward and over the white picket fence, firing harmlessly into the night. Shots rang out in quick succession as other policemen aimed into the air, surrounding the melee with a wide berth, their legs spread apart, both hands on their guns. The roar of raging men checked itself, melting into astonishment. Flexed arms stilled, battered cars ceased to rock. The gun barrels lowered to point at the crowd.

"Put the two-by-fours down!" Bates ordered. "Put 'em down now!"

Jake Lewellyn leaned into a porch pillar, breathing heavily. Uncle Frank mouthed something to him and was waved away with a fluttering hand. Thomas seized Lee's wrist and shook it as he spit out words, then abruptly turned and disappeared inside the house.

Two-by-fours slowly dropped to the ground from stiff, reluctant fingers. The rage-filled heaving of all those chests seemed to suck oxygen from my own lungs. Black dots riddled my vision again, and I shook my head, blinking. The night turned oddly quiet, blood whooshing through my ears.

Officer Bates pointed his gun at the last hold-outs. "Put . . . them . . . *down*. Torches too. And you with the gasoline. Now, back up."

"Wait!" Thomas stepped back onto the porch, hands up, palms out. "Bates! Put your guns away; let me talk to 'em!"

The policemen were stone. "You want to talk, talk!" Bates allowed curtly, eyes fastened on Al Bledger. "But the guns stay where they are."

Thomas dropped his jaw, raked in air. "Gimme a chance." His fingers trembled as if cradling explosives. "This all stops right here! Riddum *did not* set the fire. Y'all need to *think*. For God's sake, look around ya, look at what's about to happen! You who sit in church every Sunday, are y'all a bunch a *murderers?* Listen to me; I got word to you from Riddum. Word that's gonna lay this whole thing to rest, once and for all. He's not gonna work at the mill anymore. He may own it, but he'll stay away. Frank's gonna run things from now on." He looked purposefully at Lee then, as if to size him up, and they locked eyes. "And Lee's gonna be assistant manager. Also, startin' Monday, everyone's got a 5 percent raise!"

When you're barreling down a godforsaken road, mind set and teeth gritted, no amount of welcome news can immediately turn you aside, even if it's the very news you've pursued. Velocity and adrenaline demand their own time. Seconds ticked as Thomas's words tumbled over sweat-prickled heads and hulking shoulders. Uncle Frank and Lee seemed as taken aback as any.

In that moment, Thomas evidently thought he had them. Thought that, down to the last man, clear thinking would surface now that every wrong was righted, every demand met. But then, he was used to the army, all soldiers following one commander.

"Where is he?" someone called. "We wanna hear it from Riddum hisself!"

The rest took up the cry, and the policemen's fingers tightened over their guns. "All right!" Thomas retorted. "He'll come out here. Then we're all goin' home."

Carefully, slowly, as if treading through egg shells, he backed up and pushed open the heavy oak door, eyes on the crowd. A shaking, cowed Blair Riddum materialized on the threshold, escorted by Bill Scutch, grim-faced and wary. They eased onto the porch, Bill's hand on his upper arm, as if protecting a hated prisoner from lynching. Riddum swallowed, and in the wash of lamplight, I could see his Adam's apple bob. The sight of him, scared as a rabbit, coated me—and most assuredly every man in that crowd—with gloating vengeance.

His jaw creaked open. "It's true!" he wavered. "Startin' Monday."

Thomas kept a hand on his other elbow. "Bates!" he shouted, "Riddum's gonna pay for your cars. No arrests needed here tonight."

The offer caught Bates off-guard. I wasn't sure Blair Riddum expected it either. Fleetingly, I imagined the policeman's dilemma of unpurchasable justice weighed against an overpowering swell of angry men, the inevitable explanations demanded for firing upon unarmed rioters. His eyes turned indecisively to Thomas.

Do it! I wanted to scream, *before someone gets hurt!* Fresh rage pulsated my heart into overtime. How *dare* some officer—who knew nothing of Bradleyville's summer-long plight—demand retribution from these men. I pushed to my feet, swaying, mentally shaking an answer out of the man.

Uncle Frank caught Lee's eye, silently begging for agreement. Lee visibly steadied himself, pushing down his anger. Curtly, he nodded to my uncle. Together, they turned to Riddum. Approached him in three purposeful strides. Gaze drifting heavenward in gratitude, Uncle Frank reached an arm out to him. Riddum hesitated, then clasped his hand, giving it one hard shake. My uncle stepped back. Lee moved in, glaring down at his nemesis, eyes narrowing. His huge muscled arm rose slowly and hung in the air. For a moment I thought Blair Riddum would not take it. Then, flexing his jaw, he placed his fingers in Lee's. Lee grabbed them tightly, almost jerking Riddum forward, and squeezed. Riddum refused to wince. "You change your mind," Lee said, gravel in his throat, "the next time there'll be no warnin'." Riddum made no response. As if tainted, Lee dropped his hand and turned away. He and Uncle Frank walked back to the side of the steps.

"Y'all go home to your families!" he declared to the crowd. I knew he was thinking of his own mother and sister. "We got what we came for."

Nobody moved. Jake Lewellyn coughed loudly.

"Go on!" Bates yelled. "It's over."

Without warning, Riddum yanked free of Thomas and Bill. "It ain't all over!" he bellowed. "No matter *what* he says, I ain't payin' for none a that car damage!"

Thomas grabbed his shoulder and hauled him back.

What happened next is branded into my brain but in vague outline, as if seared by unsteady hands. I remember Al Bledger at the edge of the crowd, snatching up a two-by-four, brandishing it high over his head. Howling something inane—"Then pay for *this!*" Officer Bates turning back to him as if in slow motion, gun aiming, mouth dropping in a warning. Al Bledger's arm cocking back, launching the piece of wood like a missile toward Riddum. Thomas tussling furiously with Riddum, Bill pulling them apart. Jake Lewellyn gawking at the wood whistling through the air, turning to see Thomas step into its path. "Sstoppp!" roaring from Mr. Lewellyn's mouth as he pushed away from the pillar, raising pudgy arms.

Someone screaming "No!" and the sound shrieking from my mouth. My feet were running, arms flailing me toward Al Bledger, blazing anger and exhaustion sucking the air around me dry, fueling my wobbly legs. Bates swiveling my direction, distracted, other heads turning, surprised, Lee's eyes widening in amazement. My tear-filled gaze following the projectile as I ran, knowing I was too late, but unwilling, unable to stop the venting of my wrath.

Jake Lewellyn yelling at Thomas to *"Mmovve!"*

Time suspended itself as I floated across the shadowed grass, mind conjuring the consequences of Al Bledger's impulsive act. I pictured Thomas hit, guns shooting in mindless reaction, Lee falling, Uncle Frank falling. The final second ground into fast gear as Jake Lewellyn heaved himself into the path of the wood and it struck the side of his head, deflecting onto the front wall of the house and splintering with a gut-wrenching *crack!* The old man dropped like a stone.

"No!" I screamed again, aiming straight for Al Bledger, spinning into him with an unexpected force that knocked him aside, teeth rattling. In the aftermath of the man's *stupidity*, amid the unthinkable price of an innocent bystander and the terror of the moment, I churned into a whirling dervish of fury. Had I a knife, I would have used it. A gun, I would have fired it. As it was, I lit into him bare-handed, pummeling with fists and kicking with abandonment. The world went red, then unadulterated white as I fought, careening with such mania that he could not clasp hold. I screeched at him in a voice that wasn't mine. I hit him for hurting poor old Jake Lewellyn, who never meant anyone harm. I hit him for his ugly temper, which had heightened the tumultuousness of Bradleyville's summer. I hit him for all the danger that Lee had faced, and my uncle and Thomas. Then I went on hitting him. For my rib-heaving run through darkened streets. For the heartwrenching beauty of an angel lamp now diminished to ashes. For Miss Wilma's lined face and Connie's

torturous labor. I hit him for keeping me in Bradleyville these extra days, for the selfishness that had risen within me, for the kisses from Lee I would never have again. And for my lost teenage years and my drowning grief. For my poor mother's red, slapped cheek. And most of all, hardest of all, I hit him for the despair that sent her driving away from me that day. The day she died and left me so *alone*.

And when I could hit no more and shouts surrounded me and hands reached to pull me away, I staggered, sobbing, swinging half-heartedly, futilely, until nausea darkened the world. As I collapsed, familiar strong arms slid around me, gentling me to the ground. Far, far away, Lee's voice soothed me into blackness.

chapter 47

H*ey there, neighbor, what ya doin' up so early?"*
The sun had yet to peek over the distant hills, the blue-gray morning alive with bird chatter. The young man grinned, draping himself over their shared fence. "Jus' wanted to see the new day dawn, I guess."

He grunted. "Yep. Gonna be a clear day. And hot."

The mill worker ran his thumbnail along a grain in the wooden fence. "You get some rest?"

"Yeah, finally. You?"

"Well, I wasn't there, you know."

The older man scratched an itchy place on his back. "You oughta be thankin' God for that."

"I am." He gazed over the yard, out past an open field. The hills beyond were blue-purple. "Let me ask ya somethin'." His words were tentative. "You been around a long time—"

"Thanks a lot."

"No. What I mean is . . . I jus' been wonderin', ya know. Do you think everything Thomas said was true? About how the fire got started?"

He puckered his chin, considered a rosebush climbing his side of the fence.

"I mean, Thomas is a great man. You don't think he'd lie, do ya?"

He suppressed a smile. The old man would lie like a sleeping dog if he had to, he thought. "Well. Tell you somethin'. Some things in life are just as well left alone. Main thing is we got what we wanted. Plus, after all that happened, we all got to go home to our own beds."

"But settin' that fire'd be an awful big thing to git away with."

"Riddum didn't 'git away' with nothin'. He lost. We won. That's the last thing he'd want. Anyway, stop worryin' 'bout it. Thomas said he didn't set the fire; that's good enough for me."

"I s'pose."

"Well, I'm gonna go back inside. Surprise Patsy and make her breakfast before church. She ain't been real happy with me lately." He stopped on the patio, turned back. "You heared church is at the school gymnasium, didn't ya? Baptists and Methodists all together."

"Uh-huh. I'm goin'."

"Us too. Almost decided not to. Don't think I rightly deserve to face God after everything. But Patsy's put her foot down, says it's 'bout time I got my soul straight."

The young man wasn't sure how to respond.

"Hey, anyway, I'm goin' fishin' this afternoon down to the river. Wanna come?"

"Thanks, no. Mama and my sister are gonna visit Connie and her baby at the hospital. Thought I'd . . . go along with 'em."

"Oh. Kind of a woman thing, ain't it?"

"Well. She's a nice person, ya know, real sweet. Pretty too. And with everything that's happened to her and all. . . ." He shrugged self-consciously.

"Uh-huh." The older man's chin lifted knowingly. "You have a good time then. A real good time. And tell her hello for me."

He stepped inside his kitchen, closing the door softly. His eyes drifted to the yellow clock on the wall, shaped like the sun. Plenty of time before church to do it all up right. Quietly, he pulled out a heavy skillet. Went to the refrigerator for eggs and bacon. The cabinet for a mixing bowl. What do ya know, he thought, reaching into a drawer for a fork. That young kid next door, interested in Connie. Awkwardly, he broke the first egg into the bowl. And her with a brand-new baby. He broke the second egg, then fished in the yellow-white goo for bits of shell.

Interesting bit of news for Patsy.

chapter 48

I woke to birds chirping out my window, high clouds sailing a muggy sky. I stared sightlessly at the ceiling, trying to get my bearings, my body sluggish and sore. Morning meant I had only been in bed a few hours, yet my brain pulsed thickly with a perceived passage of time. My throat was parched, my stomach rumbling, and my bladder achingly full.

Scenes began spinning through my head as I padded to the bathroom. By the time I'd reached the kitchen and slumped over a steaming mug of tea, I felt sick to my stomach. In fuzzy replay I remembered awakening from a dead faint as from a nightmare, mindlessly pushing away Lee's comforting arms, stumbling with Uncle Frank to his car, shivering during the hot drive home. Jake Lewellyn had been on the ground, head streaming blood but conscious, someone's sweaty shirt pressed to his head, the police-man called Bates insisting there was no time for an ambulance; he'd take the old man to the hospital.

Mostly, I remembered the shame. And felt it now afresh, blown in on the morning breeze, heralded by birdsong. How *could* I, after all my mother had taught me? After judging the men for their own violence. What's more, as if trammeling everything I stood for into the earth hadn't been enough, I'd done it in front of all those people. Shrieking and crying, attacking a man I barely knew. Mind gone, all reason fled, no modesty, no self-restraint. The day had just begun and surely the whole town already knew. I was *mortified*. I could not bear to face anyone.

I breathed deeply, trying to steady myself. Sipped tea and burned my lips. Set down the mug too quickly and sloshed hot liquid onto the table. Reached for a napkin to clean it up and burned my wrist from steam. Shuffling to a cabinet for two aspirin, I swallowed them dry and sank back into my chair, elbows on the table, head in my hands. The sound of footsteps made me groan inwardly.

"Well. Thought I heard you."

I glanced sideways at Uncle Frank's feet in brown slippers.

"You sure slept a long time." His voice was weighted with concern. "I told your aunt maybe she should have stuck to one sleeping pill, but she said you needed a good long rest."

"It's only 7:00." My first words were rusty.

"Sunday morning."

It took a minute for the fact to sink in. I raised my head. "Sunday? I slept all Saturday?"

"Yup." He measured instant coffee into a mug, poured hot water from the tea kettle over it. I watched stupidly. Pulling out a chair, he sat across from me, slowly stirring.

Sunday. It was Sunday. My eyes blinked. "Mr. Lewellyn."

"He's okay. Coming home today."

Relief washed through me. "What happened?"

"There's a gash on the side of his head. He was lucky to be only grazed; that thing had hit him smack, he'd be dead. He had some stitches and a mild concussion, so they wanted to watch him for a while. I talked to him last night and he was already hankerin' to come home."

I managed the weakest of smiles. "Can't keep a good man down."

"Nope." He sipped his coffee. "Tell you one thing. It may not have been your intent, but you probably saved Bledger's life. If you hadn't gotten in the way, I think that policeman woulda shot him."

I made a point of trying my tea again. It was now drinkable. "How's Miss Wilma?" I asked finally. "And Connie and little Katherine May?" I could not bring myself to ask about Lee.

"All fine. Your aunt and a few other ladies from church went over to Elsa Brock's yesterday and sorted through all the baby stuff on loan. The room's all set up for Connie; even got diapers ready, Eva says. Connie's bringin' the baby home tomorrow mornin'."

"Thank you, Lord," I mumbled, vastly grateful that this duty had been lifted from me.

Uncle Frank cleared his throat briefly and drank some more coffee. "You comin' to church with us?"

Church. How could everyone just go back to church, as if nothing had happened? All the men I'd seen Friday night in a murderous rage, today piously singing hymns? The thought made me sick. Besides, I could not imagine walking into that sanctuary, all eyes turning my direction, assessing, feeding whispers. No, I could not bear to see anyone. I did not want to face Miss Wilma, who, unlike me, had managed to keep her dignity throughout her losses. And my heart lurched at the thought of seeing Lee. I could no longer trust myself near him. I'd lost control once; who's to say I wouldn't again, in a much different way? Who's to say I wouldn't fall into his arms like a shivering idiot, wanting only to block out the world with his embrace?

"I'm too tired."

He grunted, seeing through me. "It's at the school gymnasium today, everybody all together. It's a special day, Jessie, and you should be there. The Lord protected our town through the worst. And we all need to thank him for that."

"I'll think about it," was my terse reply.

We nursed our mugs in silence, eyes cruising the kitchen.

"I got your car back for you," he changed the subject.

"You *did?*"

"Yeah. Ed called yesterday afternoon. I walked over and got it."

"Oh, bless you! Thank you!" My thoughts picked up speed. "You paid for it? I'll pay you back."

"Sure," he shrugged.

Absently, I tapped my mug with a finger, surveying sudden possibilities. "Uncle Frank," I said, straightening, "I think I'll leave today. All I need to do is pack a few things in my car. I could be going by the time you leave for church."

"Oh." His gaze was a mixture of surprise and hurt. "But the moving truck's not comin' till Tuesday."

"I'll sleep on the floor till then; it doesn't matter. I'll take my bedding, some clothes. You think Aunt Eva can get Martha Plott or somebody to come over Tuesday to let the movers in?"

"I guess so." He studied me. "You sure this is what you want?"

"I'm sure."

"Ain't you even gonna say good-bye to anybody?"

My eyes wouldn't rise from the table. "I . . . can't. Really. I just need to go."

"Connie's been askin' for you."

"Maybe I'll stop and see her on my way through Albertsville."

Carefully, he pushed aside his coffee. "Gonna be mighty lonely without you. I know you been away to college and all that, but your things were still here; we knew you'd be back for holidays."

"I'll still come back for holidays."

"Sure. It'll be different, though. It finally will be just the two of us."

"Uncle Frank," I said, reaching for his hand, "I'm not doing this to leave you two, you know that. I'm doing this to . . . begin my life."

"I know. I know you believe that. But in truth, Jessie, I think you're leavin' your life behind. Because you're about to set yourself on a course that purposely leaves Christ outta the picture."

My hand slid away. "I've been on this same course for years now, Uncle Frank; you know how long I've had these plans."

"Yes, I know. And for all those years, I've prayed that God would show you the truth. I think now he has shown you, just like he's shown this town. The message is there in front of us all, if we're just willing to see it."

"And what would *that* be?" I couldn't keep the sarcasm from my voice.

He looked at me sadly. "Come to church with us, Jessie. Just do that much. People are asking about you. They want to make sure you're all right. Then go this afternoon, if you must."

"I'll *bet* they want to see me," I retorted bitterly. "'Look at the freak, ladies and gentlemen! The woman whose rage puts our men's to shame!'"

"Oh, Jessie." His eyes closed briefly. "You think anybody who was there is looking at *you*, judging *you?* You slept all day yesterday; you don't understand the guilt this whole town's feelin'. That's why the two pastors have pulled services together for today. Lots a folks have some serious thinkin' to do, and I don't mean just the men who were there Friday night. A lot a their wives supported their fightin', and others just gossiped and made things worse instead of turning to the Lord. Your aunt's even feelin' convicted because of her lack of faith that night. So don't let shame keep you away. That's one a Satan's best tools. Come with us."

Why did his words so cut to my heart? Probably because my uncle rarely asked me for anything, I told myself, and here I was, about to say no. "Well, I don't know. I have to pack."

He checked his watch. "You got two hours before the service. That's plenty a time. Go with us, come back and have some lunch, and then we'll see you off."

I studied my cooling tea. "I just can't, Uncle Frank. I'm really sorry. But I don't want to see *anyone.*"

"Forget about seeing anyone else, Jessie. You'd be goin' to see God. It don't matter what other people think. But I'll tell you anyway, they think nothin' but the best a you. They're amazed at your courage and that you ran all the way out there to try and stop what was happening."

My head jerked up. "Is *that* why they think I ran out there?"

He nodded.

For the first time that morning, I stopped to consider the details: Thomas, the piece of cut screen, the glass lamp. Blair Riddum's face. The face I saw the night of the fire. Thomas, his hands urgent on my shoulders—*Jessie, forget what you saw and listen to me.* My self-conscious worries vanished as understanding hit me in the chest, like a block of machinery jolting into place.

"Do the men still—" I stopped abruptly, choosing my words carefully. "Does everybody believe what Thomas told them? About how the fire started?"

Uncle Frank's eyes held mine. "Yes."

"Lee? Even Al Bledger? They still. . . ." The question died away.

"I'll tell you, Jessie." He lowered his voice. "And you understand this conversation is just between you and me. There'll never be another soul you can talk to about this except Thomas. That includes your aunt, who now believes that whatever you thought you saw at the fire was merely a mistake. Understand?"

"Okay." My muscles would not relax.

Uncle Frank leaned his forearms on the table. "All I can say is, in the heat of that outrage, God intervened. The men stopped long enough to hear Thomas's explanation, *and they chose to believe it.* Now, with a raise and new management promised, there's no reason not to continue believing it."

"That's right." My countenance brightened momentarily as I remembered. "I'm looking at the new manager."

"You are."

Just as quickly, the expression waned. Frowning, I thought again of Thomas, considered his cunning. "But he lied."

Uncle Frank inclined his head.

"Well, what does that mean? God *wanted* him to lie? Doesn't sound to me like God intervened at all. Thomas Bradley did."

"No, Jessie. What Thomas chose to do, I'll leave between him and God. But I do know this. God can use anything for his purpose, even a lie. And that's what he did two nights ago. I knew without a doubt when Lee was at our door that I was to go with him and cover the gatherin' a those men in prayer. By the time we got to Riddum's, I cain't tell ya how scared I was. Bein' in the midst a that rage, I could *feel* the spirit of destruction all around me. But I kept prayin' aloud in Jesus' name. And I had a sense that I was not alone. That around town, others were prayin' too."

How *awful* for Uncle Frank. I could only imagine how frightening it must have been to pray in the middle of all that rage. I'd been scared enough, guarded by a policeman and watching from a safe distance. Yet my uncle had displayed such serenity, while I'd fallen apart. Inexplicably, then, the words of Pastor Frasier from years ago sprang into my head. *When the fryin' pan meets the flame, these things alone won't sustain you. . . .*

I toyed with the handle of my cup. The tea was now too cold to drink. "Well, that's . . . good. Very good. I'm glad everything worked out."

Uncle Frank sensed my distancing from the conversation and leaned back in his chair, a sigh escaping him. "Are you going to come to church?" He was almost pleading. A pang shot through me, seeing his concern.

"I'll think about it, okay? There's still plenty of time. I'll go pack my things now."

"Okay." With a sad little smile, he pushed back his chair. "Your aunt should be gettin' up soon. She'll want to box up some dishes and pans she's decided to give you." He slid his chair back under the table with utmost care and turned away. I watched the sag of his shoulders as he scuffed out of the kitchen on slippered feet.

By 10:40 I was ready to go. My bedding, some clothes, and toiletries were in my car. I'd phoned the apartment manager and told him to expect me by late afternoon. The man must have thought me crazy, with all my changes of plans.

All languor long gone, I was intent upon leaving quickly, as if my life depended on it. And in a way, it did. So much awaited me—the fruition of my plans. And that barest whisper of doubt that had lingered after my conversation with Uncle Frank was unsettling. Church was at 11:00; my aunt and uncle would be leaving in five minutes. I'd told them I wouldn't be going with them. Uncle Frank had reacted quietly—"I'm just gonna keep on prayin' that your wheels'll lead ya there." Aunt Eva had dissolved into tears. She was now in the kitchen, packing a few last items and sniffing. "Lord help me, what a summer," she muttered. "People carryin' on and people leavin'. Can't even go to church." She banged a skillet into the box none too carefully. Any moment she could burst into fresh sobs.

Given my aunt's mood, I decided it would be better to let them drive away instead of me. At quarter till 11:00, I walked them out to the driveway, Aunt Eva theatrically clutching a tissue.

"Take care a yourself, now, you hear?" Uncle Frank hugged me hard. "Call us when you get in tonight. And, Jessie," he pulled away, holding me by the shoulders, "I know you're gonna be mighty busy with all your work and volunteerin'. But when ya get some time, pull out that Bible I gave you and read some more. We can discuss it at Thanksgivin'. Okay?"

My throat tightening, I nodded. All of a sudden, Thanksgiving seemed a very long time away. "I will. I promise."

Aunt Eva clung to me, tissue at her nose. Then they climbed into the Buick and started the slow backing out of the driveway, my aunt waving fiercely. Just before they hit the street, Uncle Frank leaned out his window. "Church starts in fifteen minutes!"

That brought a tiny smile to my face. They'd never give up.

I watched them drive down the street, Aunt Eva turned in her seat, still waving. Not until their car disappeared from sight did I heave a sigh of relief. I'd had enough good-byes.

I returned to the bedroom to fetch my keys and purse. The house was so quiet. I stood in the room that had been mine for eight years, gazing around the blank walls, trying to picture what it would look like after my furniture was gone. I wondered what they'd do to fill it. It occurred to me that Aunt Eva would have to find at least a single bed for me to use when I visited. "See you in two days," I whispered, running a finger across the headboard of my mother's old bed. "In our new home."

Home.

I was really doing it. I was really going back to Cincinnati today. Images of Hope Center spilled into my mind, and I felt a deep thrust of pain for my mother. I wondered if I'd somehow feel closer to her there—seeing Brenda Todd, the gymnasium in which the funeral was held, the kitchen in which I'd so often cooked at her side. Unexpected tears sprang to my eyes, and I sank down on the bed. *Whew.* My emotions were certainly close to the surface. I sat for a few moments with eyes closed, imagining for the thousandth time my apartment, painted and full. My desk and work files across it, meeting with families, helping them through crises. Reading to children at the Center. A quiet excitement fell over my shoulders as the pictures paraded before me. The promise of Cincinnati pulled at me while Bradleyville and all its problems began to fade.

I rose from the bed, smiling to myself, keys in hand. It was time to go.

As I reached for my purse, the doorbell rang. My hand stopped, midair. *Oh, good grief,* I thought, *now what?*

"Jessie?" Lee's voice filtered through the screen door. "I know you're still there."

I sucked in air. Slowly, I dropped my car keys on the bed. Steeling myself, I walked down the hall, rounded the corner, and saw him stepping inside the house, dressed for church in gray suit and tie, his coat off in the heat. I stopped and picked my heart up off the floor, lifting my hands in a question.

"Your aunt called."

Of course she had.

He tried to smile. "You look so good."

I glanced down my body. Jean shorts and a T-shirt. My eyes closed in remorse. "I'm sorry. I should have called you myself."

He closed the distance between us, tipping my chin up with warm fingers. "Jessie, don't do this. You don't have to do this."

I couldn't take many more of these conversations. "Yes, I do."

"What do you want? Me on my knees? I promised myself I wouldn't beg, but I know I'm runnin' outta time. So here goes. Stay here, Jessie. You love this town; this town loves you. Your family's here. Most of all, I'm here."

"My apartment is in Cincinnati, and my job, and the Center." My voice caught. "It's where I'm supposed to be; it's *my* plan for *my* life, remember?"

"Yes, I do. But that's the problem. It's *your* plan."

I shook my head, uncomprehending.

"Jessie, listen to me," he pleaded. "Give me five minutes. So much has happened since Friday night; so much has changed." Absently, he brushed a strand of hair off my cheek. "Saturday, I was holdin' Connie's little girl at the hospital, and Mama was there. And then everything really hit me. I coulda been in jail, never gettin' to hold that baby. Here was *life*, innocent new life in my hands, the same hands that were ready to *kill* a man the night before. Somethin' came over me, and I thought I was gonna crumble apart, right in that hospital room. Soon as we got to Mama's room at Miss Elsa's, I fell to my knees. Everything just flooded out of me, all the pain, the anger, all the *fear* a what I'd almost become. And what I could become again. Mama led me in a prayer, and I finally did what I'd been thinkin' 'bout for a long time. I turned my life over to Christ. Jessie, you can't imagine the peace that gave me. I feel ... different. I *am* different."

Somehow, he was. There was a gentleness about him, a calm that I'd never sensed before. "That's ... good, Lee. I'm happy for you. Really, I am." I swallowed. "But it doesn't change anything for *me*. You have your life here, and maybe now it'll be a little more peaceful. But my life is ... somewhere else."

"No, Jessie, it's not. I don't believe that because I know you're sayin' no to Christ. Instead, you're barrelin' down a road that some ... *dream* put you on."

My muscles tensed. "It was not just 'some dream.'" Pushing his arms from me, I backed away. "And I'm really tired of people trying to tell me what to do. So just stop it. You and everyone else. The whole thing's ridiculous! I've graduated from college. I'm going off to a job. It happens all the time, Lee. People grow up and move away. *Why* is this so hard for you to understand? Why are you so *stubborn?*"

He almost laughed. "*Me*, stubborn? You're one of the most stubborn people I ever met! You think your Aunt Eva sets herself in one narrow mind, or my mama, or Al Bledger, or even Blair Riddum. *Look* at yourself! Oh, sure, you're much quieter 'bout it. But you're like a bulldog, the way you won't let go." He spread his hands. "Has nothin' that's happened sunk into your head, Jessie? Cain't you see the real *you*, after you lit into Al Bledger like you did?"

My cheeks reddened. "I don't know what you're talking about. That was hardly 'the real me,' and you know it. As if you have room to point fingers. If you have nothing more intelligent than that to say, Lee Harding, I think it's time you went on to church and let me be."

He flinched as I flung the barbed words at him. I expected his brow to darken, his anger to rise, but neither happened. For a moment we faced off in silence, breathing deeply in the hot August air. Then his expression crumbled to sadness. He reached out a finger and grazed my cheek. "I didn't mean that the way it sounded, Jessie. I only wondered if maybe you saw things in yourself—old hurts and weaknesses—that you didn't realize were there. Because I sure saw those things in myself."

I couldn't reply.

"Jessie, please. I love you. I want you to stay. And I just . . . want you to find what I've found."

His tenderness broke through my anger. A lump began to form in my throat. "I love you too."

"Then why do you have to go?"

"I *told* you why. I've been planning this for years; you know that. Planning to get back to my home."

"This is your home."

Tears filled my eyes. "No, it *isn't*. It is *not*. Just because everybody *wants* it to be doesn't make it so. Why does everybody think *they* know what's best for me, what I should do with my life?"

"Forgive me," Lee said, dripping hurt, "for thinking what's best for you is to be with the person who loves you. Who wants to take care a you. Who's willing, before God, to pledge you his *life*."

The tears flowed then. He wrapped his arms around me, his chin on my head. I couldn't speak. I was crying for him, crying to my guardian angel mother, begging for her to *help* me. Ten minutes ago I'd been happy to leave; now again I was in misery. Why did it have to be so hard? If I was doing the right thing, where was the strength from her to help me through it? Where was the strength from God? All of heaven must surely have turned its back on me. Yet, even in Lee's arms, I told myself it could not be so, that my hurt over him would pass once again as soon as I was on the road, headed toward my new life. God was simply testing me, that was all. He wanted to make sure I'd follow through, no matter what. I imagined my mother on the sidelines, praying for me to understand this, her wings shimmering as she awaited my response.

"I have to go now," I said softly, pulling away. "And you do too. Church will be starting."

"Come with me. Then you can leave."

Irritation twinged up my spine. Why on *earth* was this church service so all-fired important? Seemed to me it was just one final ruse to get me to stay, as if hearing one more sermon would change my life. A part of me almost wanted to go with Lee and then drive defiantly out of Bradleyville as planned, just to shows folks I knew my own mind.

"No, Lee, I can't." My voice was firm. "I have a six-hour drive ahead of me, and I need to get going."

Deep disappointment closed his eyes. Finally, he nodded, accepting it, but with an iron weight on his shoulders. When he gathered the momentum to leave, it was with a parting shot over his shoulder. "I won't give up on you. You'll have to deal with me all over again at Thanksgiving."

Plans or not, at that moment, I longed for it to be true.

chapter 49

How I came to be in the church service happened so simply that, even looking back on it, the sequence is hard to fathom. I remember driving down our street, turning right on Main, headed toward Route 622. The same dark, desperate route I'd run two nights ago. The streets again were empty. I glided through the first light and passed the post office on my right. Then I heard the singing through my open windows, even from two blocks away. Without thinking, I slowed to listen. "Amazing Grace." It had been one of my favorite hymns since coming to Bradleyville. Something about the tune on that particular muggy August morning tugged at my heart. Before I even realized it, I'd turned left.

I rolled past the gymnasium, wondering what I was doing. The parking lot was full. Cars lined both sides of the street.

I found an empty spot one block down.

The hymn was over by the time I slipped through the open double doors. The gymnasium was standing-room-only, and I did my best to blend in with the knots of folks without seats near the back. I exchanged nods with Mr. Tull and the Clangerlees, feeling self-conscious. Pastor Frasier announced another hymn. "To God

Be the Glory." As the voices rose, an unearthly, joyous calm seemed to drift down from the ceiling. My eyes roved the beams overhead as I tried to place its source. Such a different aura from the last time the town had gathered—was it just four nights ago?

I spotted Lee and Miss Wilma near the front, next to my aunt and uncle. They must have saved Lee's seat for him. Briefly, I wondered if they'd saved one for me. Further down the row stood the Matthews, little Celia's blond head bent over her baby brother's. Thomas had a hand on her shoulder.

The hymn over, everyone sat with a squeaking of chairs and rustle of clothes. Faces tipped toward the stage expectantly as Pastor Frasier and Evan Burle, the Baptist minister, asked Martha Plott up the steps to speak. Curious whispers undulated through the crowd. No one seemed to have expected this invitation. Miss Martha's grandniece helped the old woman up the steps, both hands firmly under her arm. Once on stage, Miss Martha accepted Evan Burle's help to the podium. Pastor Frasier had to lower the mike all the way to reach the frail, white-haired woman. He and Pastor Burle then sat in chairs toward the back of the stage. Awkwardly, Miss Martha rested a thin veined hand on the wooden podium, a tissue clutched in her fingers.

"Ain't used to speakin' before such a grand assembly," she began, reacting at the reverberation of her own voice. "But I got somethin' real special to tell ya. First though, I'd like to pray for us all."

Not in all my life had I heard a prayer like what Martha Plott prayed that day. In her aged, tremulous voice she prayed for the mercy of Jehovah—the ever-gracious God of the straying Old Testament Israelites. She prayed for the gentle wind of God, like the breeze that passed before the prophet Elijah, to fill that gymnasium. She asked in Jesus' name that the forces of evil be held back and that the Holy Spirit would pour forth upon the congregation. She prayed that those who heard that small voice deep within them, calling them to the truth, would respond. And she prayed for the Great Physician's touch on Jake Lewellyn, who could not be present.

Halfway through her prayer, I opened my eyes to watch her in awe. I'd known Miss Martha since coming to Bradleyville; she was a woman the whole town respected. But the power emanating from her bent frame that day was so tangible that it seemed to fill the room.

"Amen." Her prayer done, she smiled at the congregation. "Bless y'all for comin' here today. I know you're here, like I am, to hear the Word a God and to search your own hearts now that our tragedy is behind us. Now I 'magine you're wonderin' what a little thing like me's doin' up here. Well, I could say I have a right. I heared how my own name was bandied about in front a the Riddum's house Friday night." Soft laughter rippled through the room. "But that ain't why I'm here. I'm here to tell ya 'bout an afternoon in my house over seven years ago. That afternoon, God sent me a vision. Never had one before, and I ain't had one since. And I almost didn't pay heed to it then, thinkin' I was just bein' a crazy ol' woman. But God in his mercy sent that vision *three times*, just to make sure he'd got my attention. Right away, then, he also impressed upon me who I should tell. So I called Pastor Frasier and his wife Esther, and Virginia Crofts, my dear friend who goes to the Baptist church. And the four a us been prayin' over that vision ever since then, never missed a week."

Not a sound could be heard from those listening, even with all the children in that gymnasium. I was as taken with her story as the rest. Of all people, *I* could understand the life-changing effect of a vision. I thought of my mother appearing to me in my dream, the shimmering hope that she had bestowed upon me. Oh, yes, this I could understand.

"Now here's what I saw in the vision, three times, sure as God lives. I saw the sky, black with night, stretched over a mob a ragin' men. They was yellin' and wavin' clubs. Somebody had a torch, like he's 'bout to light somethin' on fire. And there was other men pointin' guns at 'em, ready to shoot. There was a buildin' a some kind, with white pillars. Just outside that buildin' a man lay on the ground, lookin' for all the world like he was dead."

Folks' jaws were loosening. My nerves began to hum. I don't think one of us listeners dared breathe.

"And there was one more thing." Miss Martha nodded, remembering. "In that entire vision, only one face was clear. And I see ya here this mornin', dear soul. Forgive me for sayin' your name out loud to these good folk. I don't mean to embarrass ya. But this is what the Lord would have me do, to show everyone here his power and glory."

Lee, I thought. She saw Lee leading the men.

"Right smack into the middle a those violent men I saw a small figure runnin' with all her might. And that was sweet young Jessie Callum."

My knees nearly buckled. Surprise buzzed through the gymnasium, heads turning, seeking a glimpse of me. Lee and Miss Wilma and my aunt and uncle twisted around in their seats, their joy at my unexpected presence evident in their frantic searching. Aunt Eva caught sight of me first and pointed. Lee's eyes locked with mine. My heart hammered. I would have fled out the doors had my feet not been bolted to the floor.

"Listen to me, dear folks." Miss Martha waited for everyone to settle. "God, in his mercy, sent that vision so that, for over seven years, I and the three others he called specifically for his purpose, could pray. We prayed for every person in that vision—all those faceless folk we knew were from Bradleyville. God chose not to reveal the time or occasion or place a this ordeal. We could not even guess the details until the mill problems came up, and then God told me the time was near. Two nights ago, when many a you men were gatherin', Pastor Frasier got word of it, and the four a us got outta bed to pray. We met in my livin' room, pleadin' for protection and mercy over our men in Jesus' name. We prayed that whoever was on the ground in that vision would be spared. And we prayed that God would show us as a town all he needed to show us through this tragedy. Although we didn't know it at the time, God led Frank Bellingham to go and pray in the midst of the ruckus. And I know some a you wives was prayin' too. God answered our prayers. He's brought us here today, safe and sound, with Jake Lewellyn on the mend. Everyone goes back to work tomorrow. *With* a raise. Sometimes God's blessin's just overflow. I have no doubt that without God's foretellin' and without seven years' worth a prayin' the destruction two nights ago would a been a terrible sight to behold. God held back the forces a evil, folks, for this reason—*to show us all that he is Lord.* This town's been headed down the wrong road for some time now. It was a mighty dark and scary one too. I know, 'cause I was once on a road like that. Well, the Lord's got a right road for each a us. He'll cast that road before you, into glories you never could have imagined, endin' some day in heaven itself. Some sixty years ago, he set me on mine. And I believe every day he goes down that road ahead a me and blesses it."

Miss Martha spoke for another ten minutes or so, calling folks to turn their lives "100 percent" over to Christ. "Don't think settin' in church or bein' good's all ya need to do," she pleaded. "That's what we all been doin' for years now, and look where it got us. You and me, we'll never be good enough to reach heaven without the redemption a Christ."

Never good enough. For the first time, those words, coming in such context and from the lips of a woman like Martha Plott, held no chill for me. I wondered at that.

When Miss Martha finished talking, quiet weeping dotted the rows of worshipers. No one was looking at me anymore; peoples' thoughts had turned inward. The air in that hot gym hung heavy with a serene anticipation I'd never experienced. It frightened me in a vague, undefined way, as though something precious were about to be taken from me. I needed to get away from it, get out of the building. I started to turn toward the door, but my eye was caught by a familiar figure moving up the stage steps. *Thomas.* I halted, half afraid of what he would say. Surely he wouldn't confess to this crowd that he'd lied.

He nodded to the two ministers, who resumed their seats after helping Miss Martha into the hands of her grandniece by the stairs, and adjusted the microphone. "I won't be long, folks," he said almost apologetically. "I wasn't supposed to be up here at all. But I just got to tell ya, I agree with everything Martha said. Hearin' her story puts me to shame. 'Cause while she was prayin' for the Lord's intervention, I was runnin' 'round tryin' to fix things myself."

No, Thomas, I thought, holding my breath.

"Y'all know me. You know I'm a proud man. Struggled with pride all my life and probably ain't got it licked yet. My daddy always put Jesus first in his life, not his own self, so I should know better. But just seems over the years I forgot the decision I made as a boy—to let Jesus lead my life. Not that I didn't believe in the Lord, far from it. It's just that, goin' down the road, like Martha was talkin' 'bout, I was the driver. God was somewhere in the backseat. Well, by the grace a God we got through Friday night anyway. Not 'cause a anything I did, but because God pushed me outta the driver's seat and into the trunk."

He stopped for a deep breath. I could not move, listening to him. His humble words made my heart ache.

"I'm here to tell ya, I'm changin' my ways. God's gonna be my driver all the time now. I'll try to keep my high opinion a myself in the background. Okay? That's all I got to say."

I'd never seen Thomas so meek. He stepped back from the microphone, then changed his mind and moved forward again. "Jus' one more thing. Don't y'all forget that my best friend, Jake, saved my life. Now he's got his own battle scars, so I s'pose our bestin' feud is even for now." He grinned suddenly, and I saw the Thomas I knew. "But don't think our feudin's over. Somebody's got to give this town a few laughs."

That brought a chuckle as he left the podium. Pastor Burle stood to announce that we would sing a hymn, inviting those who wanted to publicly and fully dedicate their lives to Christ to come to the edge of the stage for prayer. Even as the beginning words were sung, people began to move forward. Lee was one of the first to rise. My heart turned over. For the briefest moment I longed to go with him. Then guilt flashed through me at the thought, as if I'd betrayed my own destiny. More than seven years ago, somewhere around the time Martha Plott had seen her vision, I had dreamed of my mother. Now the results of both were coming to fruition.

Ducking my head, I slipped out the door. Hot sun bounced off my forehead, and I shaded my eyes as I picked up speed, hurrying down the steps. I'd reached no farther than the sidewalk when I heard my name called. Sliding to an abrupt halt, I let my eyes slip shut, sighing in frustration.

"What is it, Thomas," I said almost accusingly as I turned. "I *have* to be going, and I don't have time for anyone else to try and talk me out of it."

"Well, then, I won't try." He drew near me on the sidewalk, standing so that a gnarled oak tree blocked the sun. "Just saw you leave and wanted to say good-bye, that's all."

Remorse washed through me. I nodded, looking at my feet.

"I'll sure miss ya. I know Celia will too."

How many times did I have to hear these words? A desperation to be gone surged through me. Only my respect for Thomas stayed a hasty farewell. "I was afraid for a moment there," I heard myself say, "that you were going to tell them the truth."

He smiled ruefully. "Couldn't do that now, could I. I can ask God's forgiveness, but not theirs. That's what I get, bein' so proudful and tryin' to fix things myself."

"How could you just make all that up?"

"Well, I didn't make it all up. That lamp did explode after the fire was set, and pieces went through the screen."

"But, Thomas, how'd you get *away* with it? Surely the fire inspectors know the truth."

"Only them. And Bill Scutch. And after it was all over, your uncle figured it out. But when the men started gatherin' that night,

I begged Bill to let me feed 'em the story. At the time, seemed it would maybe calm things down. The hard part was convincin' the fire inspectors afterward to let the story stay. It meant lettin' Riddum go. But if he went to jail, what would happen to the mill? The men could all lose their jobs—for good. If I hadn't known those inspectors personally, they wouldn't a listened. And they could sure lose their jobs too, if the truth got out. So I guess you 'n' me got one more secret between us to carry to our graves."

I smiled in spite of myself. For a moment we were silent.

"You heared what I said in there, Jessie?"

Here came the preaching. I braced myself. "Mmm-hmm."

"I hope you'll hear with your heart. There's a lot a people in there right now gettin' straight with God 'cause a all this. Their eyes have been opened, like mine." His voice was soft. "Like I hope yours'll be."

I don't know why it happened at that moment. After the years of sermons I'd heard in Bradleyville, after all the talks with my aunt and uncle and Lee. But for some reason, right then, as I stood on the hot sidewalk opposite Thomas, the quiet chorus of a hymn filtering from the school gym, I was struck by the message he was trying to get through my head. The words hit my chest, seeping into my hollow places. And suddenly I saw everything laid before me, as though a light had flicked on in my head. I was closing my eyes to the better way God was trying to show me. I was doggedly choosing my own path—my mother's path, because I could not admit she had lacked something herself. I saw this in a flash, and it scared me to death, for I could not imagine heeding this warning. I simply could not turn from the course my dream had put me on.

I shoved the thoughts away. Regrouping, I sought distraction in details of the sawmill.

"Once the men return to work, Riddum could go back on everything you forced him to say that night."

Thomas waved an impatient hand. "Don't worry 'bout that. He'll behave hisself, else he knows we'll pull a few mislaid facts outta our back pockets and come up with a 'new' theory. We finally got him right where we want him. Still, I'm gonna start prayin' he sells the mill and moves on. If I wasn't gittin' so old, I'd buy it back myself."

I remained unconvinced. "I just don't want him taking things out on the men. I want Uncle Frank and Lee to be happy."

"Your Uncle Frank'll be just fine. Lee ... well, Lee's heart's broken over your leavin'. But I s'pose he'll get used to the idea, jus' like the rest of us have to."

"It's about time I heard somebody say that. Seems like everybody in Bradleyville thinks this town's got a corner on God."

He shrugged. "Don't know 'bout that. I do know he's got a corner on us, and that's what counts. And I believe he's got a corner on you too, Jessie. I'm gonna be prayin' every day that you hear his voice loud and clear—whatever it is he needs to say to you. As for me, I got my work cut out for me, right in my own home."

"What do you mean?"

He regarded me for a moment, as if deciding how much to say. "Little Celia's a mighty sad child. I'm 'fraid she's payin' the price with Estelle for things that go back long before she was born. Those things is my fault, and I might have to spend the rest a my life tryin' to make 'em right."

Celia always had seemed so serious. I couldn't bear to think of her hurting. "I'll make sure to visit with her especially," I said lamely. "At Thanksgiving, I mean."

Sorrow flicked across Thomas's face. "You do that." He glanced over his shoulder. "Well. Better let ya go now. I gotta get back inside anyway. I need to be prayin' with folks."

I promised to call and give him my new phone number. He hugged me hard, his roughened cheek grazing mine. And then I was on my way down the street, alone, the strains of another hymn drifting behind me.

chapter 50

Things don't always happen quite the way you expect. I'd once envisioned Lee waving good-bye to me in the pouring rain, but the clouds that day were high and white, and Lee was so busy praying with the townsfolk, he probably hadn't even noticed I'd left the gym. Jealousy ripped at me as I pictured him surrounded by friends and family while I drove off alone. I'd also imagined driving out of town with spirits soaring, hardly believing that the day had finally arrived. I'd imagined it with a clear sense of my guardian angel's protection, the indomitable excitement of embarking on the plans that God, through her, had laid for me. Instead, I didn't feel sheltered at all, only solitary and vulnerable. Why, as I passed the Bradleyville sign, could I not shake that nagging feeling that, in truth, I was leaving God behind?

I drove out of town that morning with windows open, hair blowing around my face, wondering how far I had to go until the pull of Bradleyville would finally recede, and I could again feel deep within me that I was doing the right thing. The first three-and-a-half hours of my trip would be over winding Kentucky backroads. I drove as fast as I could, straining my neck out the window for a chance to pass an occasional logging truck. As the wheels of my car spun, unraveling miles between my old life and new, I turned my thoughts to my empty and waiting apartment. Tomorrow I would buy blue paint. Maybe even do the room. How much easier it would be to paint without having to cover furniture. Tuesday morning I'd rent pieces for the living room, plus a kitchen table and chairs. Arrange to have them delivered by the time the moving truck arrived, if possible. Wednesday I'd drive to Hope Center, meet the new staff, maybe pitch in for an hour or two, doing whatever was needed. Thursday I'd make a point of visiting around my apartment complex, meeting new neighbors. Perhaps go swimming. Maybe by Friday I'd have made some new friends— a couple to invite to supper, a girlfriend to see a movie with. Maybe within a week or two I'd even have a date. I tried to picture what he'd look like but could only see Lee's face.

The turnoff to the hospital in Albertsville was coming up. I passed it without slowing.

An hour from Bradleyville, I felt even more alone. As the minutes ticked by, the depression gave way to resentment. *Where are you?* I prayed to my guardian angel mother. *You're supposed to be helping me! I'm doing what you wanted; why can't you be here for me?*

It is not what I want, something deep inside me responded.

I shook my head to clear it. I breathed deeply and searched for other things to think about. In great detail, I began picturing my job. Going in the first day, wearing my yellow dress. I pictured sitting in on meetings with Edna Slate, the social worker I was replacing; being introduced to her families; going over files with her; meeting other people in the agency. I pictured the faces of the little children I'd see, imagined how my heart would go out to them, how fervently I'd want to help. I would be happy there; I'd be doing all day what my mother could only volunteer to do after work. *Plus* I'd be helping at the Center. I'd be doubly blessed. Never would I face the despair that had crossed my mother's brow as she drove away that final day of her life.

Two hours from Bradleyville I stopped in a tiny town and bought a Coke and candy bar. The girl behind the counter reminded me of a young Connie, apple-cheeked and dark-haired. Accepting change, I smiled at her lingeringly. As I left the store, I could feel her eyes on my back, wondering if she knew me.

My candy bar disappeared slowly, the Coke growing warm on the seat between my legs. The road curved and twisted, pulling me away from Bradleyville, toward my new home. Two-and-a-half hours out, I whispered aloud to my guardian angel, "Another thirty minutes and I'm halfway there." The knowledge brought no comfort.

. . . to show us all that he is Lord. Unexpectedly, Miss Martha's words flashed through my head. I saw her in front of the podium, tiny and frail, telling the town of her vision. What a remarkable thing that was. Amazing. And she and others had prayed for *seven years* about it. How strong her belief in that vision had been, to keep her praying for that long. I understood the energizing power of such unearthly knowledge, comparing Miss Martha's vision to my dream. And yet her knowledge had culminated tangibly, while mine was. . . .

The word *diminishing* sprang to mind, and I forcefully pushed it away.

At three hours the Coke was gone, the candy wrapper long since wadded onto the empty passenger floor. I had tired of actively seeking my guardian angel's comfort, now feigning nonchalance. Defiantly, I told God it didn't matter; if he was keeping her away from me, it would be no deterrent.

You know the truth.

I blinked. Where was this stuff coming from? What was wrong with me? My foot pressed a little harder on the accelerator. After all this planning, *why* couldn't I be happy today? It wasn't as if I was going off to rob banks, for heaven's sake.

I had mentally reviewed all I could of my apartment and employment and the Center. Unattended, my mind began to meander repeatedly back to Bradleyville. I found myself mulling over Thomas's lie, amazed that he'd gotten away with it. Maybe Uncle Frank was right; maybe God could use anything for his own purpose. Without God answering the prayers of Miss Martha and the rest, I couldn't imagine even Thomas Bradley possessing the fast-talking required to bend law enforcement's ancient rigidity. Then I thought of Jake Lewellyn and his immediate response to sacrifice himself for an old friend. Once I'd opened my mind to those two, other faces and names crowded in like clamoring schoolchildren. Lee's features were foremost. One by one, against my will, I remembered our evenings together, the conversations and kisses. Our fights. I told myself I couldn't imagine living under the same roof with him. We couldn't even get along three weeks straight, dating.

I counted the months until Thanksgiving, wondering if Lee's house would be rebuilt by then. Probably. The whole town would help. If I had stayed, we could've been building our own by then. I wondered how big Katherine May would be, if Connie would have lost her pregnancy weight, and if Miss Wilma's hip would be improved. I railed at myself for not having stopped at the hospital. I would make it up to Connie. Find her another angel lamp, that's what I'd do. I wondered what it would be like at the mill by Thanksgiving, with Uncle Frank and Lee almost four months at the helm. Would production be up? Would the men be happy? I thought of Miss Alice and her sewing shop, Tull's Drugstore, and the IGA. I thought of little Celia, berating myself that I hadn't said good-bye to her either.

Listen to me, a voice whispered within. *How much more must I show you?*

Please, God, I begged, *leave me alone.*

Three hours and twenty minutes since I'd left. Soon I would hit interstate, leaving behind the narrow, undulating roads that symbolized rural Kentucky. Undoubtedly, assurance from my guardian angel lay ahead, somewhere along the great stretch of asphalt leading to civilization. It did not matter that I was feeling more miserable by the minute. Everything would be all right. It had to be.

The air was hot and sticky, my back wet. When I'd stopped at the store I'd bound my hair back in a rubber band, tired of it whipping my face. I steered the car resolutely, keeping eyes on the road as I wiped the side of my face with a sleeve. I wanted another Coke. I wanted the drive over with. I wanted to see Lee one more time.

"All these commandments I have kept; what am I still lacking?"

Inexplicably, the words of the rich young man in the Gospel of Matthew popped into my mind. I pictured Pastor Frasier preaching, remembering my anger at his sermon. That was so long ago. What purpose did it serve to think of it now?

"Nothing," I said aloud. "I lack nothing."

I pressed on. Fear bubbled, then rose within me. Desperately, I prayed again for my mother. *Please let her answer me, God, please. I know you will. I know it.*

I drove through another small town. Two stoplights, just like Bradleyville. A pretty, blond little girl waved at me from the sidewalk. I waved back. Beyond the town limits, I got stuck behind a U-Haul truck, and it was a while before I could pass.

Please, Lord. I'm begging you.

The minutes ticked by, my car wheels whirring.

Finally, my dogged pretense began to tremble. Somehow, I knew that if I did not shore it up, it would crumble quickly, as a long-enduring, rain-soaked hillside slides away under that final inch of water.

So I struggled. I sat up straighter, back not touching the seat, gripping the steering wheel. My shoulders squared, and my chin raised, as though I were staring down an ancient foe. But soon my back muscles grew weary, and my fingers cramped. I felt the first pebbles begin to fall, skittering sickeningly to the depths of my soul.

My eyes smarted. I swallowed hard and drove.

They picked up speed, those pebbles, then collided with little rocks, sending them tumbling. The rocks hit larger ones. And then heavy stones. The stones rolled into motion inside me, crashing into bigger stones until, ultimately, the boulders moved. The weight of the boulders' riotous descent crushed tender soil beneath them until the very foundation of *who I was* shook, slid, then heaved itself in one mighty spill.

Anyone watching would not have known; would only have seen a young woman, tired and hot, gauging curves in the road. No one could have guessed my despair.

Not another car was in sight when I finally pulled over. My tires crunched on the graveled shoulder of a turn-about as I rolled to a slow stop. I turned off the ignition, even then trying to convince myself it wasn't true, and sank my forehead against the wheel. But I knew it was.

No "guardian angel" could give me the peace I sought.

The realization cracked my consciousness like a hammer on glass. Aunt Eva was right. My dream and all its temporary solace had led me away from God, not toward him. Somewhere, somehow, in the tumult of the last three days, I had lost the belief in my guardian angel that I'd thought would sustain me forever. Like the angel on Connie's lamp who wore my mother's smile, she had crumbled to ashes. Without her, I wanted to wail, I might as well be the baby on that lamp, scattered also into nothingness. My eyes squeezed shut as I sought my mother in futility one last time, begging and pleading to God to let her sustain me. And if not, I screamed silently, just let me die, just let me be with her. We'd rise again together, from ashes to angels. I couldn't believe that God sought to take her and my dream from me. God could not be asking this of me. I'd clung to my beliefs for so long, I didn't know how to let them go.

"God," I cried, "I can't do it! What do I have without her?"

I am all you need.

A moan escaped my lips. Hollowly, I gazed at the bends in the road before me. Minutes passed as I stared at them with locked eyes, measuring their demands, their ultimate path. As I stared, they began to reshape themselves, looming narrower, more precarious.

Fruitless.

Time flattened itself, slipping over a distant horizon. I hunched in my old Ford, oven-like under the sun, still fighting.

Soon trickling tears began to flow, a sizzle in their wake. No amount of denial could now stanch them. I do not know how long I sobbed, body rocking. Only that it was for a lifetime. The force of my tears soon shook me as jarringly as had the force of my blows against Al Bledger, a blurred succession of images deepening my grief. I cried for my apartment, its blank walls so expectant and ready. I cried for the job I'd worked so hard to earn. For Hope Center. For the dresses I'd sewed and the boxes I'd packed. For blue paint. For the years I'd spent planning, dreaming. I cried for the despair of a life "not good enough." And finally, helplessly, I cried for my mother—for a long, long time until the tears ran dry and my chest ached and my head pounded.

When I was done, I slowly raised my head. My swollen eyes could barely focus. I was weary of fighting.

"Okay, Jesus," I whispered, "here I am. I'm yours. Forgive me for not listening for so long, for putting my plans ahead of you. I promise to follow you." In desperation, then, I tried one more time. "So please, Lord, *please*, will you change your mind and let me drive on now? You can be with me in Cincinnati, *can't* you?"

I waited for the peace to come that would tell me God agreed. I waited and waited for it, then ultimately demanded it. "Why, God, *why*? They're *good* plans; I'm going to serve others; what's *wrong* with that?"

For I know the thoughts that I think toward you, saith the Lord, thoughts of peace and not of evil, to give you an expected end.

Uncle Frank's verse for Aunt Eva. The decision I faced now seemed no less calamitous than that night. I covered my eyes with both hands. For a long time I sat unmoving. Finally, in the end, I lifted my fingers away, my head tipping upward.

"Oh, Lord," my voice was barely audible, "I'm going to need so much help."

My hands trembled as I turned on the ignition. My breathing was unsteady, and I took my time, inhaling deeply. Strangely, then, the air seemed to grow alive, filling my chest, offering strength. With determination my back straightened, my fingers firming on the wheel. I put the car in gear and rolled into motion.

Then I turned around—and headed home.

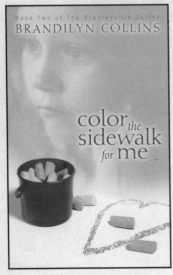

Book Three of the Bradleyville Series!

Capture the Wind for Me
Brandilyn Collins

After her mama's death, sixteen-year-old Jackie Delham is left to run the household for her daddy and two younger siblings. When Katherine King breezes into town and tries to steal her daddy's heart, Jackie knows she must put a stop to it. Katherine can't be trusted. Besides, one romance in the family is enough, and Jackie is about to fall headlong into her own.

As love whirls through both generations, the Delhams are buffeted by hope, elation, and loss. Jackie is devastated to learn of old secrets in her parents' relationship. Will those past mistakes cost Jackie her own love? And how will her family ever survive if Katherine jilts her daddy and leaves them in mourning once more?

Softcover: 0-310-24243-6

Pick up a copy at your favorite bookstore!

ZONDERVAN™

GRAND RAPIDS, MICHIGAN 49530 USA

WWW.ZONDERVAN.COM

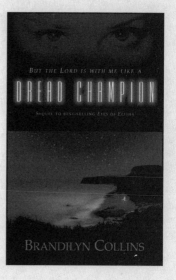

We want to hear from you. Please send your comments about this
book to us in care of zreview@zondervan.com. Thank you.

GRAND RAPIDS, MICHIGAN 49530 USA

WWW.ZONDERVAN.COM